NO-ONE EVER HAS SEX ON CHRISTMAS DAY

TRACY BLOOM

Published by Bookouture
An imprint of StoryFire Ltd.
23 Sussex Road, Ickenham, UB10 8PN
United Kingdom
www.bookouture.com

ISBN: 978-1-78681-258-2
eBook ISBN: 978-1-78681-257-5

For Tom and Sally
Wishing you both many, many great Christmases, and I hope your
dad and I never screw it up for you!

Chapter One

'Tell me there isn't an enormous inflatable reindeer on the front lawn,' said Katy as she walked into the kitchen and dumped her laptop carrier on the floor.

'There isn't a five-foot-high inflatable reindeer on the front lawn,' replied Ben without looking up from rifling through a clutch of plastic bags on the table.

Katy turned and left the room to go and check out the glowing backside of the wobbling reindeer leering at her through the lounge window. She went back into the kitchen and headed straight for the fridge, praying that Ben had pre-empted her need for a Friday night, long-week-at-work glass of wine. He had. It didn't look like the sort they usually drank, but she didn't care. She needed alcohol if she was to be enthusiastic about being greeted by an inflatable grinning Rudolph ogling her from the darkness.

'Do you like it?' Ben asked, looking up.

She gulped the wine and screwed her face up. It didn't taste good at all.

'I love it,' she lied. 'I just wasn't expecting to come home to something so big!'

'And what about Santa on the roof? Is that too much, do you think?'

'What Santa?'

'Santa on the roof. Didn't you see it? It's taken me all afternoon.'

Katy took another gulp of wine then went outside again to inspect what further festive carnage Ben had inflicted on their home.

'Bloody hell,' said Ben, coming up behind her. 'What happened? You're supposed to see Santa on the chimney next to a flashing Merry Christmas. Perhaps the fuse has gone.' He headed back into the house, disappearing to a place Katy knew she would never understand nor want to understand.

🎄

'Have they come back on yet?' he shouted from the cupboard under the stairs twenty minutes later. Katy got up out of the kitchen chair, where she had managed to get past her dislike of the wine and drink the whole glass. Outside, the Santa remained in bleak darkness, and she returned with the news to a crestfallen Ben.

'I'll have to get someone round tomorrow to help me sort it out,' he said. 'It can't have overloaded the system already. I've got a load more to go up yet.'

'What do you mean more?' said Katy, pouring herself another glass of disgusting wine.

'Of course there's more. It's Christmas!'

'But… but…' She didn't know what to say. She didn't want to burst his festive bubble. She loved the fact that Ben had a childlike level of enthusiasm about decorating their new home for Christmas. It must be the eight-year age gap between the two of them that made him so much more excitable about these things, she thought. It was just a shame that their taste levels were somewhat different. Katy would have gone for a minimal look, probably consisting of white-only sparkling lights, whereas Ben's creation looked set to rival a Las Vegas casino.

'Can we afford all this?' she asked. 'I thought we were supposed to be on a budget now that we've moved house?'

'Oh, don't worry. It was all dead cheap. I got it from that discount warehouse place in town. I got all this stuff too – look, cost virtually nothing.'

Katy watched as Ben started to pull out reams of cheap shiny paraphernalia from the carrier bags on the table.

'One hundred baubles for less than a Starbucks coffee,' he proudly showed her.

Katy thought about the gorgeous Harvey Nichols' pack of a dozen tree ornaments she'd bought a few years ago that had cost more than her party dress.

'And a sign. Every house needs a sign.' A cheeky elf now grinned back at her, holding a flag, which read 'Santa, Please Stop Here'. 'We've never had a sign before, have we? Not in the flat. You need a garden for a sign and *now* we have a garden.'

Katy nodded. It had taken a while. Nearly three years of looking and saving and sales falling through until Katy's promotion and subsequent pay rise had allowed them to think bigger and better. They had finally secured their dream home of a delightful Victorian semi-detached house in a leafy suburb of Leeds, with a garden where you could put a sign up for Santa. Katy wasn't sure whether the sign was for Ben's benefit or their three-year-old daughter, Millie.

'Aaaaaaaaand,' continued Ben, 'the best Christmas bargain of all time…' Katy closed her eyes – she didn't dare look. 'Not one, not two, not three, but *four* chocolate advent calendars all for the knock-down price of just *one* pound.'

'A pound!'

'Yeah, four for a pound! What a find.'

Katy thought she might vomit.

'You don't look impressed,' said Ben, frowning.

'Can you imagine how bad that chocolate is going to taste if they're selling four for a pound?'

Ben shrugged. 'It's not really about the chocolate, is it? It's about opening the door.'

Katy looked at Ben in shock. 'I thought you understood kids… and women for that matter. It's *always* about the chocolate! Or to be more precise, it's always about the chocolate and the once-a-year opportunity to be allowed to eat it at 7 a.m.'

Ben looked down, frowning at the four calendars. Katy wondered if it was the right time to tell him she already had a Lindt calendar stashed away in the back of a cupboard, along with a Star Wars one for him and a My Little Pony one for Millie.

'It might taste all right,' he said dejectedly. 'I mean, you're drinking the wine I got there. That must taste great given how quick you're downing it.'

'What!' gasped Katy, almost spitting out her latest mouthful. 'This is from the discount warehouse? No wonder it tastes terrible.'

'Why are you drinking it then? I tried it earlier and had to chuck it away. I have to say I'm impressed at how hardcore you are, necking that stuff. Tastes like paint stripper.'

'You could have warned me.'

'Funnier to watch you screwing your nose up! You sure you're not an alcoholic?'

'You're enough to drive me to becoming one,' she said, getting up and chucking the rest of it away.

'You couldn't live without me and you know that,' he said, laughing to himself.

'What have I done to deserve you?' She walked over and put her arms around him. She knew she must have done something really good at some point. She dreaded to think what her life would be like if she hadn't met Ben. She wouldn't have Millie for a start – their funny, brilliant, gorgeous daughter. And she wouldn't have her career. It had been Ben's idea for Katy to go back to the job she loved in advertising while he stayed at home to look after Millie. Sure, it had made sense, as she earned a lot more than he could as a secondary school PE teacher but even so, it took a special kind of man to swap traditional roles like that. He was back at work now, working at Millie's preschool as a teaching assistant. He said he enjoyed it, but it was still a compromise, Katy knew. It made everyone's life easier that he had hours that fitted in with Millie, even if it wasn't the most exciting job in the world. Still, her compromise was that she worked long hours in order to keep them in the lifestyle they were accustomed to. It worked both ways, she figured.

'I'm so excited about our first Christmas in this house,' said Ben, folding his arms round her shoulders. 'It's going to be so brilliant. I mean, we couldn't have had a reindeer that size on the balcony at the flat, could we?'

She grinned. He wasn't wrong. Let him have as many reindeers on the lawn as he wanted. Katy wanted Ben to enjoy their new house as much as she did. She might have been paying the mortgage, but he was bringing up their child. They both deserved it.

'I love it here,' said Ben, looking down at her. 'I'm half-expecting someone to come and rip it all away from us, it's so great.'

'Of course they won't, silly,' said Katy. 'We've earned this,' she added, casting her eyes round the room.

'And...' continued Ben, barely listening, he was so full of excitement and emotion, 'we even have a chimney. I have never spent Christmas in a house with a chimney – do you know that? And now we have a Santa on the chimney that lights up. Well, it will… one day.'

'I'm glad that a chimney has made your Christmas,' said Katy, allowing her head to rest on his chest. He smelt of oranges and cinnamon. 'Did you buy Christmas potpourri?' she asked.

'Is that what it is?' said Ben. 'It was free with a box of crackers. I thought you must put it on the fire or something.' Katy buried her head in his chest, not trusting herself to comment. 'Speaking of which, come and take a look at this.' He grabbed her hand and dragged her through the kitchen and the hall and into the lounge. She gasped as she walked in. 'Me and the Millster did it,' said Ben, squeezing her hand. 'Well, I did the fire, of course. Can't have a three-year-old handling matches, can we?' He laughed, and Katy knew that he had most definitely allowed Millie to play with the matches.

There were no lights on in the room, just a warm yellow glow coming from the roaring fire in the grate and the sparkle of tiny white fairy lights strung across the ornate mantelpiece. It was magical. It was the reason why she had fallen in love with the house. It was everything their designer flat in the centre of the city wasn't – it had character, it was quirky, and it had plaster ceiling roses for goodness' sake. It was a home. More than that, it was a family home. The flat had suited her well in her single days, but Ben moving in and then the arrival of Millie had made it a squeeze. They'd been more than ready to relinquish the convenience of bars and restaurants within spitting distance for the quieter pace of the suburbs. It had taken a while to find this house, but this was why it had been worth the wait: the perfect Christmas tableau right before her eyes.

'Millie put us all a stocking up,' Ben pointed out.

Katy looked at each of the three bright red stockings pinned to the mantelpiece, despite the fact it wasn't even December yet.

'I told her it was too early,' said Ben, 'but she insisted. She so takes after you.'

'Well-organised?'

'Bloody stubborn! She even made me put a carrot out for Rudolph – look. Apparently he visits the really good kids early. If I take it away she'll think he's been and not left her anything, but if I leave it she'll think she's not one of the good kids. What do I do about that? More lies I'll have to think up and remember. Christmas is packed full of lies, have you noticed? I think I'm going to have to keep a Christmas lies diary just to keep track of myself.'

'What if she finds the diary?'

'Christ, what was I thinking? You're right.'

'She can't read, Ben.'

'Oh yeah,' he said, tilting his head to one side. 'Panic over.'

'I love it,' Katy told him.

'What?'

'The fire, the lights, the stockings… it's beautiful.'

'We have another stocking,' said Ben, picking a spare one up from off the back of the settee.

'Was it four for a pound?'

'No, ten pounds actually. Me and Millie came to a decision that stockings were a sound investment for years to come and so splashed out a little and well… maybe… you know… next year we might need four stockings to go above the fireplace?'

Katy turned sharply to look at him.

'Because we said, didn't we, that once we moved, we'd get on it.' He looked serious for a moment. A rare occurrence. 'Start trying for another one, now we've got the room?'

Katy said nothing, just gazed at the extra stocking. They'd been so busy, what with the move and work being crazy as usual, she hadn't been thinking about extending their family. Ben hadn't said anything for ages either so she half-thought he'd gone off the idea. Understandable. Being a stay-at-home parent is enough to put anyone off kids. But clearly it had been on his mind, even if he hadn't talked about it. He'd been waiting for his moment; he'd bought the stocking.

'And you are getting on a bit,' he added. 'We need to get a shift on or else you'll be past it.'

'Oh, thanks a bunch!' she said, punching him in the arm. It was true; her clock was ticking faster by the minute. She'd turned forty that year so she was already leaving it late. Plenty of time for Ben of course, but maybe that's what you got when you married a younger man – a constant reminder that your body will start to wear out way before his would.

'And it would be nice to, you know, plan it this time. Have the full getting-pregnant experience,' he said, shrugging.

He said it as casually as if he'd missed the trailers before watching a movie, but Katy knew exactly what he meant. He may have sounded flippant, but he was gently reminding her of what she'd denied him when she got pregnant with Millie. Her pregnancy had come unplanned and early in their relationship. A shock to both of them – and on top of that it had taken some time to dispel confusion over who might be the father, as Katy had had a misguided and much regretted one-night stand with a childhood sweetheart around the time of conception. Fortunately they had got past it, and there was no disputing the fact that Millie's auburn locks were directly descended from Ben's ginger mop. Katy's first pregnancy had not been a time of joy and harmony, and she still felt guilty about what she'd put Ben through to this day. She looked down at the fourth stocking, absentmindedly stroking it.

'Why don't we start practising now?' said Ben gently. 'Millie's fast asleep, and I bought scented candles. They normally get you going.'

'Four for a pound?' asked Katy, smiling.

He nodded. 'Norway Spruce flavoured.'

She smiled again. The cheap wine had made her feel light-headed, so she allowed herself to be led across the lounge towards the stairs.

She'd just put her left foot on the bottom step when the phone rang.

Chapter Two

Ben gripped Katy's hand hard. They both paused on the stairs, neither saying a word as the phone continued to ring insistently. Ben prayed it didn't wake Millie. He was about to have sex with his wife, Millie demanding another read of *The Tiger Who Came to Tea* would crush any man's libido. The ringing stopped, and he heaved a sigh of relief until the answerphone kicked in. He glanced at Katy as they both stood frozen on the stairs, fearing any movement would spark the collapse of their entire evening.

'Hello, peeps. You are through to Ben, Katy and Millie. Say hello, Millie.'

'Hello.'

'We are currently partaking in a killer dolls' tea party, so please leave us a message so we can forget to call you back. Bye.'

Katy suppressed a giggle.

'Hi, love, are you there?' came a woman's voice immediately recognisable as Katy's mum.

'Of course we aren't here,' hissed Ben. 'Or else we would answer the bloody phone.'

'But we *are* here,' hissed back Katy.

Oh yeah, thought Ben. But he wasn't worried. Katy and her mum weren't that close. Rita lived in Spain, and usually Katy avoided speaking to her if she could, so there was no chance of her disrupting their ongoing journey to the bedroom.

'I really need to speak to you, Katy. Could you call me back as soon as you can? Unless your dad has already called you. I guess he might have done, but I need to give you my side of the story. He'll have blamed it all on me – I know he will – but he needs to take some responsibility. As I keep telling him, you don't walk out on over forty years of marriage for no…'

'Hello, Mum. Mum, it's me. What's happened? What are you talking about?' Katy had lunged for the phone and had already slid to the floor, clutching the receiver. Ben knew the night wasn't going to go quite as he'd hoped.

He wandered back down the hall and into the kitchen, closing the door behind him. He picked himself a cold beer from the fridge then went into the lounge and slumped down on the sofa. He turned on the TV and found some football, resting his head on the spare Christmas stocking left on the sofa arm.

🎄

He had no idea how long he'd been asleep when Katy shook him awake, her eyes red and her cheeks flushed. The logs in the grate had burnt down to embers, and the lights across the mantelpiece had switched to an upbeat flashing mode, incongruous with the sombre face in front of him. He pulled himself up to allow Katy room to slump beside him.

'So what's happened?' he asked, slapping his cheeks to try to wake himself up.

'My mother's a floozy is what's happened.'

Ben had nowhere to go with this information. If he agreed, he was doomed. If he disagreed, he was doomed. To be honest, the news wasn't too great a shock. Despite being in her seventies, Katy's mum had always petrified him. She made no attempt to hide that she was envious of Katy managing to snag herself a toy boy. She was the only person who actually called him a toy boy, and she said it in such a way that it made him feel slightly uncomfortable. It was also true, as Katy remarked many times, that despite all Katy's quite sizeable achievements in her career, her mother wasn't the slightest bit interested or proud. She was, however, very impressed that her daughter had married a handsome, athletic younger man, even if Ben did his utmost to dispel the myth he was the dream husband whenever in her company.

'Oh, how come?' he managed to ask casually.

'She's left Dad.'

'Right.' Ben scrutinised Katy. Still his path through this conversation wasn't obvious. Should he side with Katy's dad, Dennis, who for years had found the only way of dealing with his full-on wife was to pretty much ignore her? Or with Katy's mum, who should have cut her losses years ago and left him to live the life she wanted rather than moan about being trapped by her inattentive husband?

'Big decision at their age.' Ben nodded, deciding to stay neutral. 'How are they both doing?'

'Oh, Mother's like a… like a… like a dog on heat.'

This thought made Ben feel nauseous. Who would have guessed that it wasn't going to be a small child stopping him from sleeping with his wife that night but the thought of his mother-in-law panting?

'She's got a boyfriend!' exclaimed Katy, looking up at him wide-eyed.

'Really?' He tried to look surprised despite the fact that he knew the only way Rita would ever have left Dennis was if she'd found someone prepared to take her on. The fact that there *was* someone prepared to fulfil such a task did surprise him. Her addiction to appalling karaoke renditions was surely enough to make any man run a mile. 'Who is he?' he asked, trying to stop the note of wonder creeping into his voice.

'He's Spanish, owns a bar. She met him at church.'

'Church!'

'Yeah. She joined the choir.'

'Jesus! A choir? In a church?'

'It's all very confusing,' said Katy, shaking her head.

'You're telling me. No choir needs Rita, especially one in a church. Her voice is enough to frighten the Holy Ghost away.'

'She says she loves him. She says she never loved Dad like she loves Carlos. She says she wishes she'd met him before she met Dad, so she'd never have to have lived through her miserable marriage.'

Fortunately Ben realised that this was the moment to put his arm round her. And perhaps turn off the flashing fairy lights over the mantelpiece.

'I'm so sorry,' he said, when he sat back down again. 'That can't be good to hear.'

'She never mentioned me,' said Katy, her head leaning on his shoulder. 'She never said that if she hadn't met Dad then she wouldn't have had me.'

Ben put his other arm around her. He wracked his brains for the right thing to say to a daughter whose mother had repeatedly failed to show any gratitude for her existence. Words failed him. He squeezed her hard.

'He's only sixty-four,' sniffed Katy.

'Who is?'

'Carlos.'

'So she finally got her toy boy.'

'What do you mean?'

'You know she's always been jealous of you snagging yourself this young thing,' said Ben, smiling and indicating his body.

'You think she's left Dad to compete with me?'

Ben shrugged. 'Who knows? She was always going on about me being your toy boy, wasn't she? Do you think she's going through a midlife crisis?'

'She's in her seventies, Ben!'

'What do you call it in your seventies?'

'Should know better is what you call it.'

'How's your dad doing?'

'She says he's devastated.'

'Really?' replied Ben. Somehow he suspected Dennis might have even helped her pack.

'She says he keeps calling her, begging her to come back.'

He was most likely ringing her to ask how to use the washing machine when he ran out of clean clothes, Ben was tempted to say.

'I tried to call him, but there was no answer.'

He'll be down the bar with his expat mates and a big grin on his face, thought Ben. Katy was looking far into the distance, clearly in shock at the news. He squeezed her shoulders, again wracking his brains for words of wisdom to break her out of this sorrow. He wanted to tell her it was no big deal. He wanted to tell her that, in his opinion, this had been a long time coming and they would probably both be happier apart. He wanted to say they were both grown-ups and Katy had to let them get on with it, just as they had let her get on with her life. He wanted to say she hardly ever saw them anyway so the impact on their lives was going to be virtually zero. Two Christmas cards rather than one would probably the biggest change they'd see.

'They're coming for Christmas,' Katy said, reaching for a tissue.

'What! Who is?'

'Mum and Carlos.'

'What! You have to be kidding me? Tell me you're kidding me?'

'I'm not kidding.'

'But… but your mother hates Christmas in this country. Remember last time she drank rum all day to keep out the cold and passed out before Christmas dinner?'

'She says she wants to spend Christmas with us. And she wants us to meet Carlos,' said Katy, blowing her nose.

This was a disaster of epic proportions. Christmas with his deranged mother-in-law and her geriatric toy boy. This was not how he'd imagined it. He wanted to be in front of the fire all day, opening presents and eating hideously fattening food with Katy and Millie. It was the first time Millie would know what was going on, her first real Christmas. It was going to be magical. The magic certainly didn't include unwanted visitors. Christmas was well and truly ruined and it was still only November.

Chapter Three

'What are you doing up here?' asked the head that suddenly appeared out of the dormer window on the roof.

'What are *you* doing up here? You're supposed to be holding the ladder,' replied Ben.

'I got bored and I wanted to see what the view was like.'

'So who's holding the ladder?'

'No-one.'

'Great,' said Ben. He punched the inflatable Santa he'd been wrestling with for the last ten minutes then leaned forward to rest against the top rung. He was eighteen feet above the ground and level with the edge of the roof of his house. Next to him, his soon to be ex-best mate, Braindead, was leaning out the dormer window without a care in the world while he remained moments from certain death.

'You can't see much from up here, can you?' commented his friend. Ben cautiously rotated his head to look behind him over the multitude of near-identical rooftops. All he could see was grey. Grey sky, grey shiny roofs, wet with a light rain from earlier, grey tarmac roads and pathways… everywhere was grey, and it matched his mood perfectly. Darkness was just creeping in, and his fingers were raw with cold and damp from his efforts to resuscitate the stupid inflatable Santa.

'So what are you doing up here then?' asked Braindead again. 'When you asked me round to give you a hand I thought you wanted me to explain Minecraft to you for the millionth time, not you know, do something… outside!'

They had been friends since they'd started school together, aged four. Ben couldn't remember when he started calling him Braindead. Braindead had a very unique way of looking at the world that kind of lacked all sense and yet made total sense. This could make him appear both stupid and a genius simultaneously. Ben preferred to label him Braindead and keep his feet on the ground. It was a northern thing.

'I'm trying to bestow some much-needed Christmas spirit back on to this house,' Ben told him through gritted teeth.

'With that?' asked Braindead.

'It's supposed to be an inflatable glowing Santa.'

'Looks more like one of those naked pictures of people who've lost ten stone in weight and their skin's all saggy and baggy and it rolls around all over the place. Like Santa's been on the no-sugar diet and taken it too far.'

'Well, I wish he'd get fat again,' said Ben with a sigh, kicking Santa's lolloping head.

'I wonder why Santa is fat?' pondered Braindead. 'He's a terrible role model really, isn't he? *"Listen, children, if you're good then the fat man will bring you presents, and don't forget to leave him alcohol and cake so he gets even fatter."* What's that teaching our kids, eh? That the nicest, kindest, loveliest man in the world, who we allow to break into our homes every year, is a fat bastard who has a serious eating disorder. Santa has issues. He needs rebranding or rehab. I mean, in this day and age shouldn't Santa be an athletic, transsexual vegan who drives a hybrid and leaves you an educational toy along with the address of the nearest charity shop so you know where to donate it once you've finished with it?'

'He doesn't sound much fun,' responded Ben.

'He? He's transgender. Now he's a she, you dingbat! Aren't you listening?'

Ben wasn't really. Normally he found Braindead's knack of turning the world upside down entertaining, but not now. 'I think I'll just have to take him down,' he said, looking forlornly at the Santa, who was doing a head splat on to the side of the roof.

'Shall we stab him with the screwdriver, let all the air out?' asked Braindead, looking excited.

'No!' said Ben. 'Maybe if I get him on the ground I can work out why he's not glowing.'

'Yeah, let's open him up, see what's inside that huge Christmas gut.'

'How very festive,' said Ben.

'You're on a roof wrestling with an inflatable Santa. I think I'd call that festive,' pointed out Braindead.

'Well I don't know why I'm bothering. Christmas this year is going to be miserable anyway.'

'What's new?' Braindead shrugged. 'Christmas is always crap. Massive hype, massive underdelivery. It's always been like that.'

Ben looked over at Braindead.

'Not when you have a three-year-old in the family. Not when you've just moved into a house with a real chimney. Not when… not when you think the only thing that could possibly beat this Christmas will be next Christmas.'

'What are you talking about?'

'Nothing,' said Ben, looking away. 'Anyway, it's already ruined. Need to forget all that. Katy's mum is coming to stay with her new boyfriend.'

'Christmas is all about having your day ruined by unwelcome guests. From day one that's what's happened on Christmas Day. I mean take the shepherds. At least you haven't got shepherds calling in unannounced. Think of all the sheep shit.'

'I'd rather have a bunch of shepherds round than have to eat Christmas dinner with Barbara Cartland and Antonio Banderas.'

'Ooh,' said Braindead, a look of excitement flooding his face again. 'Is this like one of those dream dinner-party-guest things that can include people who are dead? Only it's Christmas dinner so you have to think really carefully.' Braindead screwed his face up for a moment. 'I've got it,' he declared. 'Surely you'd have to have Mary and Joseph? But you wouldn't want Jesus, would you? Not as a baby anyway. No-one's happy sitting down to dinner next to a high chair. But it could be interesting if he were older, then you could ask him a few things like, *"So, Jesus – did you ever question your mother on this whole immaculate conception thing?"* To be honest though the three wise men would be good. I'd want to know what they were thinking, taking gold, frankincense and myrrh. I mean who gives a baby that *and* calls themselves wise?' Braindead paused for a moment but not long enough for Ben to interrupt. 'Actually that's a really hard ask. Ideal guests for Christmas dinner, dead or alive? I mean you'd have to factor in who would bring the best presents and who would be good at the traditional post-Christmas-dinner Monopoly game. I mean would you want someone really smart who could beat you or someone stupid so you could absolutely annihilate…'

'Braindead?' Ben finally managed to interrupt.

'Yeah.'

'Shut up.'

'OK.'

Ben stared at the amorphous mass of Santa in front of him while Braindead showed no signs of returning to his post at the bottom of the ladder.

'You should be like me and have no expectations for Christmas,' said Braindead eventually. 'Everyone makes so much fuss about it. Treat it like any other day of the year and you won't be disappointed.'

'Abby agree with you on that one, does she?'

Braindead nodded. 'So far. I just give her some cash and she buys her own present. She even wraps it. Then she gives it to me on Christmas Eve, and I pop round to her mum's on Christmas night and hand it over. She always cries when she opens it. That's a bit of an overreaction, I have to say.'

'How many Christmases have you been together?'

'I don't know. Are you supposed to count?'

'Well, no but… well, let's work it out. You came to our wedding with her, didn't you? And this will be our third Christmas married so this will be your third Christmas with Abby.'

'And your point is?'

'Well, don't you think perhaps this time she might have upped her expectations?'

Braindead shrugged. 'No, if anything she's downgraded. Normally she would have bought her present by now, but she hasn't even mentioned it. Maybe we're already at the stage in our relationship where we no longer need to buy each other pointless presents?'

'Or maybe you're at the stage in your relationship when she's expecting a whole lot more.'

'What do you mean?'

'You're not getting any younger, Braindead.'

'I know that. I'm ticking the 30–35 years' age-bracket box in surveys. Although I have to admit I often tick the 15–20 years' box as my answers always seem more appropriate to that age group.'

'Third Christmas, Braindead? She'll have expectations.'

'Enough of these festive expectations,' said Braindead, starting to look cross. 'I told you I don't believe in them, whether it's the third or the twenty-third.'

'Well, if you don't produce a ring come Christmas morning, on your head be it.'

'A ring? What sort of ring?'

'For goodness' sake! An engagement ring, you bloody idiot. Mark my words, that's what she'll be expecting in her Christmas stocking this year.'

'She… she… wants to marry me? Are you insane?'

'Well, yes. I know it may seem utterly ridiculous that someone might want to spend the rest of their life with you, but it's what usually happens in normal relationships after you've been together a while, particularly at this time of year. Something weird happens to women when they start to smell the mulled wine and mince pies and watch *Love Actually* too many times. Makes them all soppy and romantic and want to walk along the River Thames holding hands.'

'What?'

'Have you ever seen *Love Actually*?'

'No.'

'I think you'd better watch it.'

'Is it about Christmas then?'

'Yes.'

'Is it like *Home Alone*?'

'No!'

Ben gave him a pained look. 'Look, all I'm saying is that it's highly likely Abby may be expecting your relationship to move on this Christmas, that's all.'

'But what if I want it to stay the same? I like it how it is now. We have a good time. Marriage puts a stop to that, doesn't it?'

'Staying the same may not be an option. I'd say three Christmases and you're out.'

'What, she'll dump me?'

'Probably.'

'But I don't want her to dump me.'

'Well you'd better go ring shopping then.'

'What? Really? Fucking hell, Ben! Why does Christmas screw everything up?'

Braindead's head disappeared back inside the house. Ben blew on his fingers and waited for his friend to appear on the front lawn to hold the ladder so he could climb down. He heard the front door open, then slam shut. Thank goodness for that. He could finally get down and warm up.

He waited.

'Braindead!' he shouted.

But Braindead was gone.

Chapter Four

'So excited about being with you at Christmas, darling. Just wanted to tell you before I forget that Carlos has high cholesterol. Skype Friday? Mum xxx'

Katy sighed and put her phone back down on her desk. She would have to deal with her mother's boyfriend's dietary requirements later; she had work to do. She looked back at her computer and continued working her way through the sixty-eight emails in her inbox. Before she could respond to an irate client who hated the visuals that the agency had produced for a poster campaign, the door to her office flew open. 'I've got a meeting in five minutes,' she said without looking up.

Daniel walked in and shut the door behind him then sat down on the sofa along the back wall of Katy's office and put his feet up. Immaculately dressed, his pale grey trousers and soft pink shirt were completed by tidy salt 'n' pepper hair and a slightly smug smile.

'Did you hear what I just said?'

'Who are you meeting with?' asked Daniel, the smile growing over his face as he made no signs of vacating her office.

Katy sighed. She loved Daniel. He was her closest friend and ally at the Butler & Calder Advertising Agency, but he also drove her crackers.

She clicked on to the calendar on her screen and searched out the name of her next appointment.

'He's a potential new German client, which is a bit strange to be honest. I'm hoping it won't take long.'

'Oh, what's his name?' asked Daniel.

'It's…' Katy hesitated. 'It looks like Wunorse Openslae.'

Daniel nodded. 'Really?' A big grin now spread across his face. 'What did you say his name was again?'

'Wunorse Openslae,' replied Katy. Daniel was laughing properly now, and she had no idea why. 'What's so funny?'

'Guten Tag,' said Daniel, leaping off the sofa and bending forward to shake Katy's hand while speaking in a very bad foreign accent from nowhere identifiable. 'So good to meet you. My name is Wunorse Openslae, ya? As in Jingle Bells, ya? Oh what fun it is to ride in a Wunorse Openslae. Or so all the boys say, ya?' Daniel collapsed back down on the sofa in fits of laughter.

Katy waited for a few moments to decide if she was annoyed and decided that actually seeing the funny side of Daniel and his badly timed and inappropriate jokes was just easier.

'I thought it was weird that a client was coming from Germany. Should have known it was you.' She sighed then got up and joined him on the sofa.

'Well it's the only way of getting any time with you these days. You are so bloody important it's like getting an audience with the Queen!'

'We're here to work, Daniel.'

'I know, more's the pity. But I have come with two very important work issues to discuss.'

'Right,' said Katy, nodding. She assumed it was the state of the current campaign they were working on for a health-food brand. As creative director for the agency, Daniel had final say on any advertising concepts that were to be presented to a client. She'd heard he wasn't keen on the suggestion of Nigella Lawson to front the campaign, but she knew that the client really wanted her. She was going to have a tough time convincing Daniel but as head of account services, that was her job – mainly to keep the peace between him and their clients. She was all ready to tell him for the millionth time that the clients paid his wages, so they were allowed to have an opinion, when Daniel came out with a whole other work issue.

'So this year's Christmas tree in reception… I'm thinking a stack of tractor tyres, reducing in size to form the general shape of a Christmas tree, sprayed brilliant white with maybe just a hint, a smidgeon of glitter. Too much and the effect will be ruined. Thoughts?'

Katy looked at her watch. She didn't have time for this.

'Fine,' she said.

'Really?'

'Yes.'

'But where do I get the tractor tyres?'

'For God's sake, that's not my problem! If you want to vent your creative genius by building a Christmas tree out of tractor tyres, you'll have to do it yourself. Anything else?'

'You're no fun any more.'

'Just because I won't do the graft and find your tractor tyres while you take all the glory when it's finished. And I mean *all* the glory.'

'Fine, I'll do it without your help. Now what about the shambles that is the office Christmas party?'

'I can't even remember what we're supposed to be doing,' said Katy.

'You do – of course you do. Do you not read my emails headed, "Why the fuck are we going to Christmas Party Land?"'

'No, I delete them.'

'What if I'm saying something important?'

'I very much doubt you are.'

'But it makes me want to cry. Seriously. Have you read the information? It's like a big huge party thing with hundreds of *other* people.'

'Heaven forbid you mix with people outside of the advertising world.'

'I think it's my worst nightmare. The amount of synthetic fabrics, cheap aftershave and hairspray alone is enough to make me want to heave. And what's Luca going to think? For the first time in my entire life I have a boyfriend at Christmas. A proper, committed, live-in boyfriend at that. Did I mention that he's Italian?'

'Many, many times.'

'He's a sophisticated Italian. For his works party the firm is taking everyone to Paris for the weekend. Where do I get to take him? Some draughty conference hall in the middle of Leeds! He seriously could leave me because of this. I'm ashamed, Katy. Ashamed.'

'You are such a snob. You never know, you might enjoy it.'

'Enjoy it? Are you real? It's themed, Katy. Themed! You know even the mention of the word makes me come out in a rash. And not only is it themed, listen to this.' He got out his smartphone, tapped it and then started to read. 'This year the exciting sounds and rituals of Africa come to Christmas Party Land with its Zulu Sundance Extravaganza.' He paused with his mouth hanging open in awe. 'It's theme is Africa? What's *that* all about? What the hell has Africa got to do with Christmas? I just don't get it, and quite frankly, heads should roll for this.'

'Wasn't there a vote on what we should do and this came out top?'

'Exactly. Everyone who voted to celebrate Christmas sweating along with the masses to bongo drums should be sacked.'

'Well, you have to go. You know what Andrew said. Three-line whip on all management attending the Christmas party unless there are extenuating circumstances.'

'I might break my leg on purpose.'

'Go ahead,' replied Katy.

'Thanks,' said Daniel. 'You're supposed to be cheering me up. Quite frankly, the thought of this party is totally ruining my Christmas.'

'Well, join the club. My mum rang last week from Spain to tell me she's left Dad.'

'You are kidding me?'

'And she's moved in with her boyfriend, who's nearly ten years younger than her, and they're both coming over to spend Christmas with us. Dancing to bongo drums rather than Slade at the Christmas party is the least of my worries. Boom,' finished Katy, pretending to drop a mic at Daniel's feet.

Daniel stared at her for a moment.

'You do know that if they play Slade I could not, will not, over my dead body in fact, ever dance to that annoying mosquito of a song that crawls out of the woodwork every year,' he stated.

Katy considered punching him, but she decided to ignore his despair regarding Christmas music and continue to press on him her own festive woes.

'I'm dreading it,' she said, suddenly finding herself on the verge of tears. 'And I'm angry. She's never been that keen to spend Christmas with us before and now, just because she's got herself a new man, she wants to do the whole happy-family thing.'

'You could say no,' said Daniel.

'I've thought about it, believe me. But she's my mum and Millie's granny. I can't say we don't want her near us at Christmas. How mean would that be? And Millie thinks she's amazing. Must be the Smarties she drip-feeds her. We'll just have to grin and bear it.'

'And what about this guy she's met?'

Katy shrugged. 'We're doing a Skype with him on Friday so we can "meet" him before he infiltrates our home and our family.'

'Presumably he's already infiltrated your mum?'

'Daniel! Please don't say things like that. She's seventy-three.'

'And how old is…?'

'Carlos? Sixty-four apparently.'

'He's Spanish! She's pulled a Spanish guy at seventy-three? My God, that's impressive. I mean I know I managed it at twenty-three, one long hot summer in Madrid, but that only happened after I plied him with an enormous amount of sangria. How exactly did she do it? How pissed did she have to get him?'

'I don't know. I doubt alcohol was involved.'

'Alcohol is *always* involved, Katy. You find me someone who cannot attribute their relationship in some part to alcohol and I will find you a Brit who is able to communicate their emotions while sober.'

'Well, she tells me they met at church in the choir.'

Daniel narrowed his eyes as he processed this latest piece of information.

'It's a lovely story, really a lovely story. It will melt hearts during the best man's speech at their wedding, but I guarantee they first locked lips after one too many sherries, you ask her.'

'I'm not asking her.'

'Ask Carlos then. When you Skype him.'

'I can't ask him that.'

'You can. He's shagging your mother – you can ask him what the hell you like.'

'Daniel!'

'What? Pure companionship, is it? You believe that if you want to, and while you're at it, why don't you write to Santa Claus and ask him for a boob job. You look like you could do with a lift!'

Katy decided to ignore the insult. If she responded to every jibe Daniel threw at her she would never have time for anything else. 'I don't need to know about that side of their relationship,' she told him.

'Well, you soon will because they'll be doing it under your roof.'

Katy gasped. 'They wouldn't, would they?'

'Why not? It is Christmas after all. Aphrodisiacs a plenty. Champagne, Buck's Fizz, Terry's Chocolate Orange, you name it. That warm fuzzy glow you get from Christmas, well, it's enough to put anyone in the mood, isn't it?'

'She wouldn't dare.'

'She's in love.'

'This is way worse than I thought!' said Katy, getting up and pacing the room. 'What am I going to do? Poor Ben. He's already distraught that my family is going to ruin this perfect Christmas he's had lined up. He's so excited that we're finally in a house rather than the flat and that Millie is utterly hyper about Santa coming. I went home to find an inflatable glowing reindeer on the lawn on Friday.'

'Oh please. Tell me he isn't going down that route.'

'I'm afraid so, but only because he wants to make it all as exciting as possible for Millie. They both went out and fed it this morning.'

'Words escape me.'

'He was just really looking forward to us having a proper family Christmas in our proper house and now…'

'Your mother shagging upstairs will put a damper on it.'

'Just a bit.'

'Big surprise present on Christmas Day will cheer him up. What does he want?'

Katy stopped in her tracks and looked at Daniel.

'All he wants for Christmas is a baby,' she stated.

'Wow! Not much then. And you? Is that what you want for Christmas?'

Katy looked away, catching sight of the picture of Ben and Millie on her desk. 'I think so.'

'I think so? Not an overwhelmingly positive answer for such a big question.'

'No. I do want another baby, I really do. And I owe him one after all. An uncomplicated one. It was all such a mess when Millie was born. He missed out on all the excitement and the build-up, didn't he?'

'Well if you will sleep with your ex as well as your boyfriend when you could get pregnant, what do you expect?'

Katy sighed. 'You don't need to remind me, Daniel. I know it's all in the past, but I feel like it would really put a seal on it. You know – if we had another child. I owe him that.'

'What's all this owing business?' said Daniel, throwing his arms out in wonder. 'You shouldn't have a baby because you owe it to someone. I mean, a baby is for life and not just for Christmas, you know.'

Katy sighed again. 'I know. I do want another baby, but there's just a tiny niggle of doubt. But that's normal, right? I mean, we've just started to get our life back a bit. We've finally moved and Millie's getting more independent by the day. She's loving preschool, especially as her dad works there.' She paused. 'But the thought of going back to nappies again and night feeds, well, it's kind of terrifying,' she told him. 'But that must be how everyone feels. I'm surprised anyone goes through it again having done it once, aren't you?'

'Don't ask me,' replied Daniel. 'Reproduction is not one of my specialist subjects.'

'The thing is, last time I had no choice, did I? I got pregnant by accident so I had none of this deciding whether or not I really wanted a child, I just got on with it. Now I can decide, well, suddenly it feels like a huge responsibility.'

'Do you have to decide now?'

Katy nodded. 'We always talked about doing it once we moved, when we had the room, but that took so much longer than expected. And I'm forty and…'

'I know,' said Daniel, literally clapping his hands together in glee. 'It was the most fun watching you go through that.'

'Well, in reproduction terms I'm pushing it. I'm old to be having a baby already. It's now or never.'

'Fuck, this is heavy stuff! Can we go back to talking about the African-themed Christmas party?'

They were interrupted before Daniel got the chance to distract Katy from her trauma by listing all the possible reasons why the party was going to be a disaster.

'Ah, here you are,' said Andrew, the MD, striding in without knocking. 'I thought you were supposed to be in a meeting with Wunorse Openslae? I've been looking for you everywhere.'

Katy glanced at Daniel, who stuffed his hand in his mouth.

'He cancelled,' said Katy quickly. 'What did you need me for?'

'Well, I've just got off the phone with the MD of Boomerang Airlines, a man by the name of Cooper White. He's starting up a new budget airline in Australia. He's seen our work on easyfly.com and he wants to come and talk to us next week.'

'From Australia? Bit of a long way to come, isn't it?'

'Apparently he's over here on business and saw our campaign. Can you muster up a pitch document by next Monday?'

Katy gulped. There went her weekend.

'Is he seriously a potential client? We can't service a client in Australia, can we?' she asked hopefully.

'I think you'll find we can,' said Daniel, leaping up. 'Bondi Beach, here we come!' He raised his hands to his sides as though surfing. Andrew glared at him. 'I didn't just do that, did I?' he asked, sitting down again.

'He owns an airline,' Andrew continued. 'If he thinks we can handle a client on the other side of the world, who am I to argue? Just give him the talk, hey? No harm in that. We'll worry about how we manage it if we get the business. Oh, and just watch Daniel around him, will you? I've seen his picture on their website. He's very good-looking.'

'Rude!' exclaimed Daniel. 'I'm very happily settled with Luca, I'll have you know. He's Italian.'

Katy sighed. 'I suppose we could dig out the old pitch documents we used for easyfly.com,' she said, thinking of the enormous amount of work a pitch took. It wasn't as easy as Andrew made it sound.

'Good idea,' he said. 'Right, I'll leave you to it, shall I?'

'We were discussing Katy's mother's sex life and the gloom that is Christmas,' said Daniel.

Andrew nodded. 'Excellent. As you were.'

'What was his name?' asked Daniel, leaping up and taking a seat behind Katy's computer and starting to tap away at the keyboard as soon as Andrew had gone. 'Cooper, was it? Boomerang Airlines?'

'I don't care what his bloody name is. He just ruined my weekend. I can't believe Andrew landed a pitch on us just like that. And just before Christmas.'

But Daniel wasn't listening. 'Bloody hell,' he said, looking up at Katy seconds later. 'Will you just look at this fine specimen of a man? Neither of us would mind finding this one in our stockings, believe me.'

Chapter Five

Matthew hummed the Chris Rea classic 'Driving Home for Christmas' as he got out of his car and stepped towards the front door. It had just been on the radio, and it reminded him that it was one of his favourite festive songs. Whenever he heard it he pictured himself driving through the Canadian Rockies in a blizzard, dodging stray moose and countless obstacles in his efforts to get home to the bosom of his loving family for the festive season. He envisaged the perfectly decorated tree twinkling in the window like a beacon of light to welcome him. He pictured his wife waiting for him at the door as he drew up, the relief and joy written all over her face that he had made it home safe. Countless children would be running around the hall in excitement at the arrival of their adored Daddy. He would hug and kiss every single one of them as they all screamed his name – such was their happiness that they were all together. Then they would make him sit down in the rocking chair and all scrabble to sit on his knee and cuddle and kiss him and tell him all about how perfect it was to be in this family at Christmas time.

He put his key in the door, noticing the elegant wreath that had been placed underneath the knocker. He smiled to himself. Christmas was coming. He couldn't wait. With three-year-old twins, a two-year-old and another baby due, it was going to be heaven on earth.

Stepping into the hall he was greeted by Rebecca lying on the floor in just her pants, screaming at the top of her voice, while George, her twin brother, hit her repeatedly over the head with a potty.

'Stop it *now*, George!' shouted Matthew, grabbing the potty, which felt suspiciously damp. 'What are you doing to your sister?' George stared back at him, indignant, and then ran off. Matthew picked up the still-screaming Rebecca and carried her into the kitchen. There should be at least two other sensible adults in the house on hand to defuse the constant ticking time bomb that was their twins' relationship. There was no-one in the kitchen. He bounced Rebecca up and down, humming to try to soothe her as he re-entered the hallway. There he found Lena, the nanny, letting herself through the stair gate at the bottom of the stairs.

'Good evening, Lena,' said Matthew. He cleared his throat. Despite the fact she had been with them for nearly two years, and despite the fact he was very well aware that they couldn't live without her, he never got past the awkwardness of sharing their home with the hired help. He tried to avoid going all *Downton Abbey* and adopting a Hugh Bonneville, avuncular and yet commanding stance, but he was actually the only role model around to deal with this situation.

'Oh hi,' she said. 'Where are your clothes?' she cried on catching sight of the near-naked Rebecca.

'I found her like this as George was hitting her over the head with his potty,' Matthew explained.

'Oh my goodness,' gasped Lena, looking flustered. 'I just popped upstairs to see if Alison was OK and to check if Harry was still napping. I was only a minute, I swear.'

'No, no, it's fine, don't worry,' said Matthew, allowing Lena to take Rebecca out of his arms. 'Is Alison OK? Is there something wrong?'

'She came back from preschool in a terrible state. She was crying, wailing and bawling, but she won't tell me what's wrong.'

'It's OK,' said Matthew, seeing that Lena was also upset. 'I'll go up and see her – you look after the kids.'

He opened the stair gate and started heading upstairs. He could feel his heart beating a little too fast. Alison was just weeks away from giving birth to their fourth child. He still couldn't believe it, to be honest. He'd never expected to have such a brood – especially given they'd had such problems conceiving the twins. Several rounds of IVF had finally produced two healthy children, a blessing they didn't expect to be repeated. After that they could enjoy sex just for the fun of it, following so many years of disappointment when it didn't result in babies.

But then one day Alison was sick. In the morning. Just like that. She'd blamed the prawns she suspected she'd left out to defrost for too long. Then she was sick again the next morning. She'd come out of the bathroom looking confused and hopeful. The doctors had warned her that women do get pregnant naturally after having had a baby via fertility treatment, but they had dismissed it as something that would never happen to them – they just weren't that lucky in the baby department. Getting George and Rebecca had been so hard-fought that to expect fate to turn round and hand over another baby, just like that, seemed a ridiculous notion.

They'd gone straight to the doctor, bypassing the chemist and a pregnancy test. There was no way they would trust an overpriced plastic stick with the news that a miracle had happened. They'd both wept when the doctor had confirmed their hopes.

Holding onto each other in bed that night, they'd whispered excitedly, unable to believe the extraordinary gift they had been given. It wasn't until the first scan that anxiety started to kick in. Seeing their baby up on screen and being talked through all the tests and procedures Alison would need to go through to monitor its health only reinforced how precious it was and how inconceivable it was that anything might go wrong. Matthew had resisted the need for a nanny, initially unwilling to share his home with a stranger, until he saw the sense of having someone to help look after Rebecca and George and take some of the workload away from Alison, who had so far thrived on being a stay-at-home mum.

Lena had been a special find. Originally from Lithuania and in her early thirties, she wasn't at all like the au pairs they had first considered. One look at the length of Catia from Portugal's skirt had confirmed to Alison that they needed a trained nanny, not a student on a gap year. Lena had been with her previous family for three years in London and was only seeking new employment as she didn't want to move with them to Dubai. She had fitted into the family brilliantly. Rebecca and George loved her, and her ever-present calmness soothed Alison. Well, normally it did. The miracle fourth baby had been perhaps even more of a shock than number three, but Alison had seemed to take it in her stride... Until now.

'What's wrong?' gasped Matthew, dashing towards the bed where Alison lay hunched over a box of tissues. He took her in his arms, and she let her head fall on to his shoulder. She started to shudder.

'Is the baby all right?' he asked. *Pray to God the baby's all right*, he thought.

'Yes, the baby's fine. It's not the baby – it's Rebecca and George,' sobbed Alison.

'What do you mean, Rebecca and George?' asked Matthew. 'They looked fine to me. Rebecca may be bruised a little on the head from the potty bashing, but I'm sure no real harm has been done.'

'Oh it has,' groaned Alison, pulling away and blowing her nose. 'We have to do something, Matthew. It's not just this Christmas that they've ruined, it's their whole future.'

'Because George hit Rebecca over the head with a potty?'

'No!' Alison sniffed again. 'No, the *Nativity*, Matthew.' She was looking cross now at his lack of understanding of this clearly very disturbing situation.

'The Nativity?' he asked tentatively.

'Donkeys, Matthew! The stupid woman has only cast them both as donkeys. What on earth was she thinking? I specifically told her that she must give them contrasting parts because they're twins, and it's imperative that their individual personalities are recognised and developed. How does casting them both as donkeys give them individual self-esteem?'

Matthew felt himself relax slightly. A Nativity casting crisis he could cope with. Probably.

'I was a donkey in the Nativity, I punched the second shepherd apparently. I got taken off the stage and sent home.'

'You'd think she'd have taken the hint, wouldn't you?' said Alison, totally ignoring him.

'Who?'

'Mrs Withers. When I said they needed contrasting parts you'd think she'd take the hint that *of course* they should be Mary and Joseph. Instead she's made Leah Mary. She has a lisp and her mother actually told me she was named after Princess Leah. I mean, how ridiculous. Brandon Eckington is Joseph. He headbutts my bump every day and his mum thinks that's funny.'

'Well I'm sure that Mrs Withers had very good reasons for casting them in the main parts. Maybe they have self-esteem issues as well and she wanted to give them a little limelight?' Matthew couldn't believe what he was saying. He really couldn't give a monkey's who played what in the preschool Nativity, but he did know that sometimes it was better to go with the general flow of Alison's thought processes, as this could lead to a conclusion far quicker. 'And besides, would you really want to see George and Rebecca cast as Mary and Joseph? Bit weird maybe, casting a brother and a sister. I know it was an immaculate conception but even so.'

'You see, this is the very problem I'm talking about, which only a mother of twins understands,' said Alison. 'So who do you choose? Does Rebecca get the part of Mary or does George get the part of Joseph? Go on – try it. Which twin gets a lead part and which gets to be a donkey? Go on, Matthew, if you're so clever, you choose!'

'Well,' said Matthew, getting up and loosening his tie to give himself a little time to think. 'Isn't the answer not to cast either of them in a lead part then?'

'No!' said Alison, thumping the top of the beautiful patchwork blanket that adorned their enormous bed. 'That sums up twins discrimination, doesn't it? So they both miss out just because they're twins. Neither of them gets to shine. That can't be right.'

Matthew walked over to the wardrobe to hang up his jacket and tie. Now he was confused. Alison made the Nativity sound so complicated. He wished he were back in the car pretending to be Chris Rea. He could feel himself start to panic. This was the type of conversation that could escalate into something big with Alison. Her pride and defensiveness over being a mother of twins was legendary. She quite rightly projected the notion that it made her special, but this often manifested itself in the idea that normal parenting rules did not apply; that she needed to rewrite the rule book, and as her husband that could make life quite difficult. He took a deep breath and said what he would say to a normal person if he were asked about this situation.

'I'm sure the teacher knows what she's doing. She can't cast everyone in the lead parts. I bet the kids don't care which part they get, and in any case it's part of life, isn't it? Learning to deal with disappointment and not letting it get you down. And after all it's *only* the Nativity play.'

As soon as he said the last line he knew he'd made a mistake. Up until then Alison had been looking at him in a weird kind of way, as though he really didn't understand what he was talking about but she was willing to forgive him, however the last line made her angry, he could tell. She swung her legs down on to the soft carpet and looked at the floor then took a deep breath before she let him have it.

'It is not *only* the Nativity,' she declared. 'It's *our* children's Nativity and the only one they'll ever be in. Do you seriously want your treasured memory of your firstborns' Nativity to be seeing them hidden under some ugly donkey head, barely able to tell them apart from the other children?'

'They'll get another chance surely? They're only three years old.'

'Well, you see that's where you're wrong. Next year they'll be in school, and the school doesn't do a proper Nativity, more a Christmas play with a moral. Because heaven forbid they might upset someone talking about Jesus at Christmas. God knows what horror lies before us then. They could both be dressing up as turkey twizzlers at this rate.'

Matthew could see that Alison was starting to get upset again. She had longed for her children so hard that she was determined that everything would be perfect for them. Matthew tried to keep her expectations realistic. Tried to stop her punishing herself when it all went tits up, as it inevitably did with three very young kids in the house, but it wasn't easy. Truth be told, to his mortification he often thought of

Ben in these situations. What would he say? How mad was that? Ben, who he'd never thought much of – particularly when they'd come to blows over Katy. He looked away in shame, scared the guilt was written all over his face. They had somehow managed to keep from Alison the stupid one-night stand that he and Katy had had, despite the chaos that had ensued when Ben found out. But he had to admit that the bizarre bonding of Ben and Alison following the birth of their children had had a very positive effect on his wife. Ben's willingness to see the funny side of everything had somehow calmed Alison down, making her so much easier to live with. It was a pity that Matthew and Katy's fraught history meant that there was no way Ben and Alison could stay friends. Still, sometimes he couldn't help wondering exactly what wisecrack Ben might be able to come out with to defuse a high-stress situation with Alison.

'Look, it's not the end of the world, is it?' said Matthew, praying the right words would come out of his mouth this time. 'They're happy, healthy kids, that's what matters. They'll get over being donkeys.'

'But what about George's anxiety issues? This won't help him at all.'

Matthew pictured George bashing Rebecca very unanxiously with the potty. But Alison had a point. Despite his rambunctiousness at home, once in the company of strangers George could be reduced to a quivering wreck. It had taken several weeks of delicate cajoling to get him used to his current preschool to the point where he didn't have to be prised away from his mother's or Lena's skirts every morning. Matthew, however, suspected that George would be delighted to be hidden behind a donkey mask, as there was no way he could picture him standing up in front of a room full of strangers to take centre stage as Joseph. In fact he suspected it could do him way more harm than good.

'Perhaps he'd prefer to be in the background?' suggested Matthew.

Alison looked at him in shock. 'In the background' was not part of her vocabulary.

'Well, I wouldn't,' announced Alison, sliding herself off the bed before closing her eyes in silent acknowledgement of her aching back. 'I'm off to see another preschool tomorrow.'

'What? You can't be serious. In your condition?'

'I'm not an invalid, Matthew. I think that's what Mrs Withers thinks, you know – just because I'm pregnant I won't stick up for my children. Well, we'll see about that. Nobody puts my babies in donkey costumes.'

'But you're about to give birth. You don't need this now.'

'My condition is irrelevant to this situation. Me having a fourth child shouldn't mean that my two eldest miss out on their rightful place in the Nativity.'

Oh God, I need to squash this, thought Matthew. She's going to drive herself completely mad. Christmas is coming. There's a new baby on the way; there are three kids already in the house. Another plate to spin was just bound to tip them over the edge.

'Maybe we should consider moving as well,' said Alison, walking over to the en suite.

'Excuse me?'

'Maybe we should think about moving house?'

Matthew glanced around the master bedroom that Alison had had redecorated maybe four months ago. The master bedroom in their five-bedroom executive home on one of the most exclusive estates in Leeds.

'Are you serious?'

'Of course I'm serious. We need to rethink our entire schooling plan, Matthew, and moving house might be the only option.' She turned and walked into the en suite, closing the door behind her.

Matthew sat down on the end of the bed and put his head in his hands. Alison had been fairly irrational in her last two pregnancies – but this? This was taking it to an epic scale. Moving house? Four kids, a nanny, house hunting, house selling… what the hell was she playing at? All he wanted was a nice calm family Christmas before they added another child to the fray. Was that too much to ask? He wished they'd never even invented the Nativity. Christmas would be a whole lot easier without it.

Chapter Six

'You want me to do the Nativity?' asked Ben, thinking he had misheard. He was glad he was sitting on a very low seat (actually a child's seat) at Millie's preschool or else he thought he might have fallen over. As it was his knees were somewhere up around his ears, and he was grateful that Mrs Allcock had a longish skirt on as child-sized chairs were not the most flattering to ladies in their fifties wearing short skirts.

'Are you sure, Mrs Allcock?' he asked his boss. She'd told him to call her Dorothy when the children were not around but one of his favourite things about working at the preschool was that he got to say 'Allcock' legitimately, many times a day. It made him smile every time. He knew it was extremely juvenile, but he couldn't help it. He'd shared this once with Katy, who'd given him such a disappointed look he'd never mentioned it again.

The kids had all just been let outside after a good fifteen-minute wrangle with coats and hats and scarves and the evil challenge of trying to get twenty-five pairs of uncooperative hands into twenty-five pairs of uncooperative mittens. There was just ten minutes of outdoor playtime left after this chaotic dance had been performed and then they would have to do it all in reverse. Ben had been looking forward to a swift cup of tea, but Mrs Allcock asked if they could have a quick chat. He should have known something was up. She never normally spoke to him like an adult, preferring to lump him in with the kids, and could often be heard yelling, 'Mr King, would you please put that child down!'

'There's nothing to be scared of, doing the Nativity,' she continued after her shock announcement. 'Especially given your previous experience.' She was smiling at him like someone who had just worked out a foolproof way to finally crack the code of how to enjoy Christmas: give some other poor idiot all the work to do. 'I think you'd do a great job,' she added.

Ben knew she didn't mean that. What she actually meant was, 'I've being doing the Nativity at this preschool for the past twenty years, and if I do another one I will quite frankly want to throw baby Jesus through the window, along with all the crying angels, the stupid wise men who won't do as they're told and the shepherds who throw up because of a bug they've all decided to pass round two days before the performance so half the cast have dropped like flies and the teachers are left to fill in the gaps.' Mrs Allcock clearly no longer wanted to pretend to be the angel Gabriel in a sea of three-year-olds.

'But I've not been here long,' protested Ben. 'I'm not sure I have the experience?' He had taken the post partly because he was bored sitting at home and needed something to do but also because he thought it would be an easy ride. Given his previous role as a PE teacher in a secondary school, gluing and painting with Millie and a bunch of her mates seemed like a doddle. But organising the Nativity? Now that was on another level entirely. That required thought and preparation. That hadn't been part of the plan.

'Nonsense! For someone as organised as you it will be a piece of Christmas cake.'

Now she's just taking the piss, thought Ben. *She's laughing at me all the way round the Christmas tree.*

'I'm really not sure it's me,' he said, frantically trying to think of a sure-fire way of saying no.

'You can make it you,' said Mrs Allcock. 'As long as the parents see the obvious bases covered. Mary, Joseph, the kings, some shepherds and an angel, that's the main thing.'

'What about Jesus?'

'Oh, you don't need to worry about him. Just make sure a baby doll wrapped in a cloth makes an appearance at some point. That's all you need to worry about. None of the parents are the slightest bit interested in Jesus. All they want is to see their child on stage under a bright star, dressed in something vaguely old and Middle Eastern. Ironic really, in this day and age. A tea towel on their head works wonders. Oh, and keep the animals to a minimum if you can. You can totally avoid any complaints if no-one's little treasure is hidden underneath the face of a camel.' She laughed to herself.

Ben scrutinised Mrs Allcock. He had seen this type of behaviour before. It was classic teacher-about-to-leave-their-school behaviour. All the hang-ups and worry about rules, and in particular worries about pleasing the dreaded parents, seem to go out the window.

'Look,' said Mrs Allcock, placing her hand on his arm. 'I've got scripts – well, I call them scripts but really it's just stage directions – and I've got songs. Just follow those. Or do it your way. Please yourself. I think you'll enjoy it. And here, I've got you something.' She reached behind her back and pulled out something made from green and red felt. 'I've worn this for over ten years during the Nativity – I thought it might suit you.' She handed it over and nodded to indicate he should try it on.

If he wasn't mistaken she suppressed a laugh when he pulled the pointy hat on to his head.

'Now you look the part,' she said. 'Shall we just call you Master Elf?' She patted his arm and smiled, clearly pleased with herself. She heaved herself up from the one-foot high chair and walked off towards the door that led to the outdoor play area. Conversation over. The Nativity was Ben's. He had twenty-five three-year-olds to shepherd through the birth of Christ and then perform in front of eager parents.

An unexpected gift at this time of year.

Chapter Seven

'Carlos can't get the Skype to work. Can you get Ben to call us?
Mum x'

'What time is it now?' Ben asked Katy.

'Five minutes after you last asked,' she replied. They were sitting next to each other on two kitchen chairs staring into the depths of Katy's laptop, waiting with bated breath for Rita and Carlos to Skype them from Spain. Ben had been on the phone for twenty minutes trying to explain how to turn the camera on, during which time Katy had felt the need to get changed and put on a smart top. The reason why was a mystery to her. Dressing up to meet her mother's new boyfriend via the internet felt all wrong, but she couldn't help herself. She felt the need to put her best foot forward, to impress, perhaps in the hope that it would signal that he needed to impress her too. That this wasn't a family with low standards and if he wanted to be a part of it, he'd better measure up.

'Oh, Millie, come back here,' said Katy as her daughter slipped off her knee for the fifth time. She had a vision that when the call arrived, the screen would flick on and there they would be: Katy, Ben and Millie, an image of the perfect family. Then maybe Carlos would realise what he was dealing with.

Ben sighed, slipping off his chair too. 'I'm getting myself a beer. You want a glass of wine?' he asked her.

'No!' She didn't want Carlos to think they were alcoholics. She didn't want him thinking he could come to their home and sit drinking all day. She wanted to tell Ben to wait until after the Skype to have a drink, but she didn't know how to ask him without sounding like a boring old woman.

She was just chasing Millie around the lounge when she heard the ringing coming from her laptop. 'Please, Millie, just come here a minute, will you?' she gasped, trying to get hold of Millie while she giggled uncontrollably. And so it was Ben who got to see the measure of Carlos first as he slung himself down in front of the screen and took a swig out of a bottle of Becks.

Katy walked back into the kitchen clutching Millie in her arms and could see Ben's face popping up from behind the screen. His eyes were wide and his mouth was hanging open. He glanced up at Katy with a look of astonishment on his face. She felt a hand grasp her heart. What had Ben seen? Why the look of shock? She started to panic and let Millie wriggle free again.

'Oh, here's Katy,' said Ben at the screen, waving at her wildly to come and take a look while leaving his chair to continue the chase after Millie. Katy couldn't take her eyes off him as she edged round the table. She creased her forehead, willing him to give her some indication, some preparation for what she was about to encounter, but he gave her nothing more than a small smile and a slight shake of his head. Contradictory and uninformative signals. She would have to go in blind.

She took a deep breath and sat down in front of the screen, automatically raising her hand in greeting.

'Hi,' she managed to splutter out as she tried to process the scene beaming live into their kitchen from the Costa del Sol.

'Oh there you are, Katy,' her mother cried in juddering Skype fashion. 'Here's Katy – look, Carlos. Say hello to Carlos, Katy.'

'Hello, Carlos,' Katy replied. Her hand was still in mid-air. She closed her mouth so it wasn't hanging open. She looked up at Ben as he walked back in the room – clearly he'd given up on pinning down Millie for her inaugural meeting with Carlos. Ben shook his head when he saw the look on Katy's face and then started to laugh. He went to the fridge and pulled out a bottle of wine, holding it up to silently ask if she would like a glass. She nodded vigorously.

'I have heard all about you from your mother,' Carlos was saying. 'And I am so happy to be meeting you at Christmas and share this very special time with you and your family.'

Katy still couldn't speak. Ben handed her the glass of wine and she took a very long gulp. He stood behind the computer screen out of sight of Carlos and Rita and scrabbled in a drawer until he found a tape measure and made a big show of silently measuring the width of the door frames and then shaking his head in despair.

'It is very kind of you to let me join you,' continued Carlos. 'I will of course come bearing gifts as well as some special Spanish delicacies to accompany your Christmas meal, which I understand you eat on Christmas Day in England?'

Katy managed to sputter out a very weak, 'Yes,' as she watched Ben walk over to the chalkboard on the kitchen wall where reminders of what food they needed were written. He picked up the chalk and wrote TURKEY x 1 then crossed the x 1 out and wrote x 3 instead.

'Ben cooks a marvellous Christmas dinner,' she could hear her mother say. 'You'll like Ben. He's a wonderful son-in-law.'

Ben beamed and polished his fingernails. Katy was tempted to stick two fingers up at him.

'I'm sure Ben would be happy to take you down to a proper English pub,' Rita told Carlos. Katy grinned at Ben and urged him to come round to her side of the screen to agree to take her mother's boyfriend down to his local.

'Absolutely,' Ben shouted without leaving his post. Instead he opened the oven door and stuck his head inside it. When he re-emerged he mouthed 'too small' to Katy.

'Have you been to England before?' Katy asked when the silence grew heavy. She had meant to be challenging, maybe even scathing of the position they had both put her in, but she was so awestruck that all of her searching questions had gone out of the window.

'Oh no,' said Carlos, shaking his head. 'Never at all.'

'Your English is very good,' said Katy.

Her mother beamed. 'Oh isn't it just.'

'Well, you don't spend thirty years running a bar in the Costa del Sol without getting good at English,' he replied. 'My first English words were "Please may I have a shandy?" but of course no-one asks for that now. It's more likely to be "Amigo! Bring me a bloody beer, pronto."' Carlos collapsed with laughter.

'And where is my granddaughter?' asked Rita. 'You must see her, Carlos. She is so gorgeous.'

'As gorgeous as you?' asked Carlos, gazing into Rita's eyes. Katy thought she might throw up. Ben scooped up a passing Millie and dangled her upside down in front of the screen.

'Hi, Granny,' screamed Millie, giggling her head off.

'Hello, darling,' replied Rita, waving frantically. 'This is my new friend, Carlos.'

Ben put Millie down on the floor so she could see properly. Millie stared at the screen.

'Hello, Millie,' said Carlos, waving cheerily.

Millie looked at Katy and then at Ben. Katy grabbed her glass and downed her wine.

'He's so big,' said Millie.

Katy wished she hadn't downed her wine so that she could busy herself downing her wine while she tried to come up with an answer. Fortunately Ben came to the rescue.

'Millie King, will you please stop saying that to everyone you meet,' he said, scooping her up and pulling her out of sight of the screen. 'It's very rude. You really upset the postman the other day.'

'I've never seen the...' Millie started to say, but Ben clamped his hand over her mouth and carried her into the living room where all that could be heard were squeals as she tried to break free. Katy was left alone again in front of the screen, trying hard not to let her jaw drop at the sight of the gigantic frame of Carlos next to her petit giggling mother. He must be at least six and a half feet tall, she figured, with a stocky broad build, whereas her birdlike mother barely skimmed five foot in heels. They reminded her of Arnold Schwarzenegger and Danny DeVito in *Twins*. An unlikely double act if ever you saw one – until you saw Carlos and Rita.

'She's at that tricky age,' explained Katy. 'Thinks it's funny to call everyone... weird things,' she trailed off, reaching for her wine glass and going to take a sip before she realised there was nothing in it.

'Well, he is a very fine specimen of a man, don't you think, Katy?' said Rita as she grasped hold of Carlos's forearm and squeezed it.

Katy couldn't bring herself to reply.

'I'm a very lucky girl,' she added.

Katy winced.

'So,' said Rita, leaning forward as if to scrutinise her daughter, 'clearly you have no good news for me then?'

'What do you mean?' She wondered if she could make a dash for the wine in the fridge and pretend they had lost reception for a moment.

'Well, I take the fact that you're drinking as evidence that you won't be announcing this Christmas that I'm to become a grandmother again.'

Katy was tempted to sneak her finger forward right now and cut her mother off.

'We've only just moved,' she replied. 'Give us a chance.'

'Well, don't leave it too long, that's all I can say. You're not getting any younger.' Katy watched in horror as Rita turned towards Carlos and loudly whispered, 'She's forty.'

'I heard that,' said Katy.

'Well you are, aren't you? You'll be past it if you aren't careful, and you wouldn't want Millie to be an only child.' Rita pulled Carlos's shoulder down so she could whisper right into his ear. 'Katy is an only child. Having a brother or a sister would have done her the world of good.'

'What's that supposed to mean?' said Katy indignantly.

'I'm just saying that being an only child isn't the best way to grow up, you know that. She's very focused on her career,' Rita said to Carlos, as though that was a major flaw in her character. 'She was lucky to find Ben.'

'Wasn't she just,' said Ben, bounding back in to grab another beer from the fridge. He brought the white wine over and poured Katy another glass. She smiled at him gratefully.

'I was just saying, Ben, that it's about time you made me a grandmother again. Katy will soon be past it. I know you won't, but she needs to get a move on.'

Ben glanced over at Katy and took her hand in his.

'We're on it, Rita, like a car bonnet. Fingers crossed it won't be long before there's good news.'

'Wonderful,' said Rita, clapping her hands. 'It would be great to think we'll be spending Christmas next year with the four of you.'

Katy and Ben looked at each other in horror. One Christmas was bad enough. She must remember to get her dad booked in for next Christmas. A strict rota system was clearly going to be the only way of avoiding her mother at least every other year. She and Ben simultaneously drank more alcohol.

'When are you actually coming then?' asked Ben, a slight strain in his voice.

'Oh, we haven't booked our flights yet,' said Carlos.

Katy and Ben squeezed each other's hands in the hope there could be a glimmer of a reprieve; that this plan was not in fact set in stone.

'We're going to tomorrow,' said Rita. 'But it will be probably be Christmas Eve. Carlos will have the bar open until then unless one of his sons can get here to open up for him.'

'Oh, you have children?' asked Katy.

'Yes,' nodded Carlos. 'Four sons and two daughters.'

'Wow,' said Katy. This was news.

'And are they all in Spain?'

'Five are, one is actually in England. Working in London. We hope to see him while we are over.'

Katy nodded. 'OK.' This was hopeful. Her mother might not be staying with them for the whole duration of her trip after all.

'I know,' said Rita, and Katy knew exactly what was coming even before she came out with it. She grabbed Ben's arm in panic. 'Why don't we invite him to yours for Christmas lunch?'

'We don't have the room, Mum,' Katy blurted out. *Especially if he has the same build as his father*, she thought.

'Oh, but he's on his own. He doesn't have family over there,' said Rita.

Great, thought Katy. This situation was just getting worse and worse.

'Hey, calm down, babe,' said Carlos.

Ben slid off his chair and resumed his position behind the screen. 'Babe?' he silently mouthed to Katy.

'He may have plans, and it is not fair to assume that your daughter can provide for him.'

Katy nodded. 'Exactly.' She was beginning to like Carlos. 'I mean, we only have one spare room.'

'You've only bought a three-bedroom house?' said her mother with a look of horror on her face.

'Yes.'

'Why?'

'Because that's all we could afford.'

'Oh. Well, that is a problem then. Of course myself and Carlos will need the spare room.'

Katy looked up at Ben. He was pretend gagging at the thought of his mother-in-law and Carlos in the spare room, which wasn't much help.

'Well, there's just the one single bed in there at the moment so we'll need to borrow another…'

'Oh no, no, no,' interrupted her mother. 'We will need at least a king-size bed.'

Ben stopped his pretend gagging motions and threw his hands up in the air. The room was barely big enough for two singles or a double, never mind a king-size.

'You cannot expect *this man* to sleep in a single bed,' added Rita. Katy winced. She wasn't sure if her mother was commenting on his size or his masculinity. She didn't want to dwell on it.

'We can't fit a king-size bed in that room, Mum, even if we could borrow one.'

'What about an inflatable?' asked Ben. 'I might be able to get hold of one of those.'

Katy looked back at Carlos and tried not to imagine him falling on to an inflatable bed while her mum ricocheted six foot in the air as he impacted.

'Don't be ridiculous, Katy,' Rita said. 'I'm seventy-three. You can't expect me to do that.'

I wasn't expecting you to be bringing home your enormous new boyfriend here for Christmas either, thought Katy. *So please cut me some slack.*

'We'll have to have your bed,' announced Rita.

'No, we cannot do that,' said Carlos. Katy really was warming to him.

'You won't mind, will you, Katy? It will only be for a few days, and it will mean we can get out of your way. Have our own space and leave you to have yours.'

Ben pretended to faint to the floor. Katy didn't know what to do. She felt trapped. It was Christmas, and it was a time of goodwill to all men, especially family – she couldn't say no, could she? She couldn't make her 73-year-old mother sleep on the floor at Christmas, could she? Did she have any choice other than to allow her mother to sleep in her bed with her enormous but seemingly nice new boyfriend?

'I think you've frozen,' came a voice. Katy could see her mother shaking her iPad as though it would defrost her. She remained absolutely still, hoping to convince her mother that she was actually frozen so they could put a temporary end to this torture. 'No, no, you're not moving,' Rita continued. 'We'll cut you off and try calling you back. Bye, bye, bye then.'

The screen went blank. Ben got up from his position on the floor. He dusted himself down and pressed the button that turned off the Skype.

'Let's just pray to God they don't shag in it,' he said. 'Or else we'll be needing a new bed for Christmas.'

Chapter Eight

Ben closed his eyes. He knew they'd been there way too long as this was now the third time he'd heard 'Rudolph the Red-Nosed Reindeer'. He'd also now seen at least four separate parties of toddlers form a line and parade around the room singing 'Happy Birthday' at the tops of their voices. But Millie was happy and not demanding his attention, so he'd gratefully read two Sunday papers, including the sports sections, while drinking two coffees that bore no resemblance to his usual injection of Starbucks but were a fraction of the price so he couldn't complain. He found himself humming along to the festive tune as he stared up at the confusion of exposed utility pipes and corrugated iron in the ceiling above. He had no idea that a stroke of genius was about to hit. If he had, he no doubt would have bought pen and paper.

Ben's eyes flew open. Reindeer Games! That was it! He looked around him as though the other parents gathered there would recognise that he had just been blasted with a lightning bolt. But they carried on chatting, eating cake and ignoring their children. He leapt up, needing to commit his plan to paper as soon as he could, and grabbed the nearest colouring-in sheet and a crayon and began to write. Suddenly being landed with the Nativity didn't seem so bad – as long as he could do it his way. That was what Mrs Allcock had said, right? The Reindeer Games – utter genius. Manhandling three-year-olds through festive-themed games would be a piece of cake surely? His ideas were just starting to flow on to paper when his mobile lit up with a message from Braindead.

WHERE R U?'
'AT SOFT PLAY.'
'WHAT'S THAT?'
'A KIND OF HELL.'
'I NEED TO TALK TO YOU ABOUT SOMETHING.'
'WHY DON'T YOU JOIN ME? YOU WOULD LOVE IT HERE.'
'OK.'
'WILL SEND ADDRESS.'

Excellent, thought Ben. He could run his genius plan by Braindead and they could stay for lunch. That would kill another couple of hours.

Twenty minutes later Braindead sauntered in, hands deep in his pockets, eyes gazing around him at the padded cells frequented by delirious children screaming at the tops of their voices.

'Is this what it feels like to be in a boy band?' he shouted over the din, taking a seat next to Ben on one of the worn, wipe-clean pleather sofas.

'Eh?'

'All this screaming… from children. Like being in a boy band?'

'Could be,' replied Ben. 'I think it's just what's known as being a parent.'

'Right,' said Braindead, nodding slowly. 'Listen, they wouldn't let me pay to get in. Is that right?'

'Yeah. You only pay for kids.'

'Oh. Does that mean I can't use any of this stuff?' he said, indicating the inflatable trampoline and the ball pit.

'Not really. Not on your own. You need to have a child with you.'

'Any child?'

'Well, preferably one you know. Or else you might get arrested.'

'Right, right,' said Braindead, taking off his coat, still looking utterly bewildered.

'Listen, do you fancy some food? I'm just about to order for me and Millie.'

Braindead took the plastic laminated menu from Ben and looked down the adult options decorated with childlike drawings of common fruits and vegetables. He looked back up at Ben, confused, then looked back down.

'What kind of menu is this?' he asked when he'd read it for the second time. 'Salad? Omelette? Quiche?'

'Mum food.' Ben shrugged. 'Kids' hangouts like this don't do real food. It's all low-carb, diet crap that women pick to make themselves feel like they've been healthy before piling on the mayonnaise and having a full-fat cappuccino for desert. I've seen them do it.'

'But where are the burgers?' exclaimed Braindead, horrified. 'You were right when you said this was some kind of hell.'

'Only on the kids' menu. It's OK to ply the kids with lard as long as you put some salad on the side, which of course they never touch. Their bins must be piled high every night with limp lettuce and cherry tomatoes covered in ketchup.'

'Tell you what, I'll have two kids' burger meals,' said Braindead, putting the menu on a table next to him as though it pained him to look at it any longer.

Ben stared at him. 'Sometimes you are an utter genius, Braindead. Why have I been suffering watery ham omelette all this time when I simply should have eaten a double kids' meal? Save our seat, I'll go and order. I'll be back in a minute.'

By the time Ben got back, Braindead was nowhere to be seen. He looked up at the brightly coloured apparatus and spotted him at the top of the highest slide with Millie. They both waved enthusiastically as Ben felt his heart leap into his mouth. Millie had never gone down that slide before. They launched themselves off simultaneously then landed laughing in a heap at the bottom before Millie dragged him off to do it again. Ben smiled to himself. He'd give him five minutes and then he knew Braindead would be begging Millie to free him from his slide-partner duties. Fifteen minutes later and Millie dumped Braindead for a small boy who dived into the ball pit with her.

'This is brilliant,' said Braindead, flopping down next to Ben. 'And it's free! I'm definitely coming again.'

'Please never come on your own,' said Ben, handing him a coffee. 'Coffee tastes shit by the way. But it's cheap.'

Braindead took a sip. 'So where's Katy?' he asked.

'Work,' replied Ben.

'On a Sunday?'

'Apparently the CEO of an Australian budget airline is coming in next week and they need to prepare a pitch for him to try to win the communications account.'

Braindead stared back at him blankly.

'Crocodile Dundee is coming from Oz and Katy needs to impress him so she keeps her job,' said Ben helpfully.

Braindead nodded. 'Hope he's not some kind of surfer dude, mate. You know them Aussies, hit your women over the head then carry them off into the outback.'

'I'm sure I have nothing to worry about. He's more likely to be some old guy who's been around the clock with leather for skin.'

Braindead nodded. 'Fair play. I was hoping Katy would be here though. I wanted to ask her something.'

'Like what?'

'You know, girl stuff.'

'Abby?'

'Yes?'

'You bought a ring yet then?'

'No,' replied Braindead. 'You were wrong there, you see. That's why I wanted to talk to Katy. Not sure I trust you and your in-depth knowledge of the woman's mind any more.'

'Why? What's happened? You haven't split up, have you?'

'No – well, I don't think so anyway. I'm not sure really. Women are so weird.'

'It's Christmas, I told you that. Sends them crazy. So what's happened?'

'So we went for a drink last night. I was driving because Abby wanted to go to The Joiners, you know that pub out in Inkleworth with the—'

'Fairy lights outside and the open fire and the mulled wine on tap,' interrupted Ben.

'Yeah, that's the one.'

'Festive, you see. Trying to get you in the mood.'

'Anyway so she has a few mulled wines and then she announces out of the blue that she's thinking of applying for a job in America.'

'Wow, just like that?'

'Yeah, no warning. Nothing.'

'What did you say?'

'I can't remember, to be honest. I think I was a bit in shock. I might have said the weather's nice over there or something. I didn't know what to say. What do you make of it?'

'She wants to get engaged,' said Ben flatly.

'No, she doesn't. Didn't you hear me? She wants to move away from me.'

'It's a threat, Braindead.'

'What do you mean, a threat?'

'What she's saying is, if you don't ask me to marry you, I'll leave the country.'

'If that's true then why the bloody hell doesn't she just say she wants to get married?'

'You'll just have to mind your language,' warned Ben when two ladies turned to give Braindead a stern stare. 'Kids present and all that.'

'Sorry,' he apologised to the two women. 'I just don't fucking understand women.'

'Shush,' said Ben, as they looked back horrified. 'So sorry,' he said to them. 'My friend is going through a tough time.' They nodded and turned away.

'Look,' said Ben, edging closer to him on the sofa. 'She's not said she wants to get married because she wants you to surprise her. She wants to see you down on one knee. She wants the full monty, Braindead.'

'I'm not stripping off!' he interrupted in horror.

'I don't mean that. She wants it to be your idea, not hers. She wants you to tell her not to go away but to stay here and marry you instead.'

Braindead stared at Ben, blinking. 'How do you know all this stuff? You never used to know about this kind of thing.'

He shrugged. 'I've been with living with Katy for nearly four years now. I watch a lot of reality TV, you pick things up.'

'So she doesn't actually want to leave me then?' Braindead asked.

'No,' said Ben. 'Ask Katy if you want but I'm sure. The last thing she wants to do is leave you. What she wants is to stay with you forever.'

Braindead continued to stare at him then to Ben's utter amazement a silent tear slid down his cheek before he heaved and fell on to Ben's shoulder.

'I thought she was going to leave me,' he sobbed while the two women behind them stared. Ben patted his back in shock. In the thirty years he had known him, Ben had never seen him like this. Ever.

'I think you're ready,' said Ben, struggling to hold the tears back himself. 'Merry Christmas, mate.'

🎄

'I'm not going to say what time do you call this, but what time do you call this?' Ben asked when Katy finally walked through the door after ten that evening. 'You been trying to import kangaroos for this bloke or something?'

'Feels like it,' said Katy, sinking down on the sofa next to him. 'I'm so sorry. Andrew didn't like the initial concepts the creatives presented so I had to rebrief and wait until they'd had another crack at it. We're getting there though. It will all be over after Wednesday and normal service will be resumed. Promise.' She bent over and planted a kiss on his cheek. 'So what kind of day have you had? Did you go to soft play?'

'Oh yes, a new all-time record. Four hours we managed. Dropped a fortune at the café obviously, but Millie thought it was Christmas staying all that time.'

'I bet she did. You must have been bored out of your skull. I'm so sorry. Promise I'll take her next week. You go off and do something.'

'It was OK actually. Braindead came over.'

'To soft play?'

'Yeah, couldn't get him off the big slide.'

'I bet!' Katy laughed, kicking her shoes off and leaning her head on Ben's shoulder.

'He's getting married, by the way.'

'What!' exclaimed Katy, sitting bolt upright. 'Since when?'

'Well, he hasn't asked Abby yet but he's going to.'

'Are you serious? I never ever thought Braindead would be the type to get married.'

'Neither did he until today.'

'What do you mean? What happened today?'

'Well I think I should take some credit. I pointed out to him last week that there was no way he was getting away with a third Christmas without it resulting in a proposal and then he turns up today saying Abby's threatening to apply for a job abroad.'

'Really?' said Katy. 'Doesn't sound like Abby.'

'Exactly. She'd no more move away from within spitting distance of the make-up counter at Boots than I would from Elland Road.'

'Your football team is the main reason why you'd stay living in the UK?'

'That and warm beer and *Match of the Day*. Abby doesn't want a job overseas. It's a threat, I told him that. Put a ring on it or she's off. Probably not abroad, but it'll be the end of them.'

'Blimey.' Katy sighed, sinking back down on the sofa and putting her head back on his shoulder. 'And you think Braindead wants to propose then?'

'You know Braindead. He takes longer to process these things than most people, but he's getting his head round it. It's dawned on him that he doesn't want to be apart from her. He actually got really upset about it. I was about to mention the "L" word but I thought I'd save that until next time. Lead him there gently.'

'He'll think you mean lesbians.'

'Of course he will,' agreed Ben. 'I'm sure he'd much rather talk lesbians than love, but I'll get him there, slowly but surely. I'll have him engaged by Christmas if it kills me.'

'Oh, how romantic!' Katy sighed. 'A Christmas engagement.'

'Bit better than mine, eh?' said Ben. 'Eleventh-hour proposal in the labour ward. I didn't even have a ring, just a banana.'

'It was the most romantic banana anyone has ever given me,' she said, flinging an arm over him. 'I will never forget it. It was perfect.'

It so wasn't, thought Ben. 'I want to make sure Braindead does it right, you know, seeing as our engagement was… well, not the blissful moment it should have been.'

Ben felt a knot form in his stomach as he remembered his last-minute dash to the hospital to claim his daughter and his future bride. Finding out about her one-night stand with Matthew had sent him off in a sulk until he came to his senses, stormed the labour ward and booted Matthew out. Ben often thought about what would have happened if he hadn't got there in time; if he hadn't proved his love for Katy and watched his daughter being born. How he would have regretted that. How glad he was that he'd proposed and been there to greet Millie into the world – he just wished it had happened in a different way. The next time he was in a labour ward he intended the experience to be poles apart.

'So, er, how about we, er, go upstairs to bed,' he said, feeling himself blush. 'Carry on what your mum interrupted the other night,' he added. 'You know, that baby-making business.'

He waited for Katy to answer. She didn't.

'Shall we go to bed and have sex?' he asked, losing patience.

But Katy still didn't reply. Instead he heard the faintest snore as her arm fell unconsciously off his chest and on to the sofa.

Chapter Nine

'I should be in by ten, Ian,' Matthew said into thin air as he sat in his car and indicated right. 'Sorry, something urgent came up,' he added, glancing over at Alison, who didn't acknowledge the slight sarcasm in his tone.

Ian's voice crackled into the car from the speaker connected to Matthew's mobile. 'No worries, mate,' he said. 'I can cope with the splendid Lorraine from Splencor until you get in. In fact, it will be my pleasure.'

'I'm sure it will,' replied Matthew. 'Remember you're there to discuss their depreciation plan, won't you, and not to chat her up.'

'Don't worry, I'll show her some depreciation. Some *real* depreciation.'

Matthew could sense Alison bristling in the seat next to him.

'In fact I thought I might ask her to the Christmas do. What do you reckon? Do you think we're allowed to invite clients? Good corporate relations surely?'

'There is no way Lorraine would come with you to our Christmas do.'

'Why not?'

'Because she's not blind. Because she has taste. Because she'll have far better invites this Christmas than coming to her tax consultants' Christmas party at Christmas Party Land.'

'But what if I tell her about the Zulu Sundance thingy theme?'

'She definitely won't come then.'

'So who am I going to bring then? I can't come on my own, can I? I'll look like a proper loser.'

'Surely you can find a date on one of the umpteen websites you're on.'

Alison was tapping her fingers on her baby bump now. Matthew knew she didn't approve of Ian, his colleague for donkey's years, but she did tolerate him – as long as he kept Ian out of her way as much as possible. He suspected this was way more contact than she would like.

'I don't think so,' he said. 'All the women on there are of a temporary nature. You know, the kind of women you don't want to give any permanent encouragement to. Not the kind of women you'd introduce your colleagues to. Not the kind of women you'd want to be in public with.'

Alison turned to stare in disgust at Matthew.

'Doesn't Alison know any MILFs?' was the next comment that came crackling over the airwaves. Matthew saw Alison's jaw drop open out the corner of his eye.

'Alison is in the car with me now,' stated Matthew.

'Oh,' said Ian. 'I'm so sorry, I didn't realise. I'll ask her myself then. Do you know any MILFs, Alison?'

Matthew hastily turned the air conditioning up to avoid Alison overheating.

'Or MILs for that matter,' added Ian. 'Anyone presentable would do.'

'If you so much as go near any of my friends, Ian, I will castrate you,' was Alison's reply.

'Fair enough,' he replied cheerfully. 'No harm in asking.'

'Did you get my email with the new figures in it?' asked Matthew, keen to change the subject. While Matthew found Ian's love life at forty-plus entertaining, he could fully understand how Alison would not.

'They're in front of me now,' said Ian. 'I'll slot them into the document before Lorraine gets here.'

'If she's still there when I get back I'll put my head round the door,' said Matthew.

'You going for a check-up?' he asked.

'No.'

'Tour of the labour ward then? Surely you know your way around there by now? Got your own room yet?'

'Bye, Ian,' said Matthew pressing his finger on the end-call button.

♣

'Hello,' said a lady in her fifties coming towards them as they waited on two tiny chairs in a corridor full of photos of angelic-looking children beaming back at them. 'You must be Mr and Mrs Chesterman. I'm Mrs Allcock.'

'Oh Alison and Matthew please,' purred Alison, getting up to shake her hand.

'Hi.' Matthew nodded briskly. He couldn't even be bothered to smirk at her name. He was hoping to set the tone for the entire tour – short, to the point, conclusive. He really didn't have time for this. They followed Mrs Allcock down a corridor that smelt of disinfectant and learning into the preschool room. A riot of primary colours and terrible artwork greeted them. Rectangles of brightly coloured card stapled on to walls displaying wedges and drips of paint as a multitude of children concluded the more the better. Unidentifiable flying objects hung from the ceiling, causing Matthew to duck as he came in close contact with a one-eyed… thing. Letters and numbers dazzled from every corner as though trying to sink into the children's minds through pure osmosis.

Mrs Allcock took them on a slow and tedious tour around the large room as Alison peppered her with question after question regarding their curriculum and policies. He didn't know why she was bothering. They were three. Surely all that mattered was that they came here and had a good time and found some mates. Before any real work started in proper school.

Matthew tried to zone out, distracting himself with writing a mental to-do list for all he had to get done before the year-end. Occasionally he would be called upon for input, at which point he would pretend to have been closely studying a piece of work on the wall and be forced to ask them to repeat the question.

Eventually it looked like the torture was over as they appeared to be standing by the door again, having taken well over half an hour to walk round the twenty foot by fifteen foot room. He looked over at Mrs Allcock and he could see she was a little shell-shocked by the level of intensity from his wife. *You want to try being married to her*, he wanted to say as he caught Mrs Allcock tentatively looking at her watch.

'So that's us,' she eventually said, putting her hand on the door handle to escort them out.

'Can I be absolutely honest with you?' Alison asked, placing a hand on her arm to show her, and indeed Matthew, that this torture wasn't over yet.

'Of course,' replied Mrs Allcock, taking a step back to release herself.

'Well, I wanted to share with you that the reason we've taken Rebecca and George out of St Mary's is because of their inability to treat them as individuals rather than twins.'

'I can assure you we have had many sets of twins through this classroom and they are all treated exactly as we would treat every child in this room. As an individual.'

Matthew thought Alison was going to weep with joy or throw her arms round the woman.

'Well, that is music to my ears I must say…' Alison hesitated then pressed on. 'St Mary's were particularly unsympathetic when it came to the casting of the Nativity. Insisting they both perform as donkeys rather than being considered for the main parts. In particular they were ruled out of the lead parts, I feel, because they're twins.'

'Well,' said Mrs Allcock, 'I can assure you that whatever their part in the Nativity, they will have a marvellous time doing it with our male member of staff, who unfortunately is busy in the main school photocopying or else I would introduce you. We feel it is very important to have some positive male role models in the environment and our "Master Elf", as we like to call him, has just taken on the Nativity this year, and I have no doubt it will be splendid and your children will be splendid in it too. The children adore him.'

'Oh that's wonderful,' gasped Alison. 'Particularly for George. Isn't it, Matthew? George has anxiety issues,' she told Mrs Allcock. 'He struggles with strangers and needs bringing out of himself. It would do him a great deal of good to have a significant part in the Nativity. He really needs to be in an environment where his confidence is being built. Would you make sure that Master Elf understands that?'

'Of course,' replied Mrs Allcock, thrusting open the door and walking briskly down the hall as confirmation of the end of the tour. By the time Alison caught up with her she was slightly out of breath.

'But you will have a word with him, won't you? The Master Elf. Make sure he understands our concerns?'

'Of course,' said Mrs Allcock with a very false smile, holding the door open for them so she could chuck them out on to the street. 'I will make sure he is fully aware of you.'

'OK,' said Alison, looking moderately satisfied with the answer. 'So our nanny, Lena, will be dropping them off next week when they start. To avoid a tricky separation scene with their mother.'

'Of course, good thinking,' replied Mrs Allcock, looking relieved that Alison wouldn't be darkening her door again. 'Goodbye,' she said, shutting the door firmly behind them.

Alison didn't speak again until she was inside the car. Matthew knew she was mulling it all over. Deciding where to place her opinion. Matthew thought he'd better point her in the right direction for all their sakes.

'I liked the school, I liked Mrs Allcock and I really liked the sound of the Master Elf,' he said. 'It's perfect, Alison. Great choice. Well done you.'

'Let's just wait to see what parts they get in the Nativity, shall we,' replied Alison. 'They'd better be good or else I shall be straight back in here to have words with Mrs Allcock and the mysterious Master Elf.'

Chapter Ten

'Hi, Katy – Carlos says to ignore my previous message about his cholesterol. He doesn't worry about it over Christmas. You are registered with a local doctor aren't you? Mum xx'

Katy put her phone away and looked into the mirror of the men's toilet on the third floor of Butler & Calder. 'Why?' she said to her reflection as she wondered how she was going to get Daniel out of there and able to stand up in front of the CEO of Boomerang Airlines and string together a coherent sentence. As she looked down at the crumpled mess crouched down beside the waste-paper basket, she had no idea what on earth she was going to do with him.

'Why now?' he sobbed into his arm. 'Why leave me now? That's what I don't understand. Who ups and leaves just before Christmas? Why would he do that?' Daniel looked up at Katy, his eyes red raw. At this rate she would be lending him some eyeliner to hide that.

'Perhaps he just didn't want to buy you a Christmas present,' she said, trying to be helpful while sneaking a look at her watch. She had precisely twenty-two minutes to sort this mess out, and she always found she very quickly ran out of sympathy when under pressure.

'But it was going to be the most perfect Christmas,' moaned Daniel. 'We'd planned it all. He even promised to cook Christmas dinner.'

'You can come and eat with us – you won't be alone,' offered Katy, stepping forward and putting a tentative hand on his back. Daniel looked up at her as though she'd offered to stab his eyes with a turkey baster.

'And have turkey!' he said with a look of disgust on his face. 'Luca was going to cook me linguine.'

'Linguine? Not very festive.'

'Who cares about bloody festive? I would have had a hot Italian cooking me pasta in my kitchen on Christmas Day! Do you seriously think eating your turkey while your mum is having sex overhead in your bed with an oversized Spaniard is going to replace that?'

'That hurt,' said Katy. 'I cook a good turkey, and I asked you not to mention my mother. I need no reminders of what we're facing this Christmas.'

'What *you're* facing?' cried Daniel. 'That's nothing compared to what I will now have to endure. Alone after the love of my life has left me.'

'Last week you said you would throw him out if he didn't stop leaving out-of-date pesto in the fridge.'

'Oh, I never meant it,' wailed Daniel. 'Of course I didn't mean it. He should have understood that I was joking. He can leave his out-of-date pesto in my fridge any day of the week if he'll just come home in time for Christmas.' Daniel's eyes suddenly flashed wide. 'Perhaps that's it. Maybe this is all a plan. Maybe he's planning a glorious Christmas Eve homecoming when he'll fall into my arms and vow to stay with me forever.' He looked at Katy expectantly.

'Does he owe you rent?' she asked.

'Yes.'

'He isn't coming back,' she said firmly.

'You are harsh,' he said, pulling himself up. 'Wouldn't hurt to just indulge me in a little Christmas fantasy in my hour of need.'

'A fantasy that isn't going to happen. Now put your face under that tap. Cooper White will be here any minute. You can't waste all the hours we've put in on this pitch just because you got dumped at Christmas.'

'Do you need to be so blunt? I am emotionally bruised right now.'

'Oh, grow up, Daniel. Pull yourself together. Do you want Cooper White to see you as the crushed ex-boyfriend of a pasta maker or as an award-winning creative director who has some seriously shit-hot ideas to share?'

'Shit hot?'

'Yeah, what about it?'

'Nobody says shit hot any more! Seriously, Katy, you need to keep up with the times.'

Katy straightened his tie and brushed some fluff off his shoulder. 'You're better. Heart mended. Now get out there and kick the shit out of this pitch.'

'Good God, Katy, you're like a dinosaur.' He looked in the mirror and pouted. 'Let's go and do a seriously sick presentation to this dude.'

🌲

It was clear twenty minutes later, when everyone was settled in the conference room and Andrew had delivered Cooper White to the head of the table, that Daniel's heart had most definitely mended. Katy watched him smooth down his hair and yes, lick his finger and smooth down his eyebrows when the tall, muscular, tanned figure of Cooper White took his seat. Katy fully understood Daniel's response, though she wouldn't go so far as to preen her eyebrows. It had to be said that Cooper White was the type of man who you took one look at and wished you were better looking.

His forget-me-knot-blue linen suit brought out the colour of his eyes, and the blonde of his hair contrasted beautifully against his healthy outdoorsy tan. But it was his smile that was the most dazzling thing about him: wide and open and warm. He went round and shook every person's hand heartily and looked you in the eye when you told him your name like he was going to remember it and it was the most beautiful name he had ever heard. Sally, the account exec who worked for Katy, was drooling almost as much as Daniel. They both sat with vacant expressions on their faces as they fantasised about a cosy Christmas spent next to a roaring fire in the company of the big, strapping, dazzling specimen of a man that was Cooper White. Even his name was dazzling.

The entire room sat in awe of this glowing man who had landed in the middle of the pasty-white bunch of British natives who fed on his sun-kissed skin like it was nectar. Andrew cleared his throat as though he was about to say a few words of welcome to the Adonis sitting at the head of the table, but Cooper interrupted and took centre stage all by himself.

'I just want to say that I'm so happy to be here, and thank you all for taking the time out of what must be very busy Christmas schedules to talk me through what you do at very short notice. I don't know whether Andrew told you, but I flew in from Sydney last week, and I happened to catch some of your work on the TV and had my assistant track you down. You are clearly extremely talented, and I just had to come and meet you for myself.' His beaming smile travelled around the room like a spotlight. 'My aim is to make Boomerang Airlines arrive into our customers' consciousness with a bang. I'm hoping that the people in this room can help me do that. And given what I've already seen, I think my hunch just may have been right.'

If Katy wasn't mistaken, he looked right at her when he said that. Not just a passing glance – a very clear, confident stare. She tried not to blush but it was hard when the best-looking man who had ever walked into the agency was staring you down. She looked over at Daniel, but he had a look on his face akin to a lovesick puppy and was clearly oblivious to anything going on around him.

'Well, we're very glad to have you here,' said Andrew, the Australian dollar signs lighting up his eyes. 'When a company as exciting as Boomerang comes along, we're very happy to turn our creative juices on and see where we could take it. The team here have really enjoyed getting to grips with the essence of the brand and the market in which it will operate, and we're delighted to share with you some initial thoughts on how we would approach the account should we be appointed lead agency. Now, as I've already taken you through the background of the agency over lunch, I'll hand over to Katy, who will kick off the presentation.'

'Oh good,' said Cooper, leaning forward expectantly. Katy felt herself blush again and had to have a quiet word with herself as she walked to stand in front of the large screen bearing the Boomerang logo. She told herself to grow up. She was forty and happily married. This was not the time or the place to have a teenage crush. She needed to get a grip and nail this presentation just as she would if the client sitting there listening was naked, which was how she often imagined them to avoid any nerves. It didn't work with Cooper, however, as imagining him naked made her feel hot and bothered rather than in control. She took a breath and instead pictured him as a small elf sitting on the table. Much better. She was back and doing what she did best. Convincing clients that Butler & Calder was the best advertising agency in the world.

Katy waited for silence in the room to build the anticipation and then picked an old-fashioned-looking book up off the table in front of her and flicked to a pre-marked page. She looked Cooper White (aka Christmas elf) straight in the eye and started to speak.

'Twenty years from now you will be more disappointed by the things you didn't do than by the ones you did do. So throw off the bowlines. Sail away from the safe harbour. Catch the trade winds in your sails. Explore. Dream. Discover.'

She said it slowly and intensely and never dropped his gaze.

'Very wise words,' said Cooper when she paused at the end.

'Indeed,' replied Katy. 'The very wise words of Mark Twain, in fact, written over one hundred years ago but never more relevant than now in this time-poor world that we live in. We are often too busy, too distracted, too exhausted to make sure that we don't end up disappointed by the things we didn't do. The trips we didn't take, the places we didn't explore, the friends and family we didn't see.'

Katy paused again for dramatic effect and to make sure she had everyone's attention. She turned to face the screen momentarily and clicked a remote control to change the image to several photographs of people enjoying great times with loved ones in various locations around Australia.

She turned back to face her audience.

'We aim to position Boomerang as the domestic low-cost airline in Australia that is there to make sure Australians and visitors to your great country do not end up disappointed by the things they didn't do.' As she said this even more images appeared on screen of people having a great time in some of the more obvious landmarks – Sydney Harbour Bridge, the Great Barrier Reef and Uluru. 'That they catch the trade winds. That they explore, dream and discover right here in this amazing, diverse and stunning country.'

Cooper White's eyes were wide open now, and he was leaning even further forward, drinking in every word. Katy looked over at Andrew, who gave her a discreet thumbs up. She let a few more pictures scroll through and once she thought the core of the idea had settled in she clicked on to the next screen and got down to the real business of what they would do to launch Boomerang Airlines in Australia.

≛

Forty minutes later, after Michelle from the insight department had shared her wisdom on demographics and customer attitudes and Daniel had flamboyantly eulogised about the creative team's ideas for TV advertising, billboards and social-media campaigns, Katy took to the floor again to wrap up and propose how the account could be managed from the UK using the latest in video-conferencing technology.

'Strong account management will be key if we win this account,' said Katy. 'The time difference and distance will of course present difficulties in communication. However, none of this is insurmountable with the right account-management personnel in place who have a close relationship with your brand and communications team. We can work together to ensure there is no disadvantage to being on opposite sides of the world. As head of account services here, I am confident we have the people and systems in place to ensure smooth running of the business and that you should not be at all concerned about geography when you pick your lead advertising agency. What you should be concerned about is sourcing the right ideas and creativity, and I hope, with what we've shown you today, that we have left you in no doubt of where you can find that. Thank you.' She sat down then asked Cooper White if he would like to ask her or anyone on the team any questions. There was a long pause as Cooper leaned back in his chair, surveying the room. A small smile played on the edges on his lips, which Katy took to be a good sign. He had listened intently throughout and thrown in the odd question, but apart from that it was hard to tell if he had heard what he wanted to hear.

He drew in his breath sharply then suddenly leaned forward.

'I love your take on the positioning of the airline. Some Australians are guilty of apathy when it comes to exploring their own country, and if we can position ourselves as the antidote to that, as the way by which you can avoid disappointment because of the things you didn't do and the places you didn't see, I can really see that having legs. I like the sound of it.'

He stared down at the floor through his legs then suddenly raised his head as though he had come to some kind of decision.

'Unfortunately we are yet to recruit a brand director. I had one lined up and then he dropped out to go and work for a confectionery company in the States, would you believe? I have headhunters on high alert, and we're about to interview two new candidates on my return to Australia, but we are committed to a launch date. Every day my airplanes aren't flying I'm losing money. Hence why I'm starting to see brand and advertising agencies myself to get the ball rolling.' He shook his head and Katy felt a compulsion to go over and give him a hug. Clearly launching your own airline was no bowl of cherries, even if you were a six-foot hunk of a multimillionaire.

'So you can understand my concern over account handling,' he continued. 'We may be launching without a brand director so the agency may have to fly solo for a while. And what with that and our relative locations—'

'Cooper,' said Andrew, interrupting, 'I can assure you that you're in safe hands with Katy. Her years of experience have made her extremely resourceful. She's used to dealing with brand managers fresh out of university who, quite frankly, can be less useful than having no brand manager. I can reassure you that the absence of a brand director is something we'll be able to deal with. Katy will make it work.'

'Mmm,' said Cooper, nodding but still looking concerned. The slightly cocky swagger had gone as the realisation of the mountain he had to climb came crashing down. He coughed. 'I would like to discuss it further,' he announced, sitting upright in his chair and looking at Andrew.

'Of course we can…' started Andrew.

'Would you be free for dinner tonight, Katy?' he said, swinging round to face her. 'Unfortunately I fly later this week and I'm only free today. But given the tremendous work I've seen, I really do believe this is the right agency, but I need to be sure that you can handle it given our circumstances. I would be most grateful if you could join me tonight so we can discuss how exactly the account can be managed.'

Katy was sure she'd heard a gasp. Probably from Daniel – appalled she had been invited out to dinner by Cooper White and not him.

'Of course she can, can't you?' said Andrew, glaring at her. 'I'm free of course as well,' he continued. 'For any reassurance you may need.'

'Oh no,' said Cooper. 'I've taken up enough of your time already. And I want to hear it direct from the horse's mouth as it were. From the people who will be on the ground dealing with the account. As long as that's OK with you, Katy. I mean, if you already have plans…'

Katy thought about the buying of the Christmas tree that would have to be put off but could see Andrew still glaring at her.

'No, of course I can come,' she said. She suppressed a yelp as Daniel kicked her, clearly expecting her to suggest that he accompany them. But she kept quiet. She didn't need Daniel droning on. A brief dinner and then she could be home and that would be that. No big deal.

Chapter Eleven

'Katy – Carlos is also diabetic but don't let that worry you. It just means we must eat early on Christmas Day so we keep his blood-sugar levels up. Shall we say lunch at noon? Bye for now. Mum xx'

How nice it must be to have nothing else to worry about other than what time Christmas lunch will be served, thought Katy when she picked up her phone to call Ben. She sighed. How on earth was she going to break it to Ben that not only were her mother and Carlos taking over their bed this festive season but they would also like to dictate what time they ate. She knew Ben would want to spend all morning slobbing around in pyjamas and playing with Millie's toys then have a late, long lunch before they all collapsed onto the sofa to watch rubbish telly. She would tell him about the proposed new timetable another time. For now she would just concentrate on informing him that she had been asked out to dinner by an attractive Australian millionaire.

'I thought you said no more late nights?' said Ben when she explained, though she held back on describing Cooper's appearance and wealth, choosing to refer to him as a pain-in-the-arse client whom she had to schmooze in order to secure the business. The trouble was that when she said it, she didn't know what version she believed. And when she pushed open the door of the restaurant later on, having left straight from work, it was clear that her heart believed the first version, given the rate at which it was pounding as she approached the table where Cooper was already waiting for her. *This is not a date*, she told herself. *Just pull yourself together. You have a job to do.*

She still had Andrew's words ringing in her ears. 'This could be huge, Katy,' he'd said when she'd popped her head into his office before she left. 'You know the drill. Promise him whatever he wants. This could be our ticket into the big time. Another airline, Katy! Just go dazzle him.'

She'd not said anything as she walked away. Talk about pressure. She'd decided to walk to the restaurant. Get her head together. Work out the key points she needed to get across. Get her head into his mindset and work out how best to allay his fears. The trouble was that every time she thought about Cooper, she felt a bit funny, which was highly distracting and wrong on so many levels.

'Give him one for me,' Daniel had shouted as Katy passed his door, obviously still smarting from the fact she'd not insisted she take him with her. She'd tried to make him understand that not every pitch was won off the back of the creative, but he'd told her she was being ridiculous and had sulked all afternoon.

Cooper had picked an Indian restaurant, explaining that he'd been told that Leeds was the home of some fantastic Indian food and he always liked to try local specialities when he travelled.

He was studying the menu as she approached the table but immediately stood up the moment he sensed her presence and rushed round to hold the chair back for her. The restaurant was mostly empty as It was only six-thirty, and as Katy explained to him, the tradition in Leeds was to eat curry late, after a skinful of beer.

'Well, we can do that,' he said. 'If that's the tradition.'

'No, no,' she said. 'Too much beer ruins a good curry – believe me. Eat it and enjoy it sober.'

He laughed and their eyes met. She looked away quickly, embarrassed, and pretended to study the cracker that was sitting in her place setting.

'Shall we?' he asked, offering her the other end of his own cracker. 'I haven't pulled one of these for a long time. And never while eating curry.'

'Seriously?' she said. 'You don't go out for a curry at Christmas purely to pull a cracker?'

'Funnily enough no. I've never done the curry and cracker Christmas combo.'

He'd taken off his jacket and the white of his shirt was almost as dazzling as his smile. She'd have to put shades on in a minute, she thought.

'Well, we'd better start as we mean to go on then,' said Katy, holding up her own cracker.

'After three,' he said, grasping hold of the other end. 'One, two, three.'

The crackers were of the slightly limp variety that came apart with a weak bang and left you holding in your hands a lot more than dropped out on to the table.

'A fortune-telling fish,' cried Cooper, picking something up from the floor. 'I'd forgotten all about these.'

She watched as he pulled the fish shape cut from red translucent plastic paper out of the packet and held it up in front of his face.

'I had no idea they still did these,' he said as if he'd rediscovered some treasured toy from his childhood. 'Hold your hand out,' he demanded.

'What?'

'Hold your hand out,' he said again. She tentatively raised her hand as he grasped it then laid the red fish in her palm. She stared at their two hands together and the wriggling, squirming fish on her skin. This was not how she had expected the evening to begin. Hand in hand inspecting a curling piece of plastic paper.

'Very interesting,' he said as he studied the chart on the packet, which told you what the movement of the fish indicated.

'What? What does it say?' she asked.

'Well, it says if it curls right up, and I think you'd agree that it's curled right up, that you are passionate.'

'Oh,' she said, pulling her hand away quickly. She could feel herself start to blush. 'I don't think it's entirely curled up,' she added, pretending to scrutinise the fish. 'It's more sort of waving its head and its tail about.'

'Well, according to this, that means you're in love.'

'Oh,' she said again, feeling herself blush even harder. She really had to stop this. She *was* in love. With her husband and her child at home. How could the company of an attractive man be sending her to mush? This wasn't on. She had to get back into professional mode. They may be out for a meal but this was still a business meeting where she had a job to do, and that was what she needed to focus on, not the stupid predictions of a red fish.

'Here, I want a try,' Cooper said, reaching over and taking the fish before she had a chance to steer the conversation back to work. She picked up the menu and pretended to study it while Cooper continued his fascination with the fortune-telling fish. After a few moments he put it down and picked up his own menu without saying anything.

'So?' she asked. She couldn't resist it. 'What did the fish say?'

He frowned. 'It said I'm false.'

'Oh. Are you?' she asked.

'Certainly not,' he said. He took a swig of his beer, not taking his eyes off Katy as a waiter somewhere clearly decided that ambience was required and turned on a Christmas-hits CD.

He put the drink down.

'In fact I pride myself on being honest and true.'

'Right.' Katy nodded, though she wasn't listening. She was mentally recalling the bullet points she'd come up with that she felt were key messages to get over to Cooper during dinner. She wanted to press upon him their previous experience with overseas accounts, the account-management structure she would put in place and her ideas for how they would build a relationship with his team on the other side of the world. She'd even put in a call to a friend from school who had emigrated to Australia ten years ago to talk about any cultural differences.

'Come and work for me,' said Cooper just as Katy was forming her opening sentence.

'What?' she replied, thinking she'd misheard over the din of Wizzard's 'I Wish It Could Be Christmas Everyday'. 'Sorry, what did you say?'

'I said come and work for me. Come and be my brand director. You are exactly what I've been looking for.' He held her gaze firm. He actually looked like he was serious.

'Are you kidding me?' she spluttered. She'd spent all afternoon preparing to wow him about Butler & Calder and now he'd thrown her this curveball.

'No,' he said, shaking his head. 'I'm deadly serious. You are exactly what I've been looking for. In fact, you're better than what I've been looking for. For the first time in months I'm pleased we haven't found a brand director. You get it, Katy. You understand my vision, and we'd never even met before you stood up and blew me away this afternoon.'

'But… what… was that some kind of interview this afternoon?'

'No, no, no,' said Cooper, shaking his head vigorously. 'I'm not that calculating, seriously. I genuinely wanted to see the agency. I wasn't expecting to meet my new brand director.'

'Just slow down,' said Katy, struggling to keep up. 'I thought I was here to talk you into using the agency.'

'Well, you are, sort of,' he replied. 'But to be perfectly honest the easiest way to talk me into using the agency is if you agree to come and work for me.'

Katy thought her head might explode. She couldn't understand what was going on.

'Are you telling me that if I don't come and work for you then Butler & Calder don't get the business?'

'No, not at all,' replied Cooper. 'I'm just saying that if you come it's a done deal. As brand director you'd want to work with your agency, right? All the problems of being on the opposite side of the world would disappear. You know everyone so the relationship is already tight. I can't guarantee that if I appoint another brand director that Butler & Calder will necessarily be the obvious choice to them. But to be perfectly honest this isn't about the agency. This is about you. I'm asking you to come and be Boomerang Airlines brand director. I think you'd be brilliant at it. And I'd start sleeping at night again.'

Katy couldn't speak. She didn't think she had ever been so shocked by anything in her life – apart from when she found out she was pregnant with Millie maybe.

'I pay well,' continued Cooper. 'And we could find you a rental property until you get on your feet. Maybe on the beachfront.'

Australia, thought Katy. Her head was spinning so fast she'd barely taken in that the job would obviously be in Australia. Australia!

'What does your husband do?' asked Cooper suddenly.

'How do you know I'm married?'

'Wedding ring,' said Cooper, nodding at her hand.

Inexplicably Katy felt her heart sink slightly. Had he known all along she was married? Was he just being nice to her because he saw her as a potential employee rather than because he fancied her? God, she was getting old.

'He's a stay-at-home dad as well as working at our daughter's preschool.'

'Perfect!' cried Cooper. 'So no real ties then. I was worried you might be married to a high flyer who wouldn't want to leave his job. Or worse that you had children in high school.'

Katy felt stung by his writing off of Ben's commitments and by the assumption that she could be old enough to have teenaged children.

'If I may say, it sounds as though you have good circumstances for taking up an opportunity to live and work overseas. It sounds like the timing could be perfect.'

It could, thought Katy, *if it weren't for one thing.*

'When would you want me to start?' she asked tentatively. She saw his face flicker slightly as he smelt victory.

'As soon as you could. After Christmas would be ideal. Of course, it would also depend on Andrew, but if the Boomerang account was secured I think he might be a little more flexible on your notice period, don't you?'

Katy said nothing, just played with her knife, trying to get her thoughts in order.

'I'll fly you over there for Christmas,' said Cooper. 'You and the family. See if you like it.'

'I can't do that,' she said. She could picture the astonishing array of fairy lights and inflatables that now adorned their home. Ben's excitement at their first Christmas in their proper house and the three stockings that he had so proudly hung on the mantelpiece. She could also picture the fourth stocking he'd bought. The one for the baby he wanted to be with them by next Christmas.

'Why not?'

'We have plans for Christmas,' she said. She could hardly tell him that the plan was to make a baby and she had no idea how that plan might fit in with this new plan of taking up the job of a lifetime. She needed time to figure that one out.

'You don't like being told what to do, do you?' said Cooper, leaning back in his chair.

'No, not really,' she admitted defiantly. He was rushing her. She needed time to process this.

'Can I just share with you something a very wise person once said to me?' asked Cooper.

Katy nodded, feeling numb.

'She said, "*Twenty years from now you will be more disappointed by the things you didn't do than by the ones you did do. So throw off the bowlines. Sail away from the safe harbour. Catch the trade winds in your sails. Explore. Dream. Discover.*"' Cooper looked into her eyes the whole time and never faltered. Repeating the lines back to her, word perfect.

Katy stared at him. It was an old trick of hers to throw quotes from great literary heroes into pitches. She knew it gave a much-needed intellectual air to what they were presenting. It made it sound like what they did was a serious and important matter not just about trying to help flog more stuff. Typically the client would smile back at her knowingly as if to say that he or she was familiar with all the great classics and how smart of her to recognise their intellectual superiority. She had never had a client throw a quote back at her and use it so cleverly.

What *would* she be most disappointed by twenty years from now? It wasn't as simple as Cooper White thought. It wasn't only moving to Australia she needed to consider, it was also the possibility of not having another child. She wondered if Mr Twain or indeed Mr White had a quote to solve that one.

Chapter Twelve

'Oh, it's you,' said Alison when she opened the door.

'Thanks for the rapturous welcome,' said Ian, sliding past the large heavy oak door into the double-height hallway. 'How are things at Dynasty Towers today, Alexis?'

'Hilarious,' she said, gliding past him. 'Matthew's in the kitchen.'

Ian watched as she departed through one of the four doors leading off the hall. He considered for a moment removing his shoes then decided against it. Real men didn't wander around other people's houses in their socks.

He picked a door and found himself in the downstairs loo and hurriedly backed out. Ian had only been to Matthew's house once before. He didn't seem to be on their dinner-party list for some peculiar reason.

'So this is where you're hiding,' he said, finally finding the door to the enormous kitchen-diner.

Matthew looked up from the paper he was reading at the table and grinned. In one fluid movement he got up, walked to the fridge and extracted two bottles of beer. He didn't normally drink during the week but he considered it an exception if they had guests even if they weren't invited.

'Unexpected,' Matthew said, handing Ian a beer and nodding for him to join him at the table.

'Mmm,' said Ian, taking a swig. 'Got sick of my own four walls, thought I'd chance it that you were around.'

'No date tonight then?'

'I'm not out every night, you know.'

'All right, touchy,' said Matthew, taken aback by Ian's grumpy reply. Ian was notoriously proud of his stamina for going out in his forties. He could keep up with the best of the twenty-something graduates who arrived every year, fresh-faced and naïve, to the firm. They soon learnt to avoid nights out organised by Ian, who would drink anyone under the table and wouldn't allow them to go home unless it was at least one in the morning.

'I was supposed to be out actually. Bernadette, a hairdresser from Otley, was keen to meet, but I just couldn't be arsed.' Ian gave him a forlorn look and Matthew wondered if he was ill.

'Unusual,' said Matthew.

'I know,' said Ian, shaking his head. 'I can always be arsed. Do you think I'm getting old?'

'You mean you don't think you're still a teenager any more?

Ian managed to raise a smile but barely.

'Has something happened?' Matthew asked. 'The Viagra stopped working?'

'No,' said Ian, not even rising to the bait. 'Carol's getting remarried.' He raised his bottle to his mouth and took a deep slug.

'Oh,' said Matthew. This wasn't how he would expect his friend to react to his ex-wife's nuptials. This was exactly the sort of thing Ian would brush off with a joke. But clearly he wasn't finding it funny. 'Well, I suppose it's to be expected. You have been divorced a long time.'

'Mmm,' said Ian, starting to peel the label off his beer bottle in a distracted fashion.

Matthew sighed heavily. He wasn't good at this. He didn't know what to say. Their friendship was not built on sharing confidences and emotions. It existed purely off the back of general piss taking.

He took a deep breath and decided he should just dive in and ask him a searching question. 'Are you telling me you still have feelings for Carol?'

'Fuck no!' exclaimed Ian, leaning back sharply as though Matthew had bitten him. 'She's still the evil bitch from hell. I feel duty-bound to warn Bob, the poor sod she's marrying, but he seems like a bit of a tosser so they're probably made for each other.'

'Right.' Matthew nodded. 'So why the long face then?'

'Because she's found someone, I guess, and I haven't.'

'You can't begrudge her that.'

'I know, I know. But it just made me ask myself what I'm doing. Why am I thinking about driving all the way out to Otley to meet a woman I don't know?'

'Because you might get a shag out of it?'

'I don't think I want that any more.'

'Oh my God! Are you feeling OK? Are you really, Ian? Has a sensible mature man swooped in and taken his place?'

'It's not funny,' said Ian. He paused then looked up. Matthew could have sworn his eyes were glistening. 'I'm spending Christmas alone.'

'Don't be ridiculous.'

'I am. The kids have plans. Catherine is going to her boyfriend's family, and Jack is off with a mate from uni to stay with his parents in Sweden. So never mind I've only seen them for half a day all these past years, now I don't get to see them at all. And Carol will be toasting marshmallows or whatever round the fire with Bob and I'll be all alone, eating a ready-meal turkey dinner in a room devoid of Christmas decorations because I can't be arsed just for me. I'll be sat there crying over *The Railway Children* and the cranberry sauce I forgot to buy. You'll find me having slit my wrists sometime in mid-January when I've finally been missed.'

Matthew was taken aback. He had never see Ian like this.

'What about your mum and dad, or your brother?'

'I can't go to Mum and Dad's,' said Ian with a deep sigh. 'I'll feel twelve again. Mum will hang me a stocking up and everything. How depressing would that be? Waking up in your childhood bedroom, alone in your forties.'

Matthew had to admit that did sound extremely bleak.

'They're going to Graeme's anyway. I could go there, but I can't bear the thought of spending Christmas with my high-achieving, happily married little brother with two kids, a dog *and* a rabbit. I mean, who has a rabbit these days? Graeme will spend all day breathing his perfect life over me.'

'Well, come to us then.'

Ian looked up at him wide-eyed. 'Seriously, mate?'

Matthew nodded.

'Alison would divorce you.'

Matthew thought for a moment.

'I have to agree that is a serious possibility.'

'Not that it would really solve the problem anyway. What I need is to... well... I don't think I have any choice but to fall in love.' Ian blew his cheeks out as though he had realised he'd finally reached the last resort.

'I think that is a very mature thing to say,' said Matthew carefully. 'But are you sure you're not just saying this because of the time of year? Loving someone isn't just for Christmas, you know. You need it to get past all the other stuff like being shouted at for not putting the loo seat down and having to remember their birthdays and your anniversaries and not getting pissed off because it turns out your view of the world is different to theirs and being patient when they drive you crackers because of their anal organisational tendencies and not agreeing on how much sport you're allowed to watch on the telly… you know, stuff like that. You need love for that.'

'I know,' replied Ian. 'I have been married before. I was in love with Carol once, although quite why escapes me. I know it's bloody hard work loving someone. You put someone on a pedestal and they can only fail you really, can't they? They're only human. It's loving them despite their flaws, that's the key. That's why Carol and me split up. She couldn't love me despite my flaws.'

'Your main flaw being that you had an affair with Marie?'

'Point taken.' He sighed. 'I'm just bored of not having someone. I go home and there's nothing. It's why I avoid going home, I guess. But I'm sick of being out. I want to go home.'

Silence fell on the room.

'Possibly the most moving thing you've ever said,' murmured Matthew.

'Fuck off,' said Ian, a grin finally creeping back on to his face.

'So what are you going to do about it?' asked Matthew.

'I'm going to find her,' said Ian, nodding seriously. 'Dating is about finding my future wife now, not just messing about.'

'Blimey! My, you've grown. And what about Christmas?'

'Oh, I'll find her by Christmas.'

'Are you insane? It's, like, really soon.'

Ian shrugged. 'Now I've made my mind up, it can't be that hard. I am a catch after all,' he said, the familiar cheeky smile returning to his face.

'There is absolutely no way you will fall in love by Christmas,' said Matthew. 'That's a stupid and naïve thing to say.'

'Oh, I'm so sorry,' said Lena, suddenly appearing at the door with a mug in her hand. 'May I?' she asked, pointing at the kettle. 'I don't want to disturb you.'

'Oh, it's no problem,' said Matthew, sitting up in his chair as though she'd caught him doing something he shouldn't. 'Please carry on.'

'Can I make you tea?' she asked.

'No, no,' said Mathew. 'Thank you, though.' He turned to ask Ian if he wanted another beer, but Ian's eyebrows had shot up to the top of his forehead, and he was looking at Matthew expectantly.

'Oh, er, Lena, this is Ian, a colleague of mine,' he said before he realised what he was doing.

Ian rose from his chair and walked over to Lena to shake her hand.

'What a pleasure to meet you,' he gushed. 'You didn't say you had a guest staying, Matthew?'

'No, no, I am Rebecca, George and Harry's nanny,' she told him.

'Oh, Lena, of course. Matthew has spoken very highly of you,' continued Ian.

'Well, that is wonderful,' she said, glancing over at Matthew.

'And remind me where you're from?' asked Ian.

'Lithuania,' she replied.

'Wow!' Ian nodded back.

He clearly had no witty comment to come out with regarding Lithuania, thought Matthew. This was not good. Did Ian actually intend to fall in love with the first woman he clapped eyes on? Surely not. Ian and their nanny had disaster written all over it. Matthew got up to go and extract two more beers from the fridge.

'And are you enjoying your time here in Leeds?' he heard Ian ask Lena.

'Most definitely,' she said. 'Especially Yorkshire pudding!'

Ian laughed. It was the laugh of a man who wanted to make someone feel like they were the funniest person they had ever met. This could not go any further, thought Matthew. Ian chatting up the nanny in casual dating mode was bad enough, but Ian searching for a soulmate could seriously damage the harmony they currently had in their home. He would have to think quickly.

'And do you get out much?' Ian asked.

Oh my God, thought Matthew, he was going for the kill. He didn't mess about, did he? Perhaps he should drop the beer on the floor, create a distraction, anything to disrupt this conversation.

Lena nodded. 'I meet up with some other Lithuanian friends every now and then.'

'Matthew?' Ian shouted over.

Matthew was just about to drop his bottle but paused. Fatally as it turned out.

'Would you mind if I asked Lena to come to our Christmas party. If she'd like to, of course,' he said, turning back to face her. 'I'd be honoured if you would accompany me. Matthew and Alison are coming so you'd be safe, no need to worry,' he joked. He turned back to face Matthew. 'That would be great, wouldn't it, if we all went together?'

Matthew looked over, stunned. Ian should have been a barrister – he was so clever and had such a way with words. Going as a foursome was a terrible idea, but he couldn't say that, could he? Not in front of Lena. Not if he didn't want to appear all *Downton Abbey*, saying that he couldn't possibly mix socially with the servants. How clever of Ian to have asked his permission in front of Lena. He'd have him for that later. He crossed his fingers that Lena was smart enough to see through Ian's slick patter.

'Of course, that would be great,' said Matthew, 'but only if Lena wants to. I mean, Ian, you can't just assume she'd want to come, can you? The last thing she probably wants to do is spend her free time with us... or you.'

'Well, I could understand that of course,' said Ian, 'but it's a party at Christmas Party Land with food and free-flowing wine, and I believe African-themed entertainment. It's supposed to be a cracking do. But if you'd rather not?' he added expectantly to Lena.

'Oh no, no,' said Lena. 'It sounds wonderful. Very British, what with its African theme?' She glanced over to Matthew, who tried To hint at disapproval, but all he managed was one raised eyebrow. 'I would love to come, as long as Matthew and Alison are OK with it?'

'Of course,' agreed Matthew. 'It's fine by me,' he said through gritted teeth.

Ian beamed. 'Brilliant.'

'Good.' Lena nodded. 'I will see you then, Lion King.'

Ian laughed again. Maybe too long and too hard. Lena picked up her tea and left the room.

'Wow,' said Ian, turning to Matthew. 'You kept that quiet.'

'No,' said Matthew, shaking his head. 'No, no, no! Take her to the Christmas party by all means but that is it. No more. If there is one thing guaranteed to make Alison divorce me more than inviting you for Christmas, it's you stealing our nanny.'

Ian smiled and shrugged. 'I can't help it if I'm irresistible.' All traces of melancholy from earlier had disappeared.

Matthew knew he was in big trouble. This might be the worst thing he had ever done in Alison's eyes: introducing Ian to their brilliant, perfect, sanity-saving nanny. He was going to have to think very hard how to tell Alison without causing her to go into premature labour.

🎄

Matthew took a low profile after Ian left. He couldn't quite summon up the words to explain to Alison that he had somehow allowed Ian to invite the wonderful Lena out on a date. She would jump straight to worst-case scenario without passing go. Lena getting involved with Ian would inevitably lead to Ian breaking Lena's heart given his dismal history with women. Lena would then hand in her notice, blaming Matthew for the terrible introduction and wanting to avoid even the vague chance that she would have to bump into Ian ever again. It was impossible to think how the household would function without her if that happened. Matthew broke out in a hot sweat just thinking about it. But it wouldn't get to that surely? It was just a date. Nothing serious. He very much hoped that Alison would see it that way.

'He's gone, has he?' asked Alison when she wandered into the kitchen after Matthew had spent about an hour trying to cook up the bravery to come clean about what he'd done.

'Er, yeah,' he replied.

'What did he want?'

Matthew was rooted to the spot. He didn't know what to say.

'I heard that Carol's getting married again. Is that why he came round? Has he decided to be upset about it?'

'Er, yeah,' replied Matthew. 'Hit him hard actually.'

'Really? But they've been divorced for years. And he's dated half the single women in Leeds since then. He's hardly played the hard-done-by divorcé card.'

'I know but even so, I think it's made him realise what he hasn't got.'

'Any sense? Any morals?' stated Alison.

'Come on, he's not that bad. He's actually quite sensitive, and he's a good guy at heart.'

'Mmm,' said Alison. 'He's got a funny way of showing it.'

'Lena took a shine to him.' Matthew tossed it out into the conversation in the hope the comment wouldn't explode like a hand grenade.

'What?' exclaimed Alison, her eyes already bulging out of her head. 'When did she see him?'

'She came down for a drink.'

'And you introduced her? Oh, Matthew, how could you?'

'I couldn't not, could I? Not when they were in the same room.'

'Well, if he comes sniffing round again, you're to take him into your study. The last thing I need right now is the thought of Ian chasing after our nanny. It makes me shudder to even think about it.'

Matthew breathed in sharply then said, 'Too late.'

'What?'

'Too late. He's asked her out.'

'She didn't say yes, did she? Oh, Matthew, how could you let this happen?'

'Ian caught me on the hop. He asked my permission and I could hardly say no in front of her, could I? But it's OK. He's invited her to the works Christmas do so we'll be there to keep an eye on them.'

'Are you serious?' cried Alison, pulling a chair out and easing herself into it. 'You're telling me that not only do I have to endure the thought of Ian trying to woo our nanny, I have to watch it too!'

'Well, we might be able to do something about it, mightn't we, if we're there. Kill the romance somehow?'

Alison bent slowly forward and put her head in her hands.

'I knew it was all going too well,' she muttered. 'We have the good fortune to have a brilliant nanny and now have a place for Rebecca and

George at a decent preschool. I thought I'd ticked all the boxes.' She sighed, sounding utterly exhausted. 'I thought we were ready,' she said, raising her head and looking directly at Matthew. 'Ready to welcome a new member of the family. I thought I could face Christmas knowing everything was in order.'

Matthew could feel his heart sinking lower and lower.

'And then Ian pops up.' She grimaced. 'Like the naughty little elf he is and threatens to bring it all tumbling down.'

'I think you might be being a bit overdramatic. He's only asked her to the Christmas party.'

'She'll take one look at the fairy lights and they'll play "Last Christmas" and that will be it. She's lost to us. People fall hard at Christmas parties, Matthew. Everyone wants to live the dream and fall in love under the mistletoe.'

'Don't be ridiculous,' dismissed Matthew. 'No-one falls in love just because George Michael is crooning in their ear.'

Alison blinked at her husband. 'I was eighteen,' she confessed. 'His name was Rex. He asked me to dance the last dance at a school disco. It was "Last Christmas". We walked outside, hand in hand, and it had snowed. Then he kissed me.'

Matthew stared at Alison. He didn't quite know how to take this information.

'Then what happened?' he asked.

'He got off with Emily Bagshaw on New Year's Eve.'

'Is that why you hate New Year's Eve?'

'Yes.'

'Because of Emily Bagshaw?'

'No, because of Rex or maybe George Michael, I don't know. I knew Rex wasn't trustworthy. I knew there was no way he wanted anything more than just a Christmas kiss, but I let myself get carried away with the music and the snow and George Michael crooning in my ear. That's what Christmas does to you. It can make you believe that a toerag like Rex is the love of your life.'

'I think that Lena has more sense than that,' Matthew offered.

'*I* had more sense than that,' said Alison desperately. 'Didn't stop me falling for him hook, line and sinker though, did it?'

Matthew was at a loss. He didn't know what to do to make it better. And quite frankly he was somewhat perturbed at the hazy expression on his wife's face when she talked about her Christmas kiss with Rex. It had clearly taken on a mythical status, and he wasn't sure how to compete with that.

'And you know what will happen, don't you, the minute the midnight bell chimes on New Year's Eve and Lena is standing all alone, broken-hearted, while Ian is heaven knows where with some floozy?' said Alison.

'I don't know,' said Matthew, despite the fact he knew exactly what his wife was about to say.

'She'll leave us, Matthew. It won't be Ian that suffers because of his philandering – it will be us. New Year's Day and she's out of here, her life in tatters and us facing a future with four children under four and no nanny!'

Matthew didn't know what to say to the tragic tale that Alison had laid out before him.

'All we can do is make sure she doesn't enjoy herself,' she added with a sigh as she hauled herself up. 'Doesn't get that Christmas feeling.'

'It *is* an African theme,' offered Matthew hopefully.

Alison nodded. 'Good. Let's hope the sound of bongo drums kills the festive spirit and an elephant lands on Ian's head.'

Chapter Thirteen

'Hi, love. Do you have a downstairs toilet in the new house? Carlos isn't good with stairs. Once he's down he likes to stay down. Let me know. Speak soon, Mum xx'

Katy put her phone on silent then placed it face down on the table. She'd sat facing the door of the café and was nursing a cup of tea that she could barely taste. In fact all her senses seemed to have gone into lockdown since her meal with Cooper White the night before. All she could think about was his job offer, and she was finding it impossible to concentrate on anything else. Luckily for her, Ben had been knee-deep in a football match on the TV when she'd returned home, having taken advantage of sole access to the remote control. He'd looked up briefly before returning his gaze to the screen, then leapt off the sofa and done a victory run round the lounge. Presumably someone had scored.

'Did you secure the entire future of Butler & Calder then?' he asked, sitting down, still transfixed by the match.

'Maybe.' She shrugged. 'Hard to tell. Do you mind if I go and have a bath?'

'Be my guest.' Ben waved towards the stairs. 'I've still got the second half to watch.'

She climbed the stairs slowly, her legs heavy, then locked herself in the bathroom. She needed peace. She needed escape. She needed to be alone with the secret she now held because the one thing she was sure about was that she wasn't ready to let Ben in on it. She was still in a state of shock at the evening's turn of events. It was the last thing she'd expected, and she had no idea what she felt about it. Partly thrilled at the idea of taking what would undoubtedly be an exciting job in an exciting city and partly horrified at what they might have to sacrifice if they took up the opportunity. Friends, family, Leeds United… And most importantly trying for another baby. She wouldn't mention it to Ben just yet, she decided. She'd check Cooper was serious the next day before she threw this possible hand grenade into their marriage.

🌲

The following morning Ben had waved her off to work as though that day was exactly the same as the one before. Only she knew it wasn't. There were life-changing decisions on the cards.

She got to lunchtime and felt like she might be about to go mad. Cooper had texted her to say he was looking forward to discussing the role in more detail whenever she was ready. Ready? She had no idea how she would ever be ready to have a sensible conversation about such a life-changing opportunity. She couldn't concentrate on anything. At every turn she fell into a trap reminding her of the consequences of her future actions. A request for a strategy-planning meeting in February. Would she be here? Budget-setting demand from Finance for the following year. She was tempted to submit something ludicrous. Tell them she needed to double her expenditure and see what they said. If they didn't like it, well then she could always leave.

She decided there was only one thing for it. She had to talk to someone, and so she was waiting patiently in a greasy spoon, fifteen minutes' walk from the office, for her confidante.

Eventually she saw Daniel peer through the steamed-up windows in his impeccable camel coat with its collar up around a cashmere scarf. She waved and he looked at her as though she'd lost her marbles. Pushing the door open, he walked across the chipped tiled floor, throwing disdainful looks like confetti.

'This had better be good, Ms Chapman,' he hissed, sitting himself down on the orange plastic chair and keeping his hands firmly in his pockets. 'What exactly are we doing here? Buying drugs?'

'No,' hissed Katy, looking around to check no-one was listening. But the old man slumped in the corner and the two men in neon worker's vests and steel-toe-capped boots didn't seem to have heard. 'I just wanted to make sure we didn't run into anyone from work.'

'I think you would normally have to administer the drugs first to get any of our lot in here. Unless they were going out to purposefully catch salmonella, of course.' He delivered this last line as a middle-aged woman in a dirty tabard approached.

'What can I get you, son?' she asked.

Daniel did not conceal his look of amazement.

'He'll have a bottle of water,' Katy said when Daniel didn't reply to the request. 'Ignore him. He's socially awkward,' she added, giving him a kick under the table.

'No worries, love,' she replied. 'We're used to that here.' She turned and walked away, appearing to completely forget about their order by continuing to read the magazine that lay on the counter.

'So what have you dragged me out to this… this… grease pit for?'

'I needed to tell you something.'

'I knew it,' said Daniel, taking his hand out of his pocket and slamming his fist on the table. The stickiness that it was met with caused another epic look of disgust. He took a thin paper napkin out of the holder and attempted to wipe it down.

'What do you know?' asked Katy.

'You slept with Cooper White, didn't you?'

'No!' exclaimed Katy. 'Of course I didn't.'

'You fancy him though, I can tell.'

Katy sighed. 'Cooper White is like Gwyneth Paltrow or Ryan Gosling or Brad Pitt. So perfect looking…'

'I assume you mean Brad Pitt without the beard?' interrupted Daniel.

'OK, yes, probably,' said Katy. 'What I'm saying is that they're so perfect looking that you'd have to be… well, weird not to fancy them, wouldn't you? It's like appreciating a work of art. Good to look at but in no way could you ever connect with them.'

'Can I add Jimmy who works in Finance to that list?'

'Yes,' said Katy. 'Exactly. He's all cheekbones and flat stomach and muscly arms, but all you want to do is look at him. You wouldn't want to spend any time with him.'

'So are you telling me that Cooper was as dull as dishwater then?'

'I'm telling you that I can appreciate his good looks but that's it, and anyway I love Ben and I'm *married*. Why are we even talking about this?'

'You dragged me here. The least you could do is confess to an affair to make it worthwhile. So what dull revelation do you have for me then?'

'Cooper offered me a job… in Australia.'

Daniel's eyes flew open. 'Could you repeat that please?'

'Cooper White wants me to go and be brand director for Boomerang Airlines in Sydney.'

Daniel continued to stare and said nothing. Katy waited for his response. After a moment he got up from his seat and walked out.

'Is he coming back?' asked the lady, who had finally arrived with his water.

'Not sure,' replied Katy, peering past her to see that Daniel was standing just outside the door with his back to her. 'Leave the water. I think he just needed some space.'

Katy stared at Daniel's back for a couple more minutes. She toyed with getting up to see if he was all right. Maybe he couldn't bear the sight of her right now. She watched as he raised his shoulders as though taking a deep breath. He turned around abruptly then came back into the café and sat down in front of Katy.

'That's utterly brilliant, Katy,' he said with a huge smile painted on his face. 'I'm really pleased for you.'

'You are such a liar,' said Katy. 'You don't mean that, do you?'

'No, I fucking don't,' screeched Daniel in a high voice and put his head in his hands.

'I'm sorry,' she said, laying a hand on his shoulder. She felt him breathe two or three more times then slowly raise his head.

'It's not that I'm not pleased for you,' he said. 'It's just that I would be even more pleased if it was me.'

'You're jealous?'

'Of course I'm jealous. You're going to work for the fine specimen that is Cooper White... in Sydney. Imagine how much fun I could have. It would make Luca leaving make sense. It would make my Christmas.' He paused, looking straight at her. 'It's just so *wasted* on you.'

'I haven't said I'll take it yet.'

'What! Are you insane? You mean you didn't snap his hand off and get him to sign something in blood there and then. Are you crazy, girl?'

'It's not as simple as that for me.'

'Tell me what isn't simple about moving to a climate where you don't need two coats?'

'I told you. Ben wants a baby.'

'Oh,' said Daniel. 'Oh,' he said again, his brain starting to whirr. 'So talk me through that one.'

'I just don't know how we can do both. How can I accept a job – a massive job – knowing I might get pregnant any day?'

'You're having sex, are you?'

'No, but that isn't the point. I can't tell Cooper I want the job and then in three months' time tell him I'm having a baby. That's not fair.'

'Why are you not having sex?'

Katy sighed. 'Can we discuss that another time? It really isn't the main issue just now.'

'If you say so.' He shrugged. 'But you will have to have sex to have a baby.'

'I know! And we will. It just isn't a priority at the moment.'

Daniel looked at her as though she'd grown two heads. 'In my experience, sex…'

'Enough with the sex talk!' said Katy a little too loudly. The two workmen turned their heads and smirked. 'We are not here to discuss my sex life,' she hissed.

'OK,' said Daniel, holding up his hands to indicate she should calm down. 'OK. So why don't you just wait then. Have a baby later, after you've bedded yourself in?'

'I'm just not sure Ben will go for that. And besides, I'm getting old. The longer I leave it, the riskier it gets. If we're going to have another one we really need to start trying now.'

Daniel said nothing. She prayed he might find some pearls of wisdom in that warped brain of his, but it wasn't looking hopeful.

'Tell him.' He shrugged. 'Tell Cooper your dilemma. You never know, he might say that's fine. Have the baby; go back to work straightaway. You might be gone what, three weeks?'

Katy bit her lip. 'I don't want to be that kind of mother,' she said. 'And I don't think that's fair on Ben.'

'So what does Ben think?'

'I've not told him yet,' she confessed. 'I wanted to get my head round it first. Let it sink in. I was struggling with the baby or career thing before this came along, and now this just makes it a whole lot worse. We could have a great life in Australia – I know we could. It could be amazing for all of us. But at what price? The price could be our next child. We could be risking that.'

Daniel stared back at her in disbelief.

'How do you do this?' he asked eventually.

'Do what?'

'How do amazing things happen to you, and yet I'm the one who ends up feeling sorry for you?'

'I don't mean to do that.'

'You must. It's just cruel, Katy. Here's me facing Christmas alone, and then you come and flash a job offer from Australia in my face. How very Christmas-spirited of you.'

'I told you – you could spend Christmas with us. You don't need to be alone.'

'Oh, how very decent of you. No doubt you will add insult to injury and rope me into packing your house up to be shipped off to the other side of the world. Merry Christmas, Daniel. You just lost your boyfriend and your best friend. The only person you work with who you can go and bitch to about everyone else on a regular basis.'

'I know you go and bitch to Rachel in HR. Don't try and tell me you don't.'

Daniel gasped. The woman in the dirty tabard looked up from her magazine.

'That is not bitching. I'm doing my duty and informing her of the inner workings of the staff at the agency. She calls me her internal barometer of the current satisfaction levels in the workplace. She reckons I save her a fortune on surveys.'

'She likes a gossip as much as you do.'

'Maybe, but I can assure you that I never, *never* reach the heights of bitchiness that I so enjoy when we get together. How can I survive the tedium of having to earn a living without you as my partner in crime?' Daniel finished his speech by taking another gasp. The woman looked up again and frowned. 'Does Andrew know?' he asked her.

'Of course not. Cooper's convinced that Andrew will be only too happy to let me go if it means they definitely secure the Boomerang account.'

Daniel gasped yet again. He was beginning to behave as if Katy was divulging the culprits of a chain of murders, right there in a greasy spoon. 'So he's blackmailing you! You let him kidnap you and we get the business. Oh my God, this is… this is corporate espionage.'

'Not quite sure what that is,' admitted Katy.

'Neither am I, but it sounds dramatic enough to describe this situation.'

'He didn't actually say that we wouldn't get the business if I said no…'

'But he didn't say we would either, did he?'

'No, he didn't. But I can't think about that. I have to decide if this is right for me, Ben and Millie, not what's right for the business.'

Daniel leaned back in his chair, his eyes fixed on Katy. He was weighing it all up. Katy hoped he was getting past his dramatic reaction and would actually offer her some sound advice, which he was surprisingly good at. She waited patiently as she watched him turn the dilemma over in his mind. Eventually he picked up the salt cellar and pretended to study it carefully. He tipped it over and they both watched the salt silently pour out of the top hole and form a small mound on the table.

Slowly, Daniel dragged his eyes up to meet hers. She thought she may have detected a minute tear in one corner of his eye, but it could just be the greasy fumes that he was reacting badly to.

'I only have the words of the greatest Christmas single of all time to say to you,' he said solemnly.

Katy wracked her brains to try and think of the festive tune that Daniel would pick. She could only think of the cheesy ones, and they didn't seem likely. 'Go on, put me out of my misery,' she finally said.

'You mean you don't know what the greatest Christmas single of all time is?'

'Cliff Richard, "Mistletoe and Wine"?' she said feebly.

'That answer is enough to make me want to send you packing straight to the other side of the world,' snapped Daniel. 'Of course it isn't "Mistletoe and Bloody Wine". That does nothing to embody the true sentiment behind Christmas.'

'Then what?' snapped back Katy, losing patience now. 'Stop talking in bloody riddles! What song does it for you at Christmas?'

'"Stay Another Day". That's what does it for me. Undoubtedly the greatest Christmas single of all time.'

'By East 17?'

'Of course by East 17. Those beautiful boys' faces encased in white fur hoods, singing to me, pleading with me to stay another day.'

'It was a surprisingly sentimental and lovely song from a bunch of hard nuts,' agreed Katy.

'It's about the prospect of losing someone,' added Daniel. 'How painful that is, and how all you want to do is plead with them to stay.'

'I'm sorry about Luca, Daniel – I really am,' said Katy.

'I'm not talking about Luca, I don't give a fuck about him. Pasta boy has well and truly gone. I'm talking about you, Katy. I don't want you to go. In the words of the legend that is Brian Harvey, "stay". Please.'

Katy stared back at Daniel and his desperate face. This was new. Their friendship mode consisted of healthy insults and banter. A declaration of neediness was unprecedented.

'Go on with you,' said Katy, finally killing the moment. 'You're just saying that because Luca left. You'll find a new boyfriend, and before you know it I'll be relegated to the friends zone and reduced to begging you to share a coffee with me.'

'No,' said Daniel, banging the table with his fist. Katy jumped. 'Is that what you think of this?' he said, waggling his finger between the two of them. 'We're just time-fillers to each other? A way of alleviating the tedium of our day-to-day lives until we can find someone more interesting to be with? And after all we've been through?'

Katy looked away in shame. She knew exactly what he was referring to. When she had come close to totally screwing up her life over the one-night stand with Matthew, it was Daniel she'd turned to for help and support. Daniel, and only Daniel, had shared her anxiety over who the father of her unborn child was.

'I don't see you as a time-filler,' said Katy, looking back up at him, her cheeks on fire.

'I think you do. In fact, I'm sure you do. Cooper comes along and dangles a beach and a barbecue in your face and suddenly our relationship means nothing?'

'But he's offering me an amazing job.'

'You have an amazing job here,' cried Daniel.

'But I'd get to develop a brand from scratch, Daniel. I get to make the decisions on what it looks like and what it stands for. I don't do any of that in my job now. Sure I can advise, I can cajole, I can even beg, but I don't get to call the shots. You know that. The client does. I'd be in charge, Daniel. Of the Boomerang Airlines brand. I'd have something to show for all my hard work. Now that's an amazing job.'

'But you don't get to work with me,' said Daniel.

Katy swallowed. Tabard lady was now openly listening in on their conversation, her head raised up from her magazine and her jaw hanging slightly open.

'Are you telling me that if Cooper had offered you a job then you would turn it down? I refuse to believe that.'

Daniel opened his mouth and closed it again. She'd got him, she thought. He didn't actually mean all this sentimental stuff – he was just being selfish. He just wanted her to stay so he would have someone to play with. If a better offer came along, he'd leave her in a heartbeat.

Daniel stood up and pulled his cashmere gloves out of his pockets and put them over his hands, refusing to look at her. When he'd finished he put his hands on his hips and finally looked her in the eye.

'I don't know what I'd do,' he said eventually. 'But the thought of leaving behind the people that I love would… well, it would break my heart.' He turned and walked out, slamming the glass door so that the Merry Christmas sign sellotaped across it fell to the floor.

Katy glanced over at tabard lady then got up and went to go and pick up the fallen letters strewn on the floor. She took them back to the counter and handed them over. 'Sorry about that,' she said. 'He was upset.'

'You just dumped him then?' the woman asked. 'Are you sure about that? He wasn't half smart-looking. He must be a bit of a catch, I reckon. I'm single if you've finished with him. You can tell him I'm on Tinder.'

Katy smiled at her. The irony was that she and Daniel would probably get on. Both blunt and to the point.

'He's gay actually,' she stated.

'Oh,' said the woman, looking disappointed, then she shrugged her shoulders. 'Never mind. Thought I'd ask.'

'But you are right though,' added Katy as she fished some money out of her wallet. 'He is a catch.'

Chapter Fourteen

What do you want for Christmas? I've got something for Ben and Millie but you are so difficult. Why don't you buy yourself something and I'll give you the money for it. Can you wrap it too? Mum xx
PS: Carlos likes cigars

Katy wondered when she would ever find the time to buy any Christmas presents as she drove home that night past the cheerful Christmas lights guiding her back to the house with the inflatable reindeer on the lawn and the Santa still hanging saggily off the roof. It was raining, obviously, but somehow that added extra sparkle to the glorious display of every colour of the rainbow lining the streets. Leeds had gone for a baubles and glitter balls theme this year, much to Daniel's disgust. The array of colours was stunning but disturbed his preference for a monotone aesthetic. Every year he wrote to the council to offer to design the city's light display, and every year they wrote back to thank him for the kind offer but they thought his 'white-light-only' rule might be too restrictive for a display on such a large scale.

She'd found Daniel's outburst earlier very unsettling. Previously her head had been merely jammed by the thought of how she would discuss the job offer with Ben and how he might feel about it. Her concerns had not stretched to the feelings of her closest but most abusive friend. He'd surprised her with his admission of... well, of love, actually. She knew they were close. She knew he was the first person besides Ben who she wanted to share the stuff going on in her head with. But they'd never defined their friendship. Never labelled it. Never discussed it in the context of needing each other or indeed loving each other. She'd never been that kind of girl. Even growing up, when many of her contemporaries craved the security of a 'best friend', Katy never did. She was happier with a wide circle. She suspected she avoided getting too close to one person for fear of relying on them too much and indeed them relying on her. Being someone's best friend felt like a massive responsibility. She might let them down. She might not live up to their expectations. So she avoided it, preferring to run in a crowd rather than as a tightly-knit twosome. The trials and tribulations of friendship shared amongst them rather than resting solely on her shoulders.

And now, at forty, she had discovered that a best friend had snuck up on her. Without realising it had happened, Daniel had come to rely on her. He was demanding that his feelings be considered regarding the decision to up sticks and move to the other side of the world. Life had just become more complicated. Exactly the reason why you didn't have best friends in the first place, Katy thought. Inevitably you'll let them down, and she hated that feeling with a passion.

It wasn't long before Katy had left the bright lights of the city and was driving towards the more open roads of the suburbs. The stately Victorian semis with icicle lights dripping from their eaves replaced the looming office buildings and stores. She took a deep breath as she pulled up outside their house and was relieved to see the reindeer still grazing the lawn and Santa still struggling to get down the chimney.

She paused before she got out of the car. She was glad to be home – it had been a hell of a day. She would sit down with Ben tonight, she thought. She couldn't bear to feel like this any longer. She'd throw it out there and see what he said. She'd sat on it too long already.

Opening the front door, she was greeted by the unlikely combination of the tinkling of Disney Christmas songs and gales of manly laughter. She opened the door to the lounge where she thought the action was taking place and was greeted by a roaring fire and two men lying flat on the floor with their hands around the base of a Christmas tree. An array of tinsel and baubles dangled precariously from its branches while Millie jumped up and down on the sofa, dressed as Snow White.

'Mummy, Mummy,' she sang out. 'We got a Christmas tree and told never to go back ever again.'

Katy walked over to gather Millie up in her arms and smother her with kisses. The familiar smell of ketchup wafted up her nostrils. She sat down and held her on her knee while she tried not to be upset that she'd missed out on the family tree-buying excursion. She was, after all, the one who'd had to work on Sunday when they were supposed to be getting it.

'Just give us a sec,' shouted Ben from somewhere under the branches. 'Just trying to stop the damn thing leaning.'

'We're barred,' cried Millie excitedly to Katy. 'Uncle Braindead did a bad thing.'

'It wasn't bad,' came a shout from under the tree. 'They just have no sense of humour.'

'It was really funny,' added Millie.

'What did he do?' asked Katy, giving Millie her full attention.

'I'll tell her, Millie,' said Ben, finally extracting himself, his jumper covered in pine needles. 'You need to learn the art of telling Mummy things in such a way that it doesn't make you look bad,' he told her seriously.

'What have you done?' asked Katy, now beginning to worry.

'It was legendary,' announced Braindead, also emerging from under the tree. 'Epic. Inspired. I do not and will not ever regret it. Please don't make me, Katy. Please.'

'Would you like a drink?' Ben asked, offering Katy his sweetest smile and winking at Millie.

'No,' said Katy. 'Just tell me.'

'So we went to buy a tree at the garden centre, you know the fancy one.'

'The one with the amazing garden furniture that's really expensive?' asked Katy.

'That's the one. So Braindead said he'd come and give me a hand to tie it to the top of the car.'

'It's the kind of guy I am.' Braindead shrugged. 'No need to thank me.'

Katy smiled. 'I'm sure there isn't.'

'So we find all the trees outside at the back and Millie picks a great one, didn't you, Millie?'

'It's called Eric,' she replied.

'Eric the tree?' questioned Katy.

'Yes.'

'OK. So you selected Eric and then what happened?'

'So it needed putting through one of those wrapper things. You know you feed the tree through and it comes out the other side sort of shrunk and wrapped in netting?' explained Ben.

'Yeees,' said Katy slowly, already sensing what was coming next.

Braindead started sniggering. Katy raised her eyebrows.

'It was bloody funny,' he said, trying to stop himself laughing.

'So there was no-one around to do it for us. We couldn't see any staff anywhere so Braindead had this idea…' Ben had to stop because he was laughing so much, which started Braindead off again. Soon they couldn't speak. They tried to get the words out to explain Braindead's idea but they were laughing so hard they couldn't spit it out.

'Daddy pushed Uncle Braindead through the tree-wrapping machine,' Millie finally said for them.

'You did what!' exclaimed Katy.

'He shrink-wrapped me like a Christmas tree,' exploded Braindead.

'You made me,' protested Ben.

'No, I didn't. The minute I suggested it, you were in. You had my feet in it before I could shout, "Save me, Rudolph."'

Katy felt shocked but not surprised. It was just the sort of thing the two of them would get up to, however it probably wasn't the type of thing you should be doing in front of an impressionable three-year-old.

'It was so funny,' said Millie again. 'He fell over!'

'I tried to walk, but I couldn't of course so I fell flat on my face,' explained Braindead.

'And then,' said Ben, now crying with laughter and struggling slightly for breath. 'You'll never guess what he did next.'

'There's more?' asked Katy.

'Of course,' declared Braindead, a look of surprise on his face as though he couldn't believe Katy thought they would have left it there. 'There were a load of trees already wrapped, leaning against a wall, so I managed to shuffle my way over to them and leaned myself alongside them as though I was an actual tree waiting to be bought. An actual tree, Katy.'

'I was killing myself, honestly,' said Ben. 'His clothes were dark so he kind of blended in and then…' He looked at Braindead for permission to proceed. Braindead nodded, putting his fist in his mouth to try to suppress the guffaws. 'And then this elderly couple came over to look for a tree and they were wandering up and down trying to pick one, and me and Millie were just watching – we didn't know what to do – and then when they got to the bit where Braindead was, he shouted this massive…'

'Boo!' shouted Millie and Braindead in unison. Katy nearly jumped out of her skin.

'They both screamed,' continued Ben. 'I thought he might have a heart attack for a minute.'

'I felt a bit bad actually,' admitted Braindead.

'The next thing we know a shop assistant comes running up to see what all the commotion is about and sees Braindead wrapped up like a Christmas tree in their display and two old biddies having palpitations.'

'The man said a very bad word,' said Millie, looking serious.

'He said, "What the *hell* are you doing?"' said Ben. 'I mean, couldn't he see there were children present?'

'And then he shouted at me to get out of the netting immediately,' said Braindead. 'I mean, how stupid was that? How was I supposed to get out? He went to get some scissors eventually and then he got his own back. He nearly cut my testicles off.'

'What are testicles?' asked Millie.

'Another name for ears,' said Ben immediately. Katy envied the speed at which he answered Millie's questions, but then again, he did have more practice than her.

'We were told never to go back,' said Braindead triumphantly.

'We're barred,' added Millie.

'From a garden centre,' said Ben, leaning forward and doing a high five with Millie and then Braindead.

'Almost as good as when we kidnapped Gloria,' added Braindead.

'Who's Gloria?' asked Millie.

Katy sighed. 'A stuffed puffin.'

'And your mother was behind that particular escapade,' added Ben.

'What's a puffin?' asked Millie.

'It's a bird, but it was a dead bird,' Katy told Millie. 'And I like to think we rescued it rather than kidnapped it.'

'From where?'

'A pub,' said Braindead. 'Actually you were there. I told your mum that I liked Gloria, and she stuffed her under her coat when you were inside her tummy and ran out the pub with you both.'

Millie's eyes were wide now. She couldn't keep up.

'You do silly things when you're younger,' Katy told her. 'Well, when you're older too,' she added, glancing at Ben and Braindead.

'It's called having fun with your mates,' said Braindead. 'And do you know what, Millie? The mates that you do the fun stuff with will always be your best mates.'

'Stealing dead birds?' she asked.

'Yes,' said Braindead. 'And pretending to be a tree that frightens old ladies.'

'And I think that's enough "meaning of life" talk for one night, don't you, guys?' said Katy, clasping Millie and hauling them both up off the sofa. 'How about I get you into bed, young lady? Say night, night.'

'Night, night,' muttered Millie, nestling her head into Katy's neck.

'Night, night, gorgeous,' said Ben, reaching over to kiss the top of Millie's and then Katy's head.

'Stay cool, Angel,' said Braindead, holding his fist up, which she gave a satisfying slap. 'Beware the human Christmas trees.'

🎄

It was nearly an hour later when Katy came downstairs having bathed Millie, detangled her hair and lain in bed next to her to read her a story. Katy knew she should be more disciplined about quicker bedtimes and should resist Millie's cries for 'one more story', but the truth was that she relished her time with her daughter, particularly given the long hours she worked. She couldn't bear to walk away from Millie when Millie wanted her to stay.

She eventually eased herself out of the bed, sensing that Millie was about to drop off. She changed out of her work clothes into tracksuit bottoms and a top then walked downstairs, already mentally sorting through the fridge to see what they could have for dinner. Before she got to the kitchen, however, she paused in the lounge to take in the tree groaning with attachments, the majority of which hung precariously at Millie height. It was the most lopsided, uneven arrangement of decorations she had ever seen. Daniel would have a fit. She went over to start rearranging then stopped herself: this was Millie's first tree-decorating experience. One that had started in the garden centre and proved so memorable that perhaps even a three-year-old would remember it for the rest of her life. The tree was perfect.

She wondered where their tree might be next year. Did they do Christmas trees in Australia? She had to talk to Ben. She'd wait until Braindead had left and then sit him down. Her heart beat quicker just thinking about it, but she knew she couldn't put it off any longer.

Walking through into the kitchen she found Ben and Braindead furiously unpacking white plastic bags and lining up silver cartons on the kitchen table.

'Thought we'd get a Chinese?' said Ben, looking up. 'Is that OK?'

'Duck pancakes?' asked Katy, suddenly starving.

'Of course,' replied Ben. 'And Beef in King Do sauce. I know what my lady likes.'

'Awesome,' she replied, sitting down, delighted that she didn't have to be creative with carrots, onions, some frozen chicken and a tin of soup.

'I never think of ducks as being very Chinese,' said Braindead, sitting down and grabbing a plate. 'I mean, you don't picture temples and dragons and ninjas along with ducks, do you?'

Ben and Katy didn't respond. They were hungry and unsure where Braindead was going with this line of enquiry.

'But did you know that there's a species of duck called the mandarin?'

'Mmm,' mumbled Ben.

'Yes,' said Braindead. 'They even named a duck after their language.'

'Or named the language after the duck,' offered Katy.

Braindead nodded. 'Good point. What came first, the language or the duck?' He shrugged and speared a chunk of crispy meat and laid it in its pancake nest.

There was silence as everyone took their first bite and chewed in satisfaction.

'I'm going to go with the duck,' said Braindead. 'I think the duck came first. Katy?'

Katy nodded her agreement. She knew better than to argue – it could go on all night.

'So are you going to ask her?' Ben said to Braindead as he grabbed another pancake.

'Ask her what?'

'You know, what we were talking about before?'

'Oh yeah,' said Braindead, suddenly going bright pink. He coughed. 'I was just building myself up to it.' He wiped the corner of his mouth and took another bite without even looking at Katy.

'What?' said Katy. 'Ask me what?' Braindead was staring down at his plate. 'What does he want to ask me?' she said, directing her question at Ben.

'Come on,' said Ben to Braindead. 'It's only Katy. You can talk to her about it, can't you?'

'It's still a bit embarrassing.'

'You just wrapped yourself up like a Christmas tree, Braindead,' stated Katy. 'I can't see what you could ever find embarrassing.'

Katy didn't think she had ever known Braindead to be shy about anything, let alone blush like he was doing now. Whatever it was, it had to be something pretty major. She wiped her fingers with a napkin and put her hand on his shoulder. 'Whatever it is I won't laugh,' she said. 'You can tell me.'

Braindead looked truly terrified. His face was now drained white. He started to try to speak then looked away in shame.

'I can't say it,' he muttered.

'He's in love,' Ben announced for him.

Katy nearly dropped her duck pancake. 'Like proper love?' she asked.

Braindead nodded, his chin sunk down somewhere over his breastbone. Ben had told her that the two of them had discussed the fact that Braindead had to take his relationship forward, but somehow the perfectly natural emotion of love didn't seem to sit well with him. Braindead didn't take life seriously enough to use such a word.

'Well, that's just brilliant,' said Katy, getting up and flinging her arms round him. 'Well done you. I'm very proud.'

Braindead hugged her back and then looked up at Ben. 'He made me see the light,' he admitted.

'Wow!' said Katy, sitting down and tucking into her duck again. 'So you do have mature conversations as well as getting banned from garden centres for wrapping yourself up like a Christmas tree.'

'I just told him,' said Ben, waving a chopstick at his friend, 'that it's not that bad, being in love.' He smiled at Katy.

'I'm going to ask her to marry me,' added Braindead.

'Right.' Katy nodded. 'And is that what you really want?'

'Yes,' said Braindead, nodding vigorously. 'Well, I think so. I don't want to be without her. The thought of that makes me sad. Like really sad, like someone's died level of sad. So I figure I must love her, right? Ben seems to think that I need to show her – I need to commit or else I might lose her.'

'And you don't want to lose her?'

'No,' said Braindead instantly. No hesitation. A look of earnestness on his face.

'Then I think Ben might be right. You need to show her if you want to keep her. Abby doesn't strike me as the drifting kind.'

Braindead nodded solemnly, deep in thought. Then he suddenly broke out into a grin.

'She'll look bloody amazing old, you know,' he said. 'I keep imagining her face all old and wrinkly next to me on the pillow with those funny brown spots you get and grey hair and all that. Makes me happy.'

'You old romantic bugger you,' said Ben, reaching out to clutch Katy's hand. She smiled back at him and squeezed his hand, knowing that she wanted to be there to see Ben's wrinkles and grey hair.

'So ask her then,' Ben urged Braindead.

The pinkness returned to his cheeks and he squirmed in his seat.

'Do you want me to help you pick out a ring or maybe plan how you ask her?' Katy said to Braindead. 'I mean, I'd be very happy to give you the female perspective if you're worried about messing it up or not doing it how Abby would want. I know you'll want to make sure it all goes to plan, and I guess that's what I do for a living so I'd be happy to give you advice and help. In fact I'd be honoured.'

Katy felt close to tears. This was a big moment. Braindead was Ben's friend, his best friend. They'd grown up together and shared a truckload of happy memories that they loved to regale her with. It had been a key moment in their relationship when Braindead had offered his approval of Katy after the Gloria-the-Puffin-stealing incident. The fact that he now wanted her to help him plan one of the most important moments in his life, well, that was endorsement of the highest order.

'Actually,' said Ben, who was now looking as awkward as Braindead. 'He was going to ask you if you would ask Daniel if he would help.'

'Daniel!' exclaimed Katy, twisting her head round to glare at Braindead. 'You want Daniel to help you plan your engagement?' She couldn't believe it. Daniel was her friend, not his. Braindead and Daniel had met a few times of course, usually on occasions when Katy and Ben were going through a rough patch and mates were dragged into the crossfire. But she never had them down as that close.

'Well, er, you know, Katy, he's good at that sort of stuff, isn't he?' said Braindead.

'What stuff?'

'You know, girly stuff.'

'I'm actually a girl, you know. Daniel is a boy, in case you hadn't noticed.'

'I know. But I think he would understand more what Abby would like than you.'

Katy leaned back in her chair, winded by the thought that Daniel had usurped her. But then she thought about Abby, and she could see what Braindead was getting at. Abby could be quite a drama queen and liked to be the centre of attention, and those attributes reminded her of someone. Oh yes – Daniel.

'I think what he means,' said Ben, 'is that Daniel is more likely to imagine what Abby would want than you.'

She couldn't argue. Abby was blunt and in-your-face and a bit of a princess. In fact, she and Braindead were an unlikely match, but somehow it worked. Braindead seemed to rise above the drama and the tantrums, bringing her back down to earth with his sideways view on life and the ability to make her laugh, the greatest aphrodisiac of all. He took none of her nonsense, and she respected him for that, and in turn her vitality and zest pushed him to embrace life in a way he never had before. Since they'd got together he had succumbed to the joys of cocktails when he'd only ever enjoyed real ale. He'd even been known to admit the quality of the odd modern pop song, when previously he'd refused to listen to anything that wasn't conceived before he was born.

'Will you ring and ask him?' said Braindead. 'Tell him what I want.'

'You could write the brief,' declared Ben. 'That's what you could do. That's what you do at work, isn't it?' he asked when Katy returned him a frown.

'I think that Daniel would prefer to work with the client direct in this instance,' said Katy. 'I'll send you his number and you can call him. Ask him if he has time.'

'Will you call him for me? Call him now?' asked Braindead.

'No,' said Katy firmly. She got up and walked over to the counter where she'd left her bag. She got out her phone. 'There, I've sent you his number,' she said. 'Call him in the morning, not now. He's always in a better mood in the mornings.' The last thing Daniel would be expecting was a call for help after the conversation they'd had that afternoon. She wouldn't be surprised if he refused to talk to her for the rest of the week. She hoped he didn't take it out on Braindead.

'Thanks, Katy,' said Braindead after she had sat back down. 'You're a mate. If she says yes, will you act as mother of the bridegroom?'

'What?'

'Well, my mum isn't going to make it, is she? Not from six feet under so I thought you might, you know, look after me on the day. Like she would have done.'

Tears again, tinged with horror that Braindead considered her to be old enough to take on such a role.

'I'd be very honoured,' she said, leaning over and squeezing his hand. And she meant it.

'She's not said yes yet,' warned Ben.

'I think she will,' replied Braindead, 'especially with Daniel in charge of proceedings. Can't fail, can I? Then come the summer we're going to have one hell of a wedding.'

'This summer?' asked Katy.

'Oh yes. We're going for it if she's up for it. This summer, come rain or shine, with the pair of you by my side.' He grinned. 'Happy days.'

'Roll on the summer,' said Ben, raising his drink to propose a toast. 'To finally seeing my best mate in a suit. Wouldn't miss that for the world. And maybe we might have some good news by then too, eh, Katy?' He leaned over and put his arm round her.

'Yeah. Roll on the summer,' muttered Katy, raising her glass half-heartedly. She wondered what he would say if he thought there was a possibility that he might be on the other side of the world, not at his best mate's wedding and without the prospect of becoming a dad again. Maybe she wouldn't talk to him tonight. He was too excited about Braindead's future. Tomorrow – she'd talk to him tomorrow.

Chapter Fifteen

'Go and play now, Millie,' said Ben as he took off her tiny gloves and then unwound her scarf in the hallway outside her preschool. 'I've got to go and get ready for our first rehearsal.'

'Can I be Mary, Daddy?' she asked, staring up at him with a look in her eyes already developed to guarantee she got anything she wanted. He looked away. He must focus; he must be impartial.

'Let's see now, shall we,' he said, unbuttoning her coat.

'But you will let me be the Virgin Mary, won't you, Daddy?'

'I said we'll have to see, Millie.'

'What's a virgin, Daddy?'

Ben stopped unbuttoning her coat. He looked around him. Fortunately there only seemed to be one other parent within earshot. A woman he didn't recognise was preoccupied with removing gloves from her little boy and girl. Mrs Allcock had mentioned there were some new starters coming; it must be them.

'It's a woman who's never had…' Ben paused to let the woman past him. 'A baby before,' he concluded.

'Oh,' said Millie. 'Like Miss Baintree.'

Miss Baintree was the other teaching assistant who helped out in preschool. She was in her mid-twenties and a bit of a looker, though Ben tried hard not to notice. He very much doubted that she was a virgin.

'Noooo,' he said slowly. 'Not really like Miss Baintree.'

'But she hasn't had a baby before. She told me.'

'I know, but it's a very special name for someone who has never even tried to have a baby.'

'So Miss Baintree has tried to have a baby?'

'Probably.'

'So she's not a virgin.'

'No.'

'But how do you know if someone has tried or not?'

'You don't.'

'So how do you know if you can call them a virgin?'

'You don't. So you must never, ever call someone a virgin. Do you hear? Or else they might get upset.'

'Apart from Mary.'

'Yes, apart from Mary. Now go away and find your mates. I need to go and sit in a darkened room.'

'OK, Master Elf,' she said, holding her hand up for a high five. He slapped her hand and pointed her in the direction of her classroom. He'd told her that from now on he was Master Elf at preschool so that the other kids weren't constantly reminded that he was Millie's dad as they prepared for the Nativity. He didn't want accusations of favouritism or Millie thinking she could twist him around her little finger.

He went off to the staff room to find some industrial-strength coffee before he was given charge of twenty-seven children and the Christmas story. Being around a bunch of three-year-olds was so much more fun than trying to herd a bunch of uninterested teenagers around a football pitch, as he used to do in his previous job. He was considering going back to college to take a course to qualify him as a primary-school teacher. They were crying out for male teachers at that level. And it would fit in well with having children. No wonder plenty of women ended up in teaching as soon as they started having kids. Where else can you work where you get the same amount of holidays as they do? He must talk to Katy about it. He hummed to himself as he waited for the kettle to boil then suddenly burst out into spontaneous laughter as the image of Braindead wrapped up like a Christmas tree crossed his mind yet again. He really hoped that if and when he got married it wouldn't mark the end of such escapades. He doubted it. Braindead thrived on the ridiculous, and he couldn't see him losing that. And if he ever became a dad, then his sense of humour would go down a storm with his kids. Ben was even harbouring thoughts that if Braindead and Abby got on with things, and if Katy got pregnant soon, then they would both have children of a similar age. How cool would that be? To watch their kids grow up together?

Glancing at his watch, he splashed boiling water into his mug and made his way to the preschool room, where the kids were involving themselves in quiet carnage before Mrs Allcock took the register. He needed to grab a word with her first to tell her he wanted to change the layout of the room before he started to talk to them about the Nativity. Push all the chairs and tables to the side and have them sit on the floor. He found her in a corner of the room talking to the woman he had spotted earlier. Two nervous-looking children were grasping hold of her hands.

'Mr Chapman,' said Mrs Allcock, beckoning him over. 'Could you come here a minute.'

'Master Elf, please,' he said, striding over and giving the two children a big grin and a wink.

'This is Ms Rubis, and George and Rebecca,' announced Mrs Allcock.

Ben shook Ms Rubis's hand while he felt a tiny alarm bell go off in the back of his head.

'Please call me Lena, Master Elf,' she said, followed by a very slight giggle.

Ben laughed. 'I've brought my hat,' he said, reaching round to pull a green pointy hat with a red pompom on the end out of his back pocket. He pulled it over his head and crouched down on his haunches in order to address the two children. The boy hid his face in Lena's skirt.

'He's very shy with strangers,' Lena told Ben.

'How do you do, my friends?' he said, holding his hand out. 'Welcome to the best playroom in the whole wide world, full of lots of naughty little elves for you to play with.' He looked over his shoulder. 'Millie, come over here and show this pair where to find the secret toys.'

'Secret toys?' asked Rebecca, her eyes wide, dropping Lena's hand.

'Have you hidden some secret Santas?' cried Millie, dashing over to the group.

'Of course,' said Ben. 'Bet you won't find them though.'

George's head peeped out and he eyed Ben suspiciously

'Bet we will,' said Millie.

'Where do we look?' asked Rebecca.

'The toilets,' said Ben, looking straight at George. 'Master Elf often puts them in the toilets. I seem to remember I definitely put a secret Santa in the boys' toilet. Shame the girls can't go in there, and I don't think any of the other boys have thought to look there yet.'

'George,' shrieked Rebecca, 'you need to go and find the secret Santa now before anyone else does.'

'Come on, I'll show you,' said Millie, tugging at his arm.

George eyed Ben again then allowed Millie to drag him off to the boys' toilet without even a backwards glance.

Mission accomplished, thought Ben. He could have been attached to that skirt all morning. He pulled himself up, basking in the approving look of Mrs Allcock.

'Nice work, Master Elf,' she said.

'I do my best,' he said, grinning at Lena.

'Your best looks good,' agreed Lena.

'Master Elf is very popular with the children – and the ladies,' said Mrs Allcock with a wry smile.

'Och, get away with you,' said Ben, laughing. 'I only have eyes for one woman and you know that.' He turned to Lena. 'I keep asking Mrs Allcock here out, but she keeps turning me down. Breaks my heart, she does.' He gave her a wink. 'I go home alone every night, crying into my pillow.'

Mrs Allcock gave a hearty laugh. 'See what I have to put up with,' she said to Lena.

'A lot of fun by the sounds of it,' she replied, beaming at Ben.

Ben detected a slight twang of an accent in her voice that he couldn't quite place. She was slim and dark and mysterious-looking, in total contrast to her children, who were blonde and bonny. Perhaps her husband was Swedish, he thought. With very strong genes. Something was nagging at him, but he wasn't quite sure what. He watched as the new trio came dashing back into the room, having had a productive trip to the loos, and headed over to the book corner to see if there were more Santas loitering there.

'Amazing,' said Lena. 'It looks like they settled already. George is normally so shy in strange surroundings.'

'Bit of healthy competition works wonders for boys forgetting where they are,' said Ben.

Lena nodded. 'I can see that. And I pick up at eleven forty-five, yes?'

'Yes, that's right,' said Mrs Allcock. 'I'm sure they'll be fine. Master Elf is starting the preparations for the Nativity with them today so it's excellent timing. Get them straight in to it.'

'Nativity,' said Lena, raising her eyebrows slightly. She looked at Ben nervously. 'Their mother is very keen on the Nativity,' she said. 'Very keen that they do not miss out because they are twins.'

So she wasn't the mother, thought Ben. That made sense now. This must be the nanny. Interesting. They had a few children with nannies at the preschool but they tended to be younger than this one. Greener. You could see the look of relief in their eyes when they handed the kids over and they could escape to a coffee shop to gossip to their fellow nannies about the state of their employers' marriages. But not this one, she didn't look like a gossip. She was older, more mature. The parents who had recruited her were either very lucky or had searched very hard for someone of her calibre.

Ben looked at Lena thoughtfully.

'Maybe we could rewrite the Nativity so the baby Jesus had an evil twin that no-one knew about? And maybe the twin becomes the devil and so our obsession with good and evil was born. How about that, Lena? Would that make their mother happy? Stars of the show, Jesus and the Devil.' He said all this with a broad grin on his face so that Lena could not help but smile back. She got that he was taking the mickey. She was smart too.

'I think that's quite enough of that, Master Elf,' said Mrs Allcock, patting his arm. 'Master Elf does have a tendency to take things too far, Ms Rubis. You can tell George and Rebecca's mother that as we discussed when she visited, they will be treated just the same as everyone else. As individuals.'

'But will they be Joseph and Mary?' asked Lena, still looking a little concerned.

'Well, that is up to Mr King, of course, but they will have exactly the same chance as everyone,' replied Mrs Allcock.

Ben saw that Lena knew this message might not placate her clearly quite overbearing employer.

'Look,' he said, 'I will make both George and Rebecca shine, I promise. Tell their mother that. Believe me, I know that mothers of twins can be very overprotective of their separate identities. I used to know a mother of twins and...' He stopped mid-sentence. He felt a cold shiver down the back of his neck as he looked over towards where George was counting secret Santas with Millie. He'd not seen Alison or Matthew for nearly three years, when the twins were still just babies. Not since he'd secretly turned to Alison in desperation for parenting advice when he found himself unable to cope and too embarrassed to ask Katy. Of course it hadn't gone down well when Katy found out, but they'd got past it. After all, he hadn't slept with Alison – not like Katy had with Matthew. He'd thought that Alison, Matthew, George and Rebecca had been placed firmly in their past, everyone hoping their paths need never cross again as disaster always struck when it did. Apart, they were two normal couples. Mix them together and they somehow turned out like some freak show on Jeremy Kyle.

Ben's heart sank to his shoes when he realised it was very unlikely there would be two sets of twins at exactly the right age in the area, both called George and Rebecca. Added to that, the insistence of the mother that they both have star parts sounded like only something Alison could contemplate demanding on their first day at a new preschool.

'You were saying, Master Elf?' asked Mrs Allcock when he failed to finish his sentence.

He turned and tried to smile back at his boss. This had doom written all over it. 'I was saying that George and Rebecca are unique children, and I will treat them accordingly.'

'Good – marvellous,' responded Mrs Allcock, shooing Lena away from Ben. 'They are going to be fine,' he heard her say. 'Their mother is going to be very proud of them.'

Chapter Sixteen

'They're running late,' Ian announced to Matthew as he dashed into the conference room, his excuses already prepared for why he was five minutes overdue for the meeting. He sat down, breathing heavily, having taken the stairs rather than wait for the lift. Christ, he was out of shape. You'd think with three kids to run after that his rapidly aging body would not need any additional physical activity. Perhaps he should think about taking up squash again. Would Alison cope with him being out of the house for a further couple of hours a week if it was for his own physical well-being? He'd tried that tack with four hours of golf every Saturday, but the suggestion was met with disdain and a scoffing remark that no-one ever broke a sweat playing golf.

'Which one is this?' asked Matthew, nodding over at the silent Ian, who was bent over his phone furiously texting.

'What do you mean?' muttered Ian without looking up.

'Which lady friend?'

'It's Baz from football. He's being a twat. Wants me to play in goal next week so I'm just giving him a piece of my mind.'

Silence fell on the room apart from Ian's tapping. Matthew opened up his notebook and found a clean page.

'Done,' said Ian, looking up with a grin. 'He won't try and put me in goal again. So how are you, sweet cheeks?' he asked.

Matthew looked over at him. A late-forties, balding man who constantly appeared to approach life as though he didn't have a care in the world apart from whether he had to play in goal or not in the Sunday league. How did he do it?

'I'd be a lot better if you hadn't cornered me the other night,' he said.

'About what?'

'Asking Lena out like that, right in front of me. What was I supposed to say?'

'Yes, of course.'

'I'd have liked to have said no,' said Matthew.

'Why on earth would you say no? I'm a catch.'

'Likely to catch something rather than being a catch, more like. Alison is beside herself. What are you playing at, winding her up when she's pregnant? You know what she can be like.'

'What's it got to do with her? It's not like I'm kidnapping Lena or anything, I'm just taking her to a party.'

'Can't you just take someone else?'

'Why?'

Matthew sighed. He could so do without this; he would have to take another tack.

'She won't sleep with you, you know.'

Ian allowed his jaw to drop slightly. 'I'm offended by that statement. I'm not expecting her to sleep with me.'

Matthew laughed. 'You always expect them to sleep with you. You choose women based on whether they will sleep with you.'

'I don't.'

'What about your six days to six months rule?' asked Matthew, recalling Ian's revelation that he never dated women whose last date was between six days and six months ago.

Ian had the decency to blush slightly. 'When I tell you these things, you're not supposed to hold them against me.'

'So is Lena in the over-six-months category?' continued Matthew. 'Not had a date in over six months so will be desperate for it – as opposed to having been on a date within the last six days so is a bit of a slapper. Either way equals sex, I seem to remember you telling me.'

'I didn't ask Lena out in order to have sex with her,' said Ian, looking uncharacteristically bothered by this line of questioning.

'So you expect me to believe that you've changed the habit of a lifetime for Lena?'

'Yes.' Ian nodded. 'Like I said, this time I'm looking for love. I'm not looking for a quick shag. And she just seemed, well, there was something about her.' He shrugged as though lost for words.

'Alison thinks you'll break her heart and she'll leave, and then we'll lose the best nanny in the north of England.'

'Oh, so it's all about you, is it?'

'Yes, it is quite frankly,' said Matthew. 'I don't know what we'd do without Lena, and if limiting her exposure to you means she doesn't leave us then I agree with Alison. In her words: you are toxic when it comes to relationships.'

'Harsh,' replied Ian.

'But fair,' said Matthew.

They looked at each other across the conference-room table. Matthew didn't like this conversation – two grown men discussing the love life of his Lithuanian nanny. It felt wrong, but he was certain his motivations were pure. He knew that Lena was perfectly capable of looking after herself, but he also knew Ian and his history with women. It was only right that he should warn him off, wasn't it? Even so, it left a bad taste in his mouth. Like he was trying to control Lena or something. He clearly wasn't descended from Victorian nobility so was unused to dealing with such a dilemma.

'Just… just look after her,' he said eventually. 'She's a good person.'

Ian stared back. The awkwardness of the conversation was not lost on him. When Ian discussed his love life with Matthew, it was usually to throw him the funny titbits of dating in the modern age. The highs and the lows, the trials and tribulations – usually at the expense of his latest faceless girlfriend. This was the first time Matthew had called into question his morals, having enjoyed them for so long as entertainment. This was awkward with a capital A.

'Of course I'll look after her,' he said as they held each other's gaze. 'She's different, I get that.'

Matthew nodded. 'Good.' He coughed and picked his pen up, pretending to write in his notebook. He hoped that would sort it. He'd tell Alison he'd had a word with Ian. That he'd promised to be on his best behaviour. He very much hoped that his wife would settle for that, though somehow he doubted it. Possibly only the castration of Ian would be enough to calm her hormone-driven mind that he wasn't going to be the downfall of their precious Lena.

🎄

To Matthew's surprise, Alison met him at the door when he returned that evening. His heart skipped a beat when she appeared before he even had time to get his key out of his pocket. He knew she'd been to see the midwife that morning. He hoped that all was fine. Typically Alison went into anxiety overdrive during this stage in her pregnancies, as a mixture of excitement and terror at the impending birth caused pure adrenaline to shoot through her veins. So much so that he feared she would make herself ill just when she needed her health the most.

But one look at her face and he could tell all was well. She was beaming as much as she was blooming. Blooming enormous, in fact. He instinctively reached out to cup the mound of her belly in awe, as always, that hidden in there was their next child.

'Come quick,' she urged, grabbing his hand and pulling him into the hall. 'You have to see this.'

He put his computer bag down and then hung up his scarf and coat as Alison disappeared into the living room. He couldn't help feeling relieved. Whatever she was dragging him to see was clearly so exciting that it was deflecting from the whole Ian trauma.

He entered the living room to find George and Rebecca chasing each other in circles round and round the coffee table. Normally this would be enough to send Alison into a flurry of instructions to 'calm down, slow down, and stop now or you'll hurt yourselves', but for some reason today she was looking on fondly as they careered headlong into the sofa.

'I will get to the stable first,' shouted George, shoving Rebecca to one side and launching himself on to the sofa.

'I'm having a baby,' Rebecca shouted back, dragging him off to take prime position next to the cushions.

Matthew looked at Alison in confusion. This sort of behaviour was usually unacceptable. What on earth had happened?

'Tell Daddy who you were at your new preschool today, George,' Alison asked him.

'Joseph!' shrieked George.

Alison looked triumphantly at Matthew. 'This is brilliant news for his anxiety,' she said. 'I simply cannot believe it. He actually told me how excited he was. George, who normally would come home weeping at the thought of standing up in front of anyone he didn't know.'

'That's brilliant,' said Matthew.

Checkout Receipt

Mooresville Public Library
(704) 664-2927
http://mooresvillelibrary.org
11/15/18 04:38PM

No-one ever has sex on Christmas Day (BO
CALL NO: F BLO
39025003027788   12/20/18

TOTAL: 1

Library Hours
Mon-Thu 9am-9pm
Fri 9am-6pm; Sat 10am-3pm
Sun CLOSED

'And tell Daddy who you were, Rebecca,' continued Alison.

'Mary, Mary, Mary, Mary,' chanted Rebecca.

'Wow!' exclaimed Matthew, scooping her up in his arms. 'How did that happen?'

'Master Elf said I could be Mary,' said Rebecca.

'I knew this was going to be a great preschool,' said Alison. 'They clearly have a great understanding of how to deal with twins.'

'They gave them the star parts?' said Matthew in wonder that Alison had managed to achieve her aim.

'Master Elf said I was the best Joseph,' said George, jumping off the sofa and pulling at his arms.

'But he said I was the best Mary,' protested Rebecca. 'Best he had ever seen.'

'Well, Master Elf sounds like quite a guy,' said Matthew, looking questioningly at Alison.

'They haven't stopped going on about him since they got back,' she said. 'He's clearly taken a shine to them. And recognised how talented they are.'

Matthew watched as George beat his favourite teddy over the head with a cushion. He sometimes wondered if Alison saw different children to him. She seemed to observe near child geniuses whereas he saw George in near constant attack mode with whatever weapon he could lay his hands on while at home but reduced to a painfully shy little shadow the minute he came into contact with strangers. And as for Rebecca, well, she seemed to occupy most of her time by thumping George with the one-legged naked doll she insisted on calling Dave.

'Well, good for Master Elf,' he conceded. 'He seems to have been a hit with these two as well as with their mummy.' He smiled and bent forward to kiss her.

'He sounds just wonderful,' said Alison. 'And you haven't heard the best of it yet.'

'Haven't you met him then?' asked Matthew.

'No, Lena took them because I didn't want any separation issues, not on their first day, and then I wanted to spend some time with Harry so she picked them up as well, but I'm so pleased she did because, well…' She paused and walked over to the door into the hall then closed it softly behind her before coming back into the room. She was grinning even more widely than before if that were possible. 'He was a hit with Lena too,' she said. 'She came back full of him – it was Master Elf this and Master Elf that. And you know what that means, don't you?'

Matthew had taken on too much information about Master Elf now. He had no idea what this meant. He shook his head.

'She's clearly taken a shine to him as well, so he could be just what she needs to throw her off the scent for Ian. Master Elf could be the answer to our prayers.'

'Master Elf?'

'Yes, Master Elf.'

'Master Elf and Lena?'

'Yes. I've told her she can do all the drop-offs and pick-ups. We need to do everything we can to encourage this one while we do everything we can to discourage Ian.'

'But… but you don't even know if this Master Elf is suitable – or even single for that matter.'

Alison stared back at him as though he were insane. As though her trying to fix their nanny up with a complete stranger only known to them as Master Elf was entirely sensible.

'I asked Lena if she thought he was married and she said she didn't think so. Apparently he was joking around about asking out Mrs Allcock and said he went home alone every night. She even told me he doesn't wear a wedding ring, and you know what that means?'

'He may or may not be married?'

'No,' said Alison firmly. 'It means she looked. It means she was interested enough in him to check out whether or not he was wearing a wedding ring. That's such a good sign. She likes him – I can tell. And she said he was a similar age to her. So if he was married, he'd be wearing a wedding ring. Everyone does these days.'

'Well maybe,' said Matthew.

'Anyway, he isn't Ian. That's what matters. Plus he works in a preschool for Christ's sake so he must be a lovely, caring human being, unlike Ian.'

Matthew sighed. He'd spent too long that day discussing Lena's love life. It's not what he expected to be spending his time doing. Let Alison deal with the whole matchmaking, matchbreaking thing.

'Well, if you really think so then by all means you encourage Lena's affection for a preschool-teaching elf. Shall we invite him round to dinner?' he said flippantly.

'Good God, no!' said Alison. 'That would be weird and a bit forward. Let it take its course. I do think we should invite Ian round for dinner though.'

'What! Are you serious? I thought you wanted him banned from getting anywhere near Lena?'

'Well, I've been thinking about it, and I've come to the conclusion that the best person to persuade Lena away from Ian is Ian. If she spends any length of time with him, especially under our supervision, she'll see the error of her ways. So I figure why wait until the Christmas party? Let's invite Ian over soon. Get it over and done with, and then I can stop worrying about it. Plus she'll now have the contrast of the wonderful Master Elf. She'll soon see why she shouldn't be wasting her time on Ian.'

Matthew thought his head might explode. Romance was complicated, especially when it wasn't your own. He shrugged. 'If you think it's a good idea, I'll ask him.'

'What about Friday?' she urged.

'This Friday?'

'Yes, this Friday.'

'All right then,' he agreed, wondering what on earth Ian – and Lena for that matter – were going to make of this latest development in the manipulation of their non-relationship.

Chapter Seventeen

'Hello, Katy. What time do they do midnight mass in your local church? Carlos was just asking. Would someone be able to take him? Mum xx PS: It would be very nice if you replied to my texts once in a while.'

Katy put her phone back down on her bedside table. What was her mum doing, texting in the middle of the night? Didn't she realise that Katy had more important things to worry about than getting Carlos to midnight mass? Besides, wasn't it obvious what time midnight mass started?

She'd been lying there going over the Christmas-tree debacle involving Ben, Millie and Braindead. She knew it would go down in history as one of the greatest Christmas memories of all time. She couldn't help but wonder also what adventures awaited them all as Braindead hopefully embarked upon married life. How could she drag Ben away from that? His friends were here; his life was here. He was a Yorkshire lad through and through. He would still only drink tea out of his Leeds United mug, and occasionally she heard him muttering prayers to God when he watched them play. That's how much he cared about this place. If they moved to Sydney it would be all for her, and she thought she'd asked him to make enough sacrifices already. He'd left his career to stay at home and look after their daughter so she could go back to work, and he'd done a stunning job of it. Much better, she suspected, than she would have done had she been the one at home all day with a baby.

He'd made it work. Even taking the job at Millie's preschool was above and beyond all expectation. He said he wanted to do it so he wasn't bored at home, but she knew he also enjoyed it, and she wouldn't be surprised if at some point he retrained to teach primary, something she knew he'd be brilliant at. How would he do that in Australia? In Australia, his prospects were probably limited to stay-at home dad to Millie with not even the thought of his longed-for second child to keep him happy.

No, it was a non-starter. She wouldn't even mention it to Ben. And truth be told, she couldn't bear the thought of the look on his face when he realised the move could jeopardise the plan to add to the family. Why put him through that? She would call Cooper White and tell him in no uncertain terms that it was a no, and if he wanted to use that as a reason to not award the business to her firm then so be it. She couldn't change her entire life for the sake of Butler & Calder.

She walked into the office that morning taking a circular route in order to avoid Daniel. She didn't need to see his sulky face just now; she didn't need another lecture. She'd much prefer to make the call to Cooper and then strut triumphantly down to his office and tell him she'd already said no. She looked forward to a tearful hug followed by an insult and then life could carry on as normal.

She sat down at her desk and took a deep breath and looked around her office. Her eyes fell on a framed photo of her with Ben and Millie sitting in a wooden frame on her desk. She looked at it and smiled: she'd made the right decision.

She jumped as her phone rang. It was Andrew, her boss.

'Can you just pop up to my office please?' he asked then put the phone down without waiting for an answer.

Her heart began to beat a little faster. *I bet he wants a debrief on my meeting with Cooper*, she thought. She'd managed to avoid him so far. What should she tell him? She'd have to bluff it out until she'd had a chance to talk to Cooper herself.

She avoided walking past Daniel's office yet again, taking the stairs up to the second floor, where Andrew had his corner office. She knocked politely on the door before walking in, and then just about managed to stop herself from gasping.

'Hi, Katy,' said Cooper, who was leaning casually back in a leather chair.

'Hello,' she replied, swallowing nervously. What was he up to now? Had he already told Andrew about the job offer? She looked over at Andrew as she took a seat. He was beaming at her. She hoped that meant that Cooper hadn't told him, as she would have hoped he'd look a lot more miserable about losing his valuable head of account services.

'Sounds like your dinner went very well,' said Andrew.

Katy glanced over at Cooper, who had the audacity to wink at her.

'Yes,' she replied. 'The dhansak was particularly delicious.'

Andrew roared with laughter.

'I can totally understand why you're so impressed with her,' he said to Cooper. 'She's such a scream.'

Katy returned the compliment with a fixed grin.

'Do you want to tell her or shall I?' continued Andrew, seemingly oblivious to her discomfort.

'Go ahead,' said Cooper. 'Be my guest.'

Andrew leaned forward across his desk, looking Katy straight in the eye.

'You,' he said, pointing at her, 'are going to Sydney.'

'What!' said Katy, whirling round to look at Cooper. 'But… but… I haven't…'

Cooper held his hand up to motion her to stop. 'What Andrew is saying is that I'd like you to come and visit us in Sydney. Look at the set-up. Meet the people. Work out how we make this work.'

'Visit you?' she questioned.

'Yes, visit. Before Christmas. Let's keep the ball rolling so that we can sort this out as soon as possible.'

'Isn't that brilliant, Katy?' said Andrew, who was showing no signs of being remotely cool about the fact that one of his staff had just blagged a trip to Sydney. You would almost believe he was going himself. 'And an enormous show of confidence in what we do here, to want you to go over,' he continued. 'Cooper is clearly a very good judge of character,' he gushed. 'He knows if there is anyone who can work out how to manage a communications campaign from the other side of the world, it's you.'

Katy looked at Andrew. How would he feel if he knew the truth? If he knew that Cooper wanted to get her out there so she would fall in love with Sydney and take the job. That was what he was up to, she was sure.

'I'm not sure I'll be able to organise childcare,' protested Katy weakly.

Andrew shot her a confused glance. 'Ben will be able to cope, won't he?' he asked.

How presumptuous, she thought. Of course he would cope, but he might have other plans. He might have a life other than being there to keep the family up and running while she was at work. Just because he was the main carer didn't mean he didn't have other stuff going on. Now she knew how it felt to be the mum at home. Assumed to be available, whatever demands the workforce placed on your other half.

'I can organise assistance for your family if that's what you need,' announced Cooper.

What was that supposed to mean? Did he have an army of nannies and chefs and drivers to hand who could swoop in and take care of all household needs?

'What I mean is,' said Katy, 'I should check with Ben's schedule before I commit to being able to go, that's all.' She shot Cooper a glare – she didn't like being manipulated in this way.

'Well, why don't you go and call him now?' said Andrew, getting up and walking round to the front of the desk.

'Now?'

'Yes, now. I think Cooper would like to know we're pressing forward before he leaves.'

'No, it's fine,' said Cooper, also getting up out of his chair. 'Just call me later today when you've had a chance to check in with your husband.' He reached into his breast pocket and took out a card and handed it to her. 'I'll be getting on a flight at around three so be sure to call me before then and we can put all the arrangements in place.'

She took the card from him and their eyes locked as she looked up at him.

'Well, that sounds like a plan,' said Andrew. 'Now I'll just go and check that Louisa has managed to get hold of those showreels I promised you,' he said and walked out of the room.

The moment he left an awkward silence descended. Katy must have looked distressed because a look of surprise then confusion flooded Cooper's face.

'What are you doing?' she spat.

'Look, I really think you would enjoy seeing our operation in Sydney,' he replied.

'You cannot manipulate me like this.'

'I'm not,' he said, looking genuinely dismayed. 'I want you to come and see it. I thought it might help persuade you. I didn't mean to trick you, I just thought it might help, that's all.'

'I *feel* manipulated.'

'Oh goodness no,' he said, looking horrified. 'I didn't mean that at all. Just come and see. Please. No pressure, I promise. Come and take a look and then decide. If you still don't think it's for you then no hard feelings.'

Katy looked him up and down. She didn't know whether to trust him or not. One minute he played the master businessman, convinced he was right and that everyone would follow, and the next minute he was this lovely, genuine guy who you might consider trusting with your life.

'Come on,' he said. 'What's the worst that can happen? At least you get to see Sydney.'

She'd always wanted to go to Australia, but could she trust herself not to fall in love with it? She'd felt so clear-headed when she'd walked into work that morning and now she felt like she had a hangover and was about to be sick.

'No pressure?' she asked him.

He held his palms up in mock surrender. 'I promise,' he said.

God, it was so tempting. 'I'll have to check it's OK with my husband,' she said.

'Of course.' He nodded. 'Totally understandable.'

She nodded back.

'Can I just say one thing?' he asked tentatively.

'You might as well,' she said.

'It's just that, well, I imagine that guilt is playing a major role in your thinking at the moment.'

She shrugged. She felt like a sulky teenager being handed well-meaning advice that she really didn't want to listen to.

'You know, if you were a man then guilt wouldn't come into it. A man would see a great opportunity and go for it. Why should you be different just because of your gender?'

She turned to look at him. She knew it was impossible to ignore her gender in this scenario. 'Are you married?' she asked.

'No, but I nearly was once,' he admitted. He looked as though he was about to elaborate, but then he stopped as Andrew walked back into the room.

'Here we are,' he said, handing a stack of showreels over to Cooper. 'Take these back and show your guys, then all being well they'll have a good understanding of what we do here before Katy gets there next week.'

'I haven't asked Ben yet,' Katy felt the need to re-emphasise.

Andrew turned his back on her as though to shut her up. 'Thank you so much for dropping in this morning.'

'My pleasure,' said Cooper. He turned to Katy, holding his hand out. 'We'll talk later then?' he said.

'Yes,' she said, limply shaking his hand back.

'Good. Well, I can see myself out,' said Cooper brusquely. 'It's been very good meeting you all.' He nodded at Andrew and turned and left the room. She heard him thank Louisa, who was sitting at her desk outside, then watched as he strode down the corridor and disappeared through a door.

'Well done you,' said Andrew, turning and grasping her shoulders in excitement. 'You must have made quite an impression! All-expenses-paid trip to Sydney? You must be chuffed to bits.'

'Yeah,' said Katy, nodding, her brow furrowed. 'Something like that.'

'Come on,' he said, 'you can be a bit more excited than that! What's the matter with you?'

'It's just a lot to get my head round, you know. And it's short notice and there's a lot going on at home, what with Christmas coming and all that.'

'Are you kidding me? It's twenty-six degrees in Sydney. You can get some sunshine and all your shopping done in Duty Free. What's not to love? Get on the phone to Ben right now. Tell him you'll bring him back a fluffy kangaroo and get your flight booked. I think we have this account in the bag.'

🎄

Katy walked back to her office in a daze. What had just happened? She'd been so certain when she'd come into work that morning. Now what was she supposed to do?

She picked up her mobile, trying to work out what she was going to say to Ben. She figured he'd be in the midst of Nativity mayhem so she would leave him a message. Ask him to call her back as soon as possible. Then in the meantime she could decide what to do.

'Hi,' he said breathlessly after two rings.

'Oh, hi. I thought you'd be busy.'

'So why did you phone?'

'To leave you a message to say call me.'

'I'm on the coffee run – you've got two minutes, so shoot.'

'Right, well, er, so remember we pitched for some business with an Australian airline?'

'Boomerang,' Ben boomed out. 'Are you serious? We hardly saw you for days because of that. How could I forget? You get the business then? Are we celebrating tonight?'

'Well, er, not quite. You see they're very keen, but they want us to go to Sydney and see the operation over there first.'

Katy heard Ben whistle. 'Wow! That's some cushy number, eh? Work trip to Oz, how cool is that? So who is the "us" then? Is it you but they need me to go and carry the bags? Tell me that's why you're calling! Are we both going to Sydney?'

'Sadly no. It's – well, it's just me they've asked actually.'

'Wow – seriously? Well, that's really cool, Katy. I'm jealous as hell though. When do you go?'

'Sometime before Christmas?'

'What! I thought you were going to say next year.'

'I guess they want to get on with it.' She paused. Ben was quiet on the other end of the line. 'I'm sorry, Ben,' she said.

'No, no, it's fine,' he said, though she wasn't sure if he meant it. 'Me and Millie will battle on without you. How long do you think you'll be away for?'

'I'll try and keep it as short as possible,' she said, 'but I don't know. I guess given how long it takes to fly there, maybe four or five days, do you think?'

'Yeah, I guess.' He sounded distant now, like he was trying to work out his reaction to the news. 'And when will you go?'

'I'm not sure yet. I've not even looked at flights.'

'Just don't miss the Nativity, will you?' he said quietly. 'Millie would be devastated.'

'Of course I won't,' she said.

'Fine,' he said. 'I suppose I'd better get back to the stable.'

'I'm so proud of you, you know,' she found herself saying.

'I'm proud of you too,' he added. 'Really proud. Will you bring me back a koala?'

'Obviously.'

'See you later.'

'Bye.'

🎄

Katy was still sitting with her head in her hands when Daniel slipped into her office about ten minutes later. She didn't think she had ever felt so confused. She wished she could turn back the clock a week, to before she had been offered a dream job in Australia – life had been much simpler then.

Daniel stood at the door and slow-clapped. Katy dragged her face out of her hands.

'I hear you've only gone and bagged yourself a free trip out to Sydney,' he said, putting his hands sulkily on his hips.

'I didn't ask for any of this,' Katy told him defiantly. 'I was just doing my job, OK?'

Daniel nodded slowly. He turned round and shut the door behind him.

'So are you going to go?' he asked, folding his arms over his chest.

She sighed; she wished she hadn't told Daniel about the job offer. It wasn't making it any easier.

'I don't see that I have any choice,' she said. 'I came in this morning ready to call Cooper and tell him it was a definite no and he's one step ahead of me. He says he just wants to show me what it's like, that's all. No pressure.'

Daniel raised his eyebrows. 'That man is used to getting what he wants, Katy.'

'I know,' she agreed. 'But what do I do? I can't refuse to go as I'll have to say why to Andrew, and then the whole deal could collapse. I might as well go. Why not? At least it will reassure me that saying no is definitely the right thing to do.'

Daniel nodded, not saying anything. He walked over to the window and looked out on the rain-sodden grey streets of Leeds. 'You're right,' he said. 'Being in glorious sunshine as opposed to this is bound to put you off.'

She didn't know what to say. He looked at her and shrugged then walked across the room to the door. He went to open it then turned just as he was about to leave.

'By the way,' he said. 'Ben called. I said I'd help Braindead work out how to ask Abby to marry him. They're going to come in here next week.'

'Thanks,' said Katy. 'I appreciate that.'

'No problem, that's what friends are for.'

He walked out and Katy put her head back in her hands.

Chapter Eighteen

'I'm not so sure about this idea,' Matthew said to Alison as he entered the kitchen. 'Lena has been in the bathroom for a very long time. Like she's going to a lot of effort.'

Ever since Alison had suggested inviting Ian for a meal to display all his failings to Lena, he'd had a bad feeling about it. After all, he knew Ian a lot better than Alison did. She barely socialised with him, having built her opinion of him from the stories Matthew had shared with her regarding his relationship history. Alison had never experienced Ian's full charm offensive, and Matthew had a sneaking suspicion that her cunning plan was about to backfire spectacularly.

'Oh, I'm not worried about that,' said Alison, stirring a pan of home-made soup. 'In fact the more effort she makes the better. The disappointment of discovering what Ian is actually like will then only be harder to bear and completely throw her off.'

'Well, I hope you're right,' he said, reaching up to take wine glasses from the cupboard and putting them on the counter. 'This is a hell of a lot of trouble to go to just to stop two people falling for each other.'

'As I said before, better for it to happen here than at the Christmas party. And I can be here for Lena when she realises what a mistake she's making. Now, can you make sure we have enough wine in the fridge?'

'Do you think Lena drinks?' he asked. 'I don't think I've ever seen her, have you?'

'Oh,' said Alison, turning towards him. 'I'm not sure actually.'

They looked at each other, confused.

'Then again I don't think I've ever offered her a glass of wine in the house,' Matthew continued. 'I guess there's never been the occasion for it.'

'Well no,' said Alison. 'She is our employee at the end of the day so I guess there wouldn't have been any reason to offer her wine.'

'Until now.'

'Until now,' agreed Alison. She turned away.

Another reason Matthew was inclined to think the evening would not go as expected was the unique occasion of having their live-in nanny as a guest to dinner. As much as he liked and appreciated Lena, he always felt awkward somehow eating with her. If you sat down with a guest, you would make an effort with polite conversation. A member of the family you could just ignore. But an employee sitting at your breakfast table in their dressing gown? What does one do? His answer was typically to skip breakfast, meaning Lena was costing him a fortune in cereal bars at work, which were no good for his waistline either.

There were two bottles of white in the fridge. More than enough surely, especially as Alison wasn't drinking and Ian would be driving. He felt suddenly panicked. That would mean possibly only he and Lena would be drinking. It didn't feel like a night for getting pissed with the nanny. That couldn't be right, and yet the mere thought of the evening ahead made him want to get very drunk indeed.

He took one of the bottles out of the fridge and put it back in the wine rack.

'Can I do anything?' he asked as Alison opened the oven door.

'I think it's all in hand,' she said, steam billowing out in her face. 'I've gone simple, soup and then a goulash. I thought we'd eat in here actually. Could you set the table?'

'Of course,' he said, glad of a job. He wanted to be busy when Lena came down; he didn't want to be inactive and so forced into idle chatter. What would he talk about? A wave of panic passed over him yet again.

He was just trying to do what Alison normally did with napkins when Lena tentatively entered the room. She slid in so quietly that Alison didn't even notice that she was hovering nervously by the door.

Matthew swallowed. The second he saw her he realised the night was doomed.

'You look er… very smart,' he faltered. This was a lie. She looked stunning. A midnight blue dress swathed her slim frame, complementing her dark hair, which she'd let fall loose around her shoulders rather than scraping it up into a ponytail as she usually did. It was her eyes that took your breath away, though. She must have put a lot of make-up around them, thought Matthew, because they looked enormous compared to normal. She clearly knew what she was doing in that department, though they had never seen this skill emerge before. Beautiful green eyes looked at him nervously, and he wanted more than anything to be able to cancel the entire night's proceedings.

'Wow!' he heard Alison say. She was standing over the hob, wooden spoon paused in mid-air. Alison looked surprised and alarmed. She clearly hadn't expected Lena to scrub up this well either. There was an awkward silence as they both continued to stare at her.

'May I help?' she asked, walking towards Alison. 'Please. What can I do?'

'Oh, er, well, er, I'm not sure,' replied Alison, clearly thrown.

'Let me wash those pans?' she said, heading towards the sink.

'Oh no,' cried Alison. 'Your dress!'

'It's OK,' said Lena, pulling open a drawer and putting on an apron. 'This is so kind of you, I must help.' She tied the apron round her waist then turned to the sink.

Alison glanced over at Matthew and they exchanged bewildered looks. Now she was starting to panic, he could tell. He tried not to give her an 'I told you so' look back.

The doorbell rang. 'I'll get it,' he gasped and dashed out the room, pleased to have the chance to gather his thoughts and readjust his approach to the evening.

He pulled open the door ready to greet Ian but for a moment he couldn't see him as he was obscured by an enormous bunch of blood-red roses.

Oh for fuck's sake, thought Matthew. *He's really going for it.*

'How do,' said Ian cheerily, stepping into the hall. 'How's it going?'

'Brilliant, just brilliant,' said Matthew with a forced grin. 'Couldn't be better. Those for me?' he said, nodding at the flowers.

Ian laughed uproariously. 'No, for someone special. Not you, you worthless waste of space.'

Matthew sighed. 'You'd better come through.'

'Hold on a minute, chap,' said Ian, pulling on his arm. 'Just need to check something. It is Lena, isn't it? Her name, I mean. Don't want to get it wrong.'

'Seriously?' said Matthew.

Ian shrugged. 'Just checking.'

'Yes, it's Lena,' replied Matthew, pulling his arm away and walking through the kitchen door.

'I'm here,' announced Ian as he waltzed through after him. Alison looked up and grimaced. Lena turned her head over her shoulder to look at him, her arms still submerged in the washing-up bowl. 'What a beautiful sight to behold,' he continued.

'Two women slaving in the kitchen to cook a meal for men,' sneered Alison, glaring at the roses.

'No,' said Ian. 'Just two beautiful women.' He advanced towards Alison and bent to kiss her on the cheek. 'These are for you,' he said. 'So very kind of you to invite me over, I really appreciate it.'

Matthew nearly laughed out loud at the look of surprise on Alison's face. Ian truly was a genius when it came to playing women.

'For me?' she said in surprise.

'Of course,' he replied. 'Matthew told me this was your idea, and I wanted to show you how grateful I was.'

Alison put down her spoon and took the flowers from Ian, staring down at them in amazement.

'Well thank you,' she said, looking back up at him and giving him a small smile. 'They're beautiful.'

'My pleasure,' he replied before glancing over at Matthew. Matthew expected Ian to give him a crafty wink, but he didn't succumb.

'Drink?' Matthew asked him.

'That would be great, but let me lend a hand while you're sorting that out,' replied Ian. He leaned past Alison and picked a tea towel off the rail and went to stand next to Lena at the sink. She looked at him in surprise before handing him a suds-soaked saucepan.

Matthew was in awe. Even for Ian this was a stellar performance: flowers for the lady of the house currently plotting his downfall and volunteering for drying duties alongside Lena. Matthew put the second bottle of white back in the fridge.

🌲

After the washing-up had been completed, Matthew guided them to the table to be seated, only for Alison to rearrange everyone to make sure Ian and Lena were sitting diagonally across from each other. She'd looked accusingly at Matthew, as if to imply he should have guessed the correct seating arrangement for the occasion. Despite the re-organisation, however, it was still impossible to prevent Ian from openly staring at Lena. He'd not glimpsed her full-on until she'd turned from the sink and taken off her pinny. Her stunning make-up, flowing hair and figure-hugging dress had all but caused him to drool as his jaw dropped as he'd watched her glide gracefully over to the table. So entranced had he been that he nearly missed his mouth with his first mouthful of soup, forcing him to try and gather himself and attempt some kind of conversation.

'So how was your day?' Ian asked her.

'It has been lovely,' she replied. 'I took George and Rebecca to the park. They love it there.'

Matthew felt like he was in a Jane Austen novel as he oversaw the dating rituals of his charges over dinner. It was stiff and awkward, unlike any other dinner he had attended in the name of sociability. He wished he were anywhere but here.

'George loves to play hide and seek but Rebecca's favourite is the slide.'

'The slide!' exclaimed Ian. 'I love a good slide too.' He said this as though this thing in common with the daughter of her employer made them the perfect match. Matthew grimaced at Ian. This was new. He was tongue-tied in the face of this exotic beauty. She'd knocked his confidence and his chat-up lines were coming out worse than anything Matthew might have tried in his heyday.

'George and Rebecca have started a new preschool,' said Alison, stepping into the conversation. 'It's absolutely wonderful. They absolutely adore their new teacher, don't they, Lena? What is his name again?'

She shrugged. 'I only know him as Master Elf. He is so very good with the children. He made them comfortable immediately.' She giggled as if remembering something. 'He made them go and find secret Santa in the toilet.'

'What?' exclaimed Alison, looking suddenly horrified.

'It was just a joke really,' reassured Lena. 'But it made them happy. And it gave George his confidence. He so quickly forgot about me in his race to find the Santa.'

'He sounds like a wonderful man,' said Alison, grinning broadly at Lena.

'He is kind,' she said. 'I can tell. Especially with the young.'

'I expect you can tell a lot about a man from how he is with children?' Ian asked her.

'Oh yes,' said Lena. 'And how children are with them. Children don't hide their thoughts.'

'How are your children by the way?' Alison asked Ian. 'Have you seen them lately?'

Ian swivelled his gaze to Alison, who was sitting beside him.

Thirty points to Alison, thought Matthew.

'Well they've both been at uni of course for the last few weeks,' replied Ian. 'I was married very young,' he said to Lena. 'I know you can't believe that I'm a father of kids at college.'

'And your wife?' asked Lena, her brow furrowed.

Thirty points to Lena, thought Matthew.

'We divorced six years ago,' he replied.

'I am sorry,' she said.

'Not as sorry as she was,' muttered Alison.

Ian glanced at her uncomfortably then looked back at Lena.

'Like I said, we married too young and then grew apart. Only I wasn't mature enough to tell her straight. I had an affair and she found out. I'm not proud of it.' He put down his spoon and patted his mouth with his napkin before he continued. 'What I did was a terrible thing, but we needed to split up because we were making each other miserable. I would never, ever put someone through that again, but I'm glad it happened. She's about to remarry actually, and he makes her happier than I ever could. We got two fantastic children out of the marriage, which I will never regret.'

A silence fell around the table. Matthew was stunned. That was the most Ian had ever revealed about the end of his marriage. It was almost as if he'd expected to be asked.

'Honesty, even when the news is bad, is a good thing,' said Lena. 'Honesty goes a long way.'

Matthew looked over at Alison, who was staring at Ian and then at Lena. He had no idea who was winning now.

'And will your children be with you for Christmas then, Ian?' asked Alison.

'Sadly no,' he replied. 'Catherine is spending it with her new boyfriend – in Slough, of all places. And Jack is with the family of one of his posh mates in Sweden. That's what happens when you go to uni in Newcastle apparently. It's where all the toffs go, so you end up celebrating Christmas naked in a sauna!' He started to laugh then stopped, realising he'd slipped into normal Ian mode.

'What are toffs?' asked Lena.

'Posh people,' replied Ian. 'People with money and aristocratic connections, bit like Alison.' He winked at her. Matthew didn't care for Ian's chances now; this was dangerous ground.

'But Alison is a good person,' said Lena, before Alison could protest. 'You make toffs sound like bad people.'

Alison leaned back in her chair, awaiting Ian's answer.

'You're right,' agreed Ian fervently. 'Alison is a good person, so you could never call her a toff. I guess it means someone who has more money than sense. Certainly not something you could accuse Alison of at all.'

'And your son's friends, do they have more money than sense?' asked Lena.

'Some maybe. But I trust Jack to see through that. Despite his father, he has a sensible head on his shoulders. He must get that from Carol.'

'But you will miss them so at Christmas?' Lena asked.

'Desperately,' replied Ian. 'It'll be the first time ever I haven't seen them both on Christmas Day. But they have their own lives to lead, I can't tell them what to do. Who wants to spend Christmas with their old man when they can be in Sweden with their mates or with the love of their life in Slough?' He shrugged. 'I have to leave them to it and let them get on with it. It's their life, not mine. I'm just happy they're happy. That's all that matters.'

Lena leaned forward, looking at Ian intently.

'They are lucky,' she told him. 'That you think that. My father would not say that. He thought he knew what was good for my happiness, but all he wanted was for me to do what made him happy, not what made me happy.'

'I'm very sorry to hear that,' replied Ian.

If he had been sitting next to her he would have reached over and taken her hand. Matthew could tell that would have been his next move – Alison had been right about the seating arrangements.

'Oh, it is all in the past. Nothing really. He was just very ambitious for me. He wanted me to study, study, study all the time. Go to university. Be a doctor or a lawyer or something. But it was not for me. All I could do was disappoint him.'

Matthew could hear Ian's response before it had even come out of his mouth.

'There's no way on earth you could be a disappointment,' he said with a look of astonishment. 'Could she, Alison?'

Alison looked trapped, forced into collaboration on this conversation with nowhere to go. 'Of course not,' she said. 'Lena's brilliant. I honestly don't know what we'd do without her.' She directed this at Ian. He didn't read the underlying threat in her voice.

'That is very kind of you to say,' added Lena. 'I feel very lucky to be in such a good house with such good company.' She smiled and raised her glass.

'Well, I will drink to that,' announced Ian, beaming at Lena. 'To a good house in good company,' he said, chinking his wine glass against her's. Alison half-heartedly raised her water glass while Matthew tapped his glass against Lena's and Ian's before taking three generous gulps.

🎄

'So tell me more about where you come from,' Ian asked Lena as Alison cleared away the dessert plates.

'Would you get the coffee on?' Alison asked Matthew before Lena could reply. Matthew looked back at her in a daze. The meal had progressed with Ian continuing to play an absolute blinder. He'd judged the situation perfectly, dialling down his usual raucous patter to become a funny, charming man who was sympathetic to all his fellow diners. He'd gently cajoled Lena into opening up about her background, making her reveal more in an hour than Matthew and Alison had learnt in over eighteen months of her living under their own roof. Not forgetting he was there at Alison's invitation, he splashed lavish praise on all the food, clearing up every scrap and asking for seconds as he lamented that living alone had made him lazy in the home-cooked food department and stressed how grateful he was to be enjoying a proper meal. He positioned himself perfectly as the struggling bachelor while being honest about the fact that he wasn't short of girlfriends. 'Loneliness' apparently drove his constant need to seek out female company. Matthew did splutter at this slightly, as he was always under the impression that sex had something to do with it as well.

'Dating in this day and age is like being in the toyshop but not being able to find your favourite toy. Lots of things to play with but nothing that you crave to have constantly by your side,' he'd said at one point.

'Are we supposed to feel sorry for you?' Alison had asked in astonishment.

'Yes,' said Ian firmly. 'Yes, you are. Look at you, you've got it all – a full house, literally. Whatever you think of me, Alison, I still go home to an empty house.'

Matthew could sense Alison getting increasingly frustrated at Ian's ability to charm and extract sympathy. She'd tried everything, asking him a list of probing questions that should have been guaranteed to expose his loose morals and suspect lifestyle, but somehow he'd managed to slip through her fingers. Every time he'd turned her questions into an opportunity for Lena to cock her head to one side and give him a look that dripped with compassion.

'Do something,' Alison hissed to Matthew when they collided at the sink, her dumping dishes and him filling the coffee pot with water.

'Like what?' Matthew hissed back. Ian had performed a masterclass in charm, and Alison had been totally outmanoeuvred. He'd warned her, and she hadn't listened.

'I don't care,' hissed back Alison. 'Anything!'

Matthew returned to the table in a daze. He'd drunk too much as his nervousness for the outcome of the evening had grown. He was in no fit state to take on a sober Ian. However, he knew that if he didn't at least give it a shot, his life wouldn't be worth living.

He slumped down into his chair and took another slug of wine. There was one last thing he could think of; he would have to give it a try.

'How's the waterbed?' Matthew asked Ian. 'Still fun?' Ian paled slightly, and Alison, standing behind him getting cups out, gave Matthew a thumbs up. He felt a wave of relief – he might just get out of this evening alive. Ian had bought a waterbed to please both himself and his last serious girlfriend, having tried one on a dirty weekend away in Blackpool.

Ian picked up his glass of water and took a gulp before he spoke. He put the glass down and opened his mouth then closed it again.

It was all over, thought Matthew. Finally a symbol of his lifestyle Ian couldn't explain. Matthew reached for his glass to congratulate himself with more wine. Only somehow his hand wasn't quite connecting with his eye line and he knocked a full glass of white flying, all over Ian.

'Oh no!' gasped Lena, immediately getting up and dashing round the table to hand him a napkin.

'It's OK,' said Ian, taking the napkin from her and pressing it down on his leg to try and soak up the liquid. 'It's only wine, I've had worse chucked at me.'

'Sorry, mate,' said Matthew, handing over another napkin.

'Not a problem,' replied Ian. 'I know you didn't mean it.' He glanced up, giving him a meaningful look.

'Here's a wet cloth,' said Alison, dashing over. 'Press it over it.'

'Are you sure you are OK?' asked Lena, putting a hand on his shoulder.

'I'll live,' he replied, covering her hand with his. He looked into her eyes and smiled. 'Look, it's probably time I went anyway. I'll go home and get these wet things off, if you don't mind. It's been lovely, though – thank you so much, Alison.'

'I'm sorry,' said Matthew feebly. Alison glared at him.

'Oh, I nearly forgot,' said Ian. 'I made you something, Lena.' He walked out into the hall, soggy-legged, and came back a moment later with a small paper bag and handed it over to Lena. She looked at him with a confused smile then peered in. When she looked back up, her face shone.

'How?' was all she said.

'YouTube,' he replied.

She laughed and carefully pulled out what looked like some kind of snowflake made of white tubes. She held it up to the light as it dangled from a string.

'It's what they do in Lithuania at Christmas,' Ian told Matthew and Alison. 'They make decorations out of paper straws. Thought I'd give it a go.' He shrugged as though this was totally normal.

Lena was enchanted, rotating the slightly wonky snowflake in her fingers. Matthew and Alison shook their heads in disbelief.

'It's amazing,' said Lena. 'Brings back such memories.'

'Good ones, I hope?' Ian asked.

'Yes,' she said. 'Thank you, it is so very kind and thoughtful.'

Ian grinned. 'Would you see me to my car?' he asked.

'Of course,' replied Lena, and Matthew and Alison watched as they left the room, closing the door softly behind them.

'You nearly had him,' said Alison.

'I know, I'm sorry.'

'I'm not sure that Master Elf can beat Lithuanian Christmas tree decorations,' she added, leaning back in her chair and shaking her head. 'But he's going to have to try. We need him now more than ever.'

Chapter Nineteen

'I've got it,' said Daniel, standing up and walking around the agency's boardroom the following Monday afternoon. He stopped dramatically in front of Ben and Braindead.

'She'll want to be the centre of attention, right?' he asked.

Braindead nodded.

'She'll want to be made to feel like a princess, right?'

He nodded again.

'Belle of the ball?'

'Yes.'

'Fireworks, strobe lighting, music throbbing, a smoke machine perhaps?' he continued.

'Sounds like Abby,' agreed Braindead, 'but there's no way on earth I can afford all that.'

'You don't have to,' Daniel told him. 'That is the genius of this plan.'

'You're scaring me now,' said Braindead. 'What are you talking about?'

'Just tell him, Daniel,' said Ben, looking at his watch. He had to pick Millie up in half an hour. He hadn't expected it to take this long.

'You propose at Christmas Party Land!'

'Come on, Braindead,' Ben had said earlier as they stood outside the offices of Butler & Calder. 'We only have an hour, and we're already late.'

'Are you sure this is a good idea?' asked Braindead as the automatic doors slid apart before them. 'When you suggested we ask Daniel for help, I thought we'd be having a pint down at The Feathers with him while he gave me a few pointers. Stopped me making a fool of myself. Told me how to impress Abby. I wasn't expecting this,' he said, throwing his arms wide to indicate the vast and modernist reception space.

'What do you mean, "this"?'

'I mean, a meeting,' explained Braindead. 'You don't come here for a casual chat, do you? Nothing casual happens here. I mean, look at the chairs. Designed to be uncasual.'

Ben looked across to the clear acrylic dining chairs lining one wall. They did look like the most uncomfortable thing on the planet.

'This is the only time Daniel could fit us in. When I suggested a cheeky pint, he said the last time he'd had a cheeky pint was in 1984 when he was fifteen and thinking he had to impress women. He'd grown out of cheeky pints very quickly, he said.'

'As well as women.'

'Exactly. Look, we'll probably just sit in his office or something. Nothing to be scared of.'

'Ben King and Brain— I mean Martin Freeman for Daniel in Creative Services,' Ben told the receptionist.

'*The* Martin Freeman?' the receptionist asked with a friendly smile.

'Do I look like a hobbit or a midget detective?' spat Braindead.

'Just asking,' she said, frowning and picking up the phone.

'Just chill, will you,' advised Ben.

'It's just there's a lot riding on this, and tired jokes about Martin Freeman are not helping.'

'Ben King and Martin Freeman are in reception,' said the woman into the phone. 'No, not *the* Martin Freeman.' She paused to listen to the response before cupping the receiver with her hand. 'Are you the Martin Freeman otherwise known as Braindead?' she asked.

'Precisely,' agreed Braindead, marching off and sitting himself down in an uncomfortable acrylic chair.

🌲

'Martin?' Daniel exclaimed as he came out of the lift a few minutes later. 'Seriously? Martin?'

'Yes, what of it?'

'No wonder you prefer Braindead.'

'Shall we go to the pub? There's one next door.'

'No,' said Daniel. 'I'm supposed to be at work. You and Ben are here for research purposes, if anyone asks. Now come upstairs and try not to draw attention to yourselves.'

🌲

'It's a very big dining room,' said Braindead, when they reached their destination.

'It's a boardroom,' said Daniel, switching lights on and pulling up blinds.

'I knew that,' said Braindead. 'I watch *The Apprentice*.'

'Well, unlike *The Apprentice* no-one gets fired in here. They have a pokey little HR office for that. The windows are cheaper to replace if they get smashed, and it's on the ground floor if anyone decides to jump.'

'Really?' exclaimed Braindead.

'No,' said Daniel. 'It's on the first floor. But with locked windows. Now sit down and let's get on with this, shall we?' He indicated for the pair of them to sit down then went over to a large glass screen on wheels and dragged it over.

'You building a greenhouse?' asked Braindead.

'No, this is a smart screen. We can write on it – see.' Daniel grabbed a pen and scribbled fluorescent yellow on the glass.

'Wow,' said Braindead, 'very *Minority Report*! Are you sure this is all necessary, Danny boy?'

'Do you want my help or not?' asked Daniel.

'Yes, but—'

'Yes, but nothing. You came to me to make sure this job gets done properly so we'll start as we mean to go on. Now let's talk about our target customer.' Daniel grabbed a pen and wrote Abby in capital letters across the top of the screen.

'Even I think you might be going a bit over the top here, Daniel,' muttered Ben.

'That's where you're wrong. The key to success in most things is always to put the customer at the centre of the experience, whatever that is. Whether it's buying beans or test-driving a Porsche. You understand your target market and you'll be successful, I promise you. Now, tell me about Abby. Let's start with her likes.'

'Me,' said Braindead.

'Well yes, that does speak volumes and tells us things about her that are best left unsaid – but what else?'

Braindead went quiet.

'What apart from me?' he eventually asked.

'Yes, apart from you.'

'Well, all the usual girly things really. She loves make-up – I mean, really *loves* it, spends hours with it. Don't get it myself. And fake tan, what's that all about? Her mate goes round with a tent every week and she stands in it stark bollock naked while she gets sprayed with dirty water. I've told her that if an alien landed and watched her handing money over for the privilege, he'd pack his UFO up and get off the planet as soon as he could.'

'What if an alien landed and saw thousands of people watching a tiny little ball bounce around a field every week? What would he do then?' asked Daniel.

'Probably ask someone to explain the offside rule?'

Daniel stared at him. 'Back to Abby... What else switches her on?'

'Bit personal eh, Danny Boy?'

'You know what I mean. What else does she get excited about?'

'Apart from me?'

Daniel blew his cheeks out.

'She likes her music, doesn't she?' said Ben. 'And dancing. You can often find Braindead at the edge of a dance floor while Abby really goes for it.'

'I don't do dancing,' said Braindead, shaking his head.

Daniel wrote music and dancing on the glass board in lime green.

'What do you enjoy doing together?' he asked.

'Again, a bit personal!' exclaimed Braindead.

Daniel put the top on his pen, put it down on the table and went to walk out.

'No, don't go, I'm sorry,' said Braindead, leaping up and pulling on his arm. 'Please, I'll stop taking the piss, I promise.'

'I have much better things to do with my time than be messed around by you.'

'Sorry. Really sorry,' blustered Braindead. 'It's just nerves,' he said. 'You know. It's kind of embarrassing, that's all.'

'Braindead, you're about to reveal your innermost feelings to the woman you love. This is no time for embarrassment. Now, what do you enjoy doing together?' He took the top back off his pen.

'Why don't you tell him, you know, about that thing you told me you do?' said Ben.

'What thing?'

'You know, your Thursday-night thing.'

Braindead didn't reply just turned slightly pink. 'When did I tell you about that?' he asked.

'Chris's stag do. You passed out soon afterwards, you were very drunk.'

'I am *never* drinking again,' he said solemnly.

'You always say that.'

'I mean it this time.'

'Oh for God's sake!' cried Daniel. 'What is your Thursday-night thing?'

'Beer, balti and *Beauty and the Beast*,' muttered Braindead.

'Excuse me?' asked Daniel. 'Could you repeat that please?' He had his pen paused ready to write it down on the screen.

'He said beer, balti and *Beauty and the Beast*,' said Ben helpfully. 'They drink beer, have a curry and watch *Beauty and the Beast*, and depending on how drunk he is then they do a slow dance round the living room at the same time as the ballroom scene.'

'I am never, ever drinking again,' said Braindead, staring at Ben with a horrified look on his face.

Daniel was staring at Braindead with his mouth open.

'Every Thursday?' he asked.

'Pretty much,' muttered Braindead.

'For some reason this ever so slightly raises you in my estimation,' said Daniel. 'Wait. I trust you mean the original animated version?'

'The cartoon one, yes. I'm afraid so,' said Braindead, hanging his head. 'If you tell anyone else I will kill you both. It's just… it's just, she likes it, and she made me watch it, and it's quite a good story actually so we just got into this weird habit. We always watch *The Premier League Show* straight after. Without fail. Always. I am very firm about that.'

Daniel shook his head. 'If somebody else told me about their beer, balti and *Beauty and the Beast* habit I would be appalled, but somehow from you, Braindead, it's kind of romantic.'

Braindead shrugged. 'Like I said, we watch *The Premier League Show* straight after.'

Daniel was staring at the screen, tapping his mouth with the pen.

'It's your story, isn't it?' he said suddenly. 'You think you're *Beauty and the Beast*. Abby likes to think she's a princess who has discovered this great man hidden underneath this beastly exterior. It's a metaphor for your entire relationship.'

'A what?'

'A metaphor.'

Braindead looked back at him blankly.

'It's kind of a thing that is representative of something else.'

Braindead still looked blank.

'Abby thinks she's Beauty and you think you're the Beast,' Ben said helpfully.

'Well, he's pretty cool, I have to say. Goes a bit soft at the end, but I like the fact that he says what he thinks.'

Ben and Daniel looked at each other.

'So this could be it,' Daniel told Braindead. 'This could be the inspiration for your proposal.'

'What could?'

'Your Thursday-night ritual.'

Braindead thought for a minute.

'What, take her out to a proper curry house and propose over a proper Indian beer?'

'No!' cried Daniel. 'Sweep her off her feet like the Beast did. Make her feel like a princess, like the belle of the ball. Do you get it?'

'Get what?'

'Belle of the ball. Isn't the girl in *Beauty and the Beast* called Belle?'

'Yes.'

'Well that's what I meant – you need to make Abby feel like the belle of the ball.'

Braindead furrowed his brow. 'How the fuck do I do that?' he eventually exclaimed. 'Where do I get hold of a ball, for goodness sake? I can't just conjure up a ball out of nowhere, can I? I'm not the soddin' Queen. We're not living in the eighteenth century, when there were grand balls every soddin' weekend. You aren't helping at all, Daniel.'

'We may not be living in the eighteenth century, but we do have something on our side.'

'And what might that be?' replied Braindead with a sigh. He was fidgeting and casting Ben sideways glances as if he wanted to leave.

'Christmas,' said Daniel and laid down his pen.

🎄

'Christmas Party Land!' exclaimed Braindead some time later when Daniel had explained how he could easily access a ball at this time of year.

'Yes,' he said decisively. 'It's the perfect stage for you to make Abby feel like the only woman in the world.'

'But I don't even understand what it is,' protested Braindead.

'It's at the Pride Court Arena, and it's like one big massive party night for local companies. You can book as many tables as you want. Personally when I heard we were going there I was absolutely appalled. I cannot imagine anything worse than celebrating Christmas with a load of estate agents and construction workers... well, maybe construction workers would be OK,' said Daniel, pausing to think about this for a moment. 'Anyway, the theme for some unknown reason is Zulu Sundance or something. I know what you're thinking. A theme? Really? Anything that has a theme is by its very definition crass and appalling and bound to be a disaster, but given it's Christmas, I guess you need to forgive their poor taste levels. Anyway, what I'm saying is that a big event like that strikes me as the perfect occasion to play out your little *Beauty and the Beast* fantasy and propose to Abby.'

'Can you run that by me again in plain English,' asked Braindead. He looked over at Ben, who was trying hard to disguise a smirk. Braindead wasn't sure whether what was coming was utter humiliation or something quite brilliant.

Daniel got up and started pacing up and down the room deep in thought, his chin cupped in his hand.

'What are you doing?' Braindead asked.

'Shhhh,' he said, 'I'm thinking.'

'What's he doing?' Braindead whispered to Ben. 'I'm scared. Why have you brought me here?'

'You heard. He's thinking,' replied Ben. 'It's going to be good, but I think you need to prepare yourself. It's going to be big.'

'What do you mean, big?'

'I don't know, but you asked Daniel to help because you thought he'd be on the same wavelength as Abby, right?'

'Yeah.'

'Would Abby want a subtle, quiet, personal proposal or an in-your-face-everyone-look-at-me proposal?'

Braindead leaned back in his chair. He screwed up his face.

'I see what you're saying,' he said. He cast a terrified glance in Ben's direction. 'What have we done?' he asked nervously.

'I've got it!' exclaimed Daniel before Ben could reply. 'Are you ready for this?'

'No,' said Braindead, shaking his head vigorously.

'Well, prepare yourself because this is good. This is going to blow her socks off.' He pushed the glass screen out of the way and cleared his throat as he took centre stage. 'Ball guests are milling around; pre-dinner drinks are being sipped. There is light-hearted chatter to the gentle background of Christmas music. The ladies are splendid in their gowns while the men are dashing in their dinner suits.'

'What has this got to do with me?' interrupted Braindead.

'Hang on a minute, I'm getting to that,' said Daniel. 'Just be patient. A giant gong announces the commencement of dinner and the guests move to find their tables. Abby is worried. You're nowhere to be found. You've promised to meet her here, but it seems as though you haven't showed, or perhaps you're hidden behind one of the fake African trees and you haven't made yourself known yet.' Daniel raised his eyebrows. Braindead and Ben rolled their eyes.

'Just as the guests are seated, the music pipes up. The first bars of the Disney classic, "Beauty and the Beast", sang by the glorious Céline Dion can be heard throughout the auditorium.'

'Now hang on a minute, there's no way I'm doing anything to Céline Dion!' said Braindead.

'But she sings the song,' said Daniel.

'Which song?'

'"Tale as old as time, Beauty and the Beast." She sings it,' replied Daniel.

'Fuckin' hell,' said Braindead, a look of total outrage on his face. 'Why did no-one ever tell me I was doing it to Céline Dion?'

'There's no shame in doing anything to Céline Dion,' said Daniel. 'Now calm down and let us continue.' He closed his eyes momentarily to get himself back in the zone.

'When Abby hears the familiar music she smiles to herself as it reminds her of you,' continued Daniel. 'She looks around for you again and sees that people are pointing towards the ceiling. It appears as though it has started to snow as delicate flakes cascade to the ground. There is excited chatter and then gasps as a lone figure begins to descend from the ceiling on a rope. A man dressed in the sharpest of evening suits, a mask covering his face and holding a lone yellow rose. He stares out across the packed room until a hush descends as he hits the floor. He is unhooked from his harness and walks straight over to Abby, offering her the single rose and his hand. She follows him to the dance floor, where they spin and twirl, round and round until the music ends and then the masked man reveals himself.'

'Who is it?' gasps Braindead, now entranced.

'You, you bloody idiot!'

'Me?'

'Of course it's bloody you!'

'What the hell am I doing all that for?'

'Because then, after you've swept the girl of your dreams completely off her feet, made her feel like an utter princess, that is when you'll drop down on one knee in front of all those people. Everyone will be thinking that you, Martin Freeman – not *the* Martin Freeman, the other one – are the most romantic person on the planet.' Daniel paused to check he still had their attention. 'And that the woman you're proposing to has to be the luckiest woman alive. An utter miracle and a feat of quite extraordinary stage management that we could convince anyone that Abby is lucky to be proposed to by you, Braindead,' he continued, pointing at him. 'And when she nods and throws her arms round you, then you'll have the whole room in the palm of your hand. There will be clapping and cheering and smiling and everyone will talk about you for days and weeks after. The man who pulled off the most romantic proposal ever, you'll be an absolute legend.'

Daniel sat down, exhausted.

There was a shocked silence as they absorbed what Daniel had just said.

'I don't know what to say,' said Braindead eventually.

'How about thank you?' answered Daniel.

'It's just so, so, so much bigger than what I was expecting to do.'

'You see, that's the problem with men,' said Daniel, getting up and wiping the screen clean. 'They're about to do the single most life-changing thing in their lives and all they want is to play it down. Come on, Braindead. This is big, asking someone to marry you is huge. So go big! Don't skimp. Make it a big deal because it *is* a huge fuckin' deal.'

Braindead swallowed. 'But how – how do we make all that happen? It doesn't seem possible.'

'I am the creative director of the north of England's most successful advertising agency,' replied Daniel. 'This is what I do. This is easy-peasy. If I can get a bull in a china shop, quite literally, then I can get you dangling on a piece of string and proposing. We just get Katy to call the production company for the event and set it up. Brilliant publicity for them, they'll love it.'

'But won't we need tickets at least?' asked Ben. 'Don't they sell out in like, June? I remember Katy asking me to pick my menu months ago.'

'I've already thought of that,' said Daniel. 'I'm not sure if Katy mentioned it – probably not knowing her – but Luca, my boyfriend, and I split up very recently, leaving me with a spare ticket that I haven't inflicted on anyone yet. And it's possible Katy won't be here either if she ends up going to Australia by the end of the week.'

'What?' asked Ben.

Daniel paused. 'She has told you about her trip to Sydney, hasn't she?'

'Yes, but last I heard she didn't know when she was going.'

'Oh,' said Daniel, pretending to stare at something on the floor. 'Well, she mentioned this morning that she might be flying out at the weekend. Maybe she'd just got the details through when I saw her.'

'Right,' said Ben, nodding slowly.

'Katy's going to Australia!' exclaimed Braindead.

'Sounds like it,' said Ben tightly.

'What? With work?'

Ben shrugged. 'Something to do with a new client.'

'Jesus!' said Braindead, glancing around him. 'When can I get a job here, drawing pretty colours on glass screens?'

'I'm sure she must only have found out this morning,' said Daniel, looking nervously at Ben. 'I bet she wants to talk to you about it tonight.'

'Yeah,' said Ben. 'I guess so.'

'So Katy might not be there to see me fly through the night dressed as a penguin?' said Braindead.

'Does that mean you want to do it?' asked Daniel, clapping his hands together.

Braindead looked at them both. Ben looked thoughtful, as though he were in another place. Daniel looked eager, like a puppy.

'Fuck it,' said Braindead. 'In for a penny, in for a pound. I'm only going to do this once, aren't I?'

'Yes,' said Daniel, jumping up and hugging Braindead. 'This is going to be the talk of the night, this is going to make everyone's Christmas.'

Chapter Twenty

'Hiya,' Ben heard Katy shout as she came through the door later that night.

'Is Millie in bed?' she asked, as she walked into the kitchen and started to take off her coat.

'She's just gone down,' he replied.

'I'll pop in and give her a kiss then,' she said. 'Sorry I'm so late, been a hell of a day.'

He watched as she left the room then turned to start laying the table ready for dinner. He tried to calm his breathing, but he was struggling. He wasn't feeling himself; he wasn't feeling himself at all. He was having feelings that he didn't like, feelings he didn't really recognise.

He was used to living in the here and now. He couldn't be arsed to look too far ahead – or too far back, for that matter. He preferred to just live in the moment. But all afternoon his head had been elsewhere. He wasn't there when he picked Millie up from her friend's house. He forgot her coat, and he was sure he forgot to thank Freya's mum for looking after Millie while he was with Braindead and Daniel. When they got home he'd just stuck the TV on and stared at Peppa Pig blankly, taking in none of the story or the hijinks that usually did a pretty good job of entertaining him as well as Millie.

He just couldn't stop his mind wandering towards the reality of Katy flying to Sydney next week. It gave him a pain in his stomach just to think about it. He couldn't understand why it made him feel so bad. She didn't have a choice after all: she was going with work, it was part of her job. And yet the resentment he felt was burning him up. It was screwing with his mind. He wanted to say things that he never expected he would ever say.

Things like:

'And what am I supposed to do while you're in Australia enjoying yourself?'

And:

'Oh, you just leave me to do all the Christmas preparations. Of course I don't mind being dumped with all the present buying and the food shopping and the card writing.'

And:

'What do you mean, you're travelling on a weekend? That's my downtime. That's your time with Millie. How am I supposed to go to footie training?'

But most of all what was utterly killing him was the fact that by travelling this weekend it surely put at risk Katy's ability to be back in time for the Nativity. Had she forgotten all about it? And if she had, why did it matter so much? It was just the Nativity, after all. But the thought of her not being there – well, that just felt wrong.

The implications of Katy's imminent trip kept spinning round and round in his head and were not helped by the phone call he'd taken from her mother, just as he was about to put Millie to bed.

'Hello.'

'Hello, Ben, it's Rita. Are you OK?'

'Yes, fine, thank you. Katy's not here, I'm afraid.'

'Oh dear, where is she?'

'Still at work.'

'Seriously? What is she doing still there? She works far too hard, that girl. Anyone would think she didn't want to come home.'

'Mmm,' Ben had said.

'Well, can you ask her to give me a ring? I need to talk to her about Carlos's son. He lives in London – remember we talked about him?'

'Yeees,' Ben had said, not really listening.

'You really do need to invite him for Christmas dinner. He was thinking of going back to Spain and spending it with his mother, but he doesn't really want to. She's a terrible bitch, so if you were to ask him then he could stay here and spend Christmas with his father, which would be wonderful, wouldn't it?'

Ben had said nothing. Just sighed.

'He wouldn't be any bother. He's an architect. Very intelligent.'

Bloody hell, Ben had thought. An over-educated egomaniac – just what they needed. 'Shall I tell Katy to call you when she comes in?' he'd said.

'Yes, well, as long as it's in the next half hour. We're off out to dinner at Carlos's brother's. Do you think she'll be back before then?'

'I have no idea,' he'd replied. All he'd received was a text after lunch saying she had to attend an account meeting but was hoping it wouldn't be too late. That could mean anything.

Now he could hear her moving around upstairs, and he wanted her to stay there. He wanted her to stay there so he didn't have to talk to her, because he didn't know what to say. Every time he tried to formulate in his mind how to explain why he was pissed off because she was going to Australia, it just sounded petty and pathetic and small-minded, and he prided himself on being none of those things. He'd spent a lot of time over the last three years listening to mums complain about their husbands. Complain that they didn't take enough responsibility with the children, that they were always home late, that they didn't lift a finger in the home, that they got to go away on business trips and stay in a hotel bed and eat food in restaurants. He tried to nod understandingly whenever a woman shared her rage that her husband had called drunk during the mayhem of kids' teatime while he was on the other side of the world, having been out with customers eating and drinking the finest foods and wines.

Often the women making these complaints were the stay-at-home mums whose husbands' high-flying careers made it possible for them to not have to work. They complained of the freedom that their husbands had, to be able to waltz off to New York at a moment's notice to attend an urgent meeting. Yet Ben often felt that they failed to recognise the freedom bestowed on them – that they could afford to be at home raising their children.

And could they really be so mean-spirited that they would object to their husbands enjoying some aspects of having to travel with work? If he'd ever had a job like that then he would have made sure he made the most of it, because he was certain that anyone in that kind of position was working their socks off as well.

The thing was, he had made the choice. He could have been at work rather than taking care of Millie. He had come to value the fact that he had been able to choose, that Katy had a sufficiently high-paid job to enable him to opt for being the one to stay at home. He knew exactly where he'd rather be. Some of the mums just didn't seem to realise how lucky they were.

So he didn't want to moan about Katy going to Sydney. He was jealous, but he was also happy for her. Probably. What an opportunity. Just why did it have to be next week and would she even realise what she was missing?

🌲

'She said that George gave her a kiss today.' Katy came into the kitchen giggling to herself. 'She said he's a twin. I didn't realise there are twins in her class.'

'Oh, I forgot to mention it.' *Oh shit*, thought Ben. *I forgot all about George and Rebecca.* 'Funny story, actually. You'll never guess who they are.'

'Who, the twins? No idea.'

Ben took a deep breath. 'It's George and Rebecca, Matthew and Alison's kids.' Katy turned to look at him with her mouth open. 'So much has been going on, I forgot to tell you about it,' he continued.

'How could you forget to tell me that? Last time we saw them… last time we saw them…'

'We vowed never to set eyes on them again.' Ben nodded. 'I know, but they just turned up.'

'Matthew and Alison did?'

'No, George and Rebecca. They have a nanny. I've not seen Matthew or Alison at all – the nanny does all the drop-offs and pick-ups.'

'They have a nanny? I thought Alison was some kind of supermum, I never thought she would have a nanny. I can't believe you didn't tell me,' said Katy, looking visibly shaken. 'What if they decide to send the twins to Millie's school? We'll have to see them all the time. This is a nightmare.' She sat down and put her head in her hands.

'I just forgot, that's all,' said Ben defensively. 'What with Christmas and you working all hours, it doesn't seem like we've had the chance to talk properly in weeks. And now, with you going to Sydney.' He paused. Just come out with it, he thought. She can't accuse me of forgetting to tell her things when she failed to consult me on the timing of her trip. 'At the weekend, is it?'

'Oh, yes, sorry. They've booked the flights today. I tried to call you to check, but I couldn't get hold of you. I fly out Sunday and come back Friday. It's the quickest I can do it before Christmas. Is that OK?'

'I know it's not an ideal time to be going away,' Katy continued. 'I'm so sorry, I'm making it as short a trip as I possibly can.'

'When do you get back?' he asked.

'Friday.'

'What time Friday?'

'Er, I'm not sure. Early, I think. Hang on a minute – I'll check.'

He watched as she got up and went to fish her phone out of her bag. She tapped at it, occasionally glancing up at him.

'I actually get in at five in the morning to Heathrow,' she said. 'Blimey, I won't know where I am!'

'How will you get back up here?' asked Ben. He couldn't believe it. She was bound to say something any minute, wasn't she? She couldn't have forgotten. Perhaps it wasn't important. Perhaps he shouldn't be getting so wound up.

'I don't know. Train maybe? I haven't got that far yet.'

She was going to force him to say it, and he wouldn't say it right. He would sound pathetic and whiny when he'd vowed never to be that. She was staring at him now. They were both uncomfortable. There appeared to be a lot of unsaid words hanging awkwardly in the air. Who would crack first? Ben couldn't stand it any longer.

'But what about Millie's Nativity?' he said, looking away, embarrassed. He'd wanted to say 'my Nativity' but stopped himself.

Katy gasped. 'I totally forgot. I'd blocked out Friday morning as a meeting to make sure I didn't put anything in, but I couldn't remember what it was for.' She sat down on a chair with a thud. 'Things have just been so busy it went clean out of my mind. Oh my God, what do I do? What time does it start?'

'Ten,' said Ben flatly.

They looked at each other, both trying to do the maths. Whichever way you looked at it, it was tight.

'I'll take the car,' she said. 'Drive straight up.'

'You can't drive from London to Leeds after that kind of flight, you'll kill yourself.'

'I'll look at trains or see if I can get a connecting flight up to Manchester. Yes, that's what I'll do. Fly up to Manchester and then get a taxi or something.'

Ben looked across at her. They both knew there was a high risk she was going to miss it.

'I'll be there,' said Katy. 'Whatever it takes, I'll be there.'

He nodded. His eyes felt hot and prickly. He needed to change the subject fast. 'Your mum phoned,' he said. 'She wants you to invite Carlos's son for Christmas Day.' He watched as she screwed her face up then a look of concern appeared.

'It's not the Christmas you envisaged, is it?' she said. 'I'm so sorry.'

He breathed long and slow several times, praying the prickly eye thing would go away.

He shrugged. 'Maybe.'

Katy looked horrified. 'I'll make it up to you, I promise,' she said.

'Make up for what?'

'For it not being the Christmas you imagined. When I get back from Australia, I promise we'll do Christmassy stuff.'

Like make a baby, he wanted to say. But something stopped him.

'I said I'd meet Braindead and Abby down the Crown,' he said. He suddenly needed to get out.

'Right,' said Katy. 'OK. I'll, er, give Mum a call while you're out. See if I can deflect Carlos's son.'

'Whatever you want,' he replied and turned to walk out the door.

Braindead and Abby found him an hour later nursing his third pint. He'd been hideously early leaving for their rendezvous, but he didn't tell Katy that. His disappointment at her forgetting about the Nativity was weighing so heavy on his shoulders that he didn't feel he could even be in the same room as her.

'How do,' said Braindead, slapping him on the back. 'You want another?'

Ben nodded and tried hard to smile at Abby, despite the fact he didn't feel like smiling.

'Large white?' Braindead asked Abby. She nodded then he loped off to the bar.

'Braindead said you needed to ask me something?' Abby said as soon as she sat down.

Ben nodded. 'Shall we wait until he gets back?' They'd agreed to meet that night so they could invite Abby to join the Butler & Calder table at Christmas Party Land as instructed by Daniel. He'd called HR before they'd left, who said they had a spare ticket because Colin in Accounts had just been fired for getting caught in the audience of a TV Christmas special when he was supposed to be off sick.

'Is it about Katy? Have you got woman troubles?' asked Abby.

'No,' he replied defensively. Him and Abby had had a rocky start. She had arrived in their lives via her best mate, Charlene, who had been in the same antenatal class as Ben and Katy. Initially Abby had taken a shine to Ben, thinking he was fair game as a stay-at-home dad, casting Katy as the evil bitch who had put her career first. Ben had never reciprocated, and thankfully as soon as Abby had met Braindead, it proved to be an unlikely match made in heaven. It was clear, however, that Katy and Abby were never going to be the best of friends, and as such, Abby was always keen to lap up any crumbs that might be to Katy's detriment.

'No, it has nothing to do with Katy,' he repeated. 'Well it has, but only indirectly. If you see what I mean.'

'Not really,' replied Abby.

Ben sighed. 'Let's just wait until Braindead gets back,' he said.

Abby shrugged and got out her phone, staring into it to check her reflection. Her make-up must have taken hours and was flawless in that caked-on kind of way. Ben wondered for the hundredth time what she actually saw in the scruffy ragbag that was Braindead.

'There we go,' said Braindead, landing two pints and a large glass of white wine on the table. 'Have you asked her?' he said to Ben.

'No,' he replied. 'We were waiting for you.'

'What for?'

'The suspense is so killing me,' said Abby. 'Just spit it out, whatever it is.'

'Will you come to Katy's office Christmas party?' asked Ben.

'Why?' said Abby after a moment's thought. 'That is the weirdest thing you have ever said to me. What are you talking about?'

'Because er…' He looked at Braindead for help.

'Because I'm going,' said Braindead.

'Oh, how come?'

'I'm going with Daniel.'

'Gay Daniel.'

'Yes.' Braindead nodded. 'Though don't call him that on the night, eh? He really doesn't like it. Well he doesn't mind it from me, but he's used to my refusal to be intimidated into being politically correct. He may take offence at you, though – he's a bit touchy like that.'

'Why are you going with Gay Daniel – sorry, Daniel?' asked Abby.

'Because er...' said Braindead, now looking for Ben to help him out.

'Because his boyfriend just dumped him and so he has a spare ticket and he doesn't want to go on his own.'

'So he invited him?' she asked, pointing at her boyfriend.

'Yes.'

'Does he fancy him then or something? None of this makes much sense. Are you trying to tell me you're gay?'

'No,' said Braindead, shaking his head. 'You're totally overthinking it. Right, let's start again.' He took a deep breath. 'Abby, would you like to go to Christmas Party Land next Saturday night with me and Ben and Gay Daniel and Katy?'

'I'm already going, you numpty!' she exclaimed. 'It's our works do. I've told you a million times. I asked you to come and you said no.'

'Did I?' said Braindead, clearly having no recollection.

'Yes! But clearly if Daniel asks you then you leap at it. Are you sure you don't want to tell me something?'

'No!' said Braindead. 'I'm sorry I just—'

'You just forgot she asked you, right,' Ben added helpfully. 'I bet it was months ago.'

'We did book it in June, I think,' admitted Abby.

'Of course you did,' said Braindead. 'How am I supposed to remember that?'

'Daniel was desperate,' continued Ben. 'Braindead really had no choice. But he insisted you were invited along as well.'

'Did he?'

'I did,' said Braindead, nodding vigorously. 'I said there's no way I'm going unless Abby can come too.'

'Aaah, did you?' said Abby. 'That's sooo nice.'

Ben watched in horror as Abby leaned forward and landed a full-on smooch on Braindead's lips.

'So exciting,' she declared when she had finally pulled back. 'I can't wait to tell Chloe. She's been lording it over me all year because her boyfriend's going with her, and now I can tell her that you're coming with your gay best friend who works in advertising. Beat that, Chloe Simcox! In fact I'm going to ring her now. That will crush her mince pies. I'll just pop outside where I can get a better signal.'

'Am I making a massive mistake?' Braindead asked as they watched Abby walk out of the pub. 'I'm going to look like a complete tit flying through the air in a penguin suit, aren't I?'

Ben nodded. 'Absolutely.'

'I imagine that would be the cause of much mirth for you.'

'You're not wrong.'

'You knew with Katy though, didn't you? You knew you had to get married.'

Ben took another gulp of his beer. He knew he couldn't talk about his utter certainty that he wanted to spend his life with Katy. Not at this moment. This moment had more pressing issues to face.

'Katy forgot about the Nativity,' he said, putting his pint down. 'She might not be back in time from Australia to see it.'

'Millie's Nativity?'

Ben paused. 'It's my Nativity too,' he said quietly. 'I'm running the show.'

'I'll come, mate – if you like,' said Braindead after a moment.

Ben looked up at him gratefully. 'Thanks,' he said. 'I don't know why I feel so emotional about it. It's only a bloody Nativity, isn't it, after all? A bunch of kids running around with tea towels on their heads, singing out of tune.'

'You spend a lot of time with women,' said Braindead. 'It was bound to happen.'

'What was?'

'That you start behaving like them.'

Ben nodded. 'Right.'

'But it isn't a bad thing. It's just that you start caring about stuff you didn't used to. That's all.'

'Like kids in Nativity plays?'

'Yeah, stuff like that.'

'So what do I do?' asked Ben.

'There's only one thing you can do, mate.'

'What's that?'

'Claim back your inner man.'

'How do I do that?'

Braindead shrugged. 'Get pissed.'

'I'll certainly drink to that,' said Ben, raising his glass.

Chapter Twenty-One

'Rudolph!' cried Ben, stumbling up his garden steps three hours later.

He lurched towards the leering inflatable animal and threw his arms round its neck. Rudolf was surprisingly soft and squishy, caving in easily to Ben's affections and leaving them rolling around on the floor in some bizarre festive wrestling match.

'What are you doing?' someone hissed behind him.

Ben tried to struggle to his feet but couldn't get a grip as the wobbling reindeer thwarted his efforts at every turn. Eventually he gave up, falling back into a giggling heap.

Katy peered down at him through the darkness. 'Are you all right?' she asked.

'This is fun,' he said, laughing. 'Come on, you try it.'

Katy folded her arms across her dressing gown and pursed her lips. It didn't look like she fancied reindeer wrangling at this time of night. He made another effort to get to his feet, and this time he managed to find safe ground and hauled himself up.

'Is everything OK?' she asked. 'You've been gone ages, I was worried.'

'Everything is great, brilliant in fact. Me and Braindead got stuck into a session and put the world to rights.'

'I can see that,' replied Katy as Ben lost his footing slightly and had to grab hold of the fence. 'It *is* a school night, you know,' she pointed out.

Ben felt his high spirits leak out of him, making him feel as deflated as poor Santa on the roof. He didn't want a lecture; he was well aware it was a school night but needs must. He'd needed his escape for a while, and now Katy had dragged him firmly back to reality.

'I am very aware it's a school night,' he said stroppily. 'You're not my mother, you know. If I want to go out and have a few beers with my mate, I can. I don't need to ask your permission.'

'I never said you did. You just could have texted me to say you were staying out late, that's all,' replied Katy.

'Oh, like you let me know every minute of every day what you're doing,' bit back Ben.

Katy stared back at him for a moment.

'Is this about the Nativity?' she asked.

'Yes, it's about the Nativity,' said Ben, raising his voice. He didn't care any more. The beer had undone him, and it was all about to spill out.

'I've spent all night online trying to work out what to do,' said Katy. 'I've managed to change my flight to get me straight into Manchester rather than London, and I've booked a car to pick me up from there. I should make it, really I should. I'm doing everything I can – honestly.'

'Oh, well done you,' replied Ben. 'Doesn't make up for the fact that you forgot about it in the first place, you were so excited about going on *holiday*!' He was leaning into her now, their faces inches apart. He felt himself sway and had to pull himself back quickly.

'I'm not going on holiday,' she said. Her hands were screwed up tightly into balls and she looked on the verge of tears.

'Really? Really?' cried Ben, swaying even more. He turned and paced round Rudolph, trying to gather his rapidly unravelling thoughts.

'Let's go inside and talk about this properly,' said Katy. 'There's something—'

'There's nothing to talk about,' declared Ben. 'Cooper What's His Face has clicked his fingers and you're off. Just like that without a backward glance at me and Millie.'

'What's that supposed to mean?'

'You tell me,' said Ben, leaning forward to look her closely in the eye again. 'First dinner, and now a free trip to Australia. Just sayin', that's all.'

'What are you "just sayin"' said Katy, a look of horror on her face.

Ben took a deep breath. 'Just sayin' that this man seems to have you wrapped around his little finger. I'm starting to wonder what's so special about him.'

'Nothing,' replied Katy a little too quickly.

'Are you sure?'

'Sure about what?'

'That there's nothing going on between the two of you.'

'Between me and Cooper?'

'Yes, between you and Cooper!' shouted Ben.

'Of course there's nothing going on!' shouted back Katy. 'How could you accuse me of that? You know I would never, *ever* do anything like that.'

Ben narrowed his eyes. He paused.

'But you did, didn't you – once?' he said quietly.

Katy snapped her head back as though she'd been slapped. Ben watched as her eyes filled with tears.

'And that's exactly why I would never do anything like that ever again.'

She turned and he watched her flee back into the house.

Chapter Twenty-Two

'I know it's late, darling, but we are at a Christmas party on the beach. Such fun! Just about to head home to bed. To sleep obviously ;) Did you call Carlos's son to invite him for Christmas? Mum xx'

Katy slammed the phone on the kitchen table before she ran upstairs and buried her head in the pillow. The tears came with force as the tension of the last few days and the devastation that Ben could think she was capable of an affair came flooding out. Could he really still be carrying around such a deep resentment over her stupid one-night stand? It was nearly four years ago. She'd thought he was over it. They had been through so much since then. Did he actually trust her at all?

Eventually she cried herself to sleep and didn't hear him come to bed. She woke up the next morning to the sound of him in the shower, trying to revive himself ready for his day at preschool. She sat on the bed, waiting for him to come out. Thinking what to say. Trying to make sense of the mess she seemed to have got herself into over Cooper White and his job offer. She knew she had totally screwed up her timing, but she had to tell Ben the secret she'd been hiding. She just prayed he understood why she hadn't told him before and could understand why she was finding it so hard to make a decision.

He finally emerged, and she stood up to begin to talk to him, but he stopped her in her tracks, holding his hand up.

'I'm sorry for what I said,' he announced. 'I know you wouldn't do anything. Can we just pretend last night didn't happen?' he asked.

'Of course we can,' replied Katy, engulfed with relief that he hadn't meant what he'd said. 'I wouldn't, couldn't—'

'I know,' interrupted Ben. 'You don't have to say anything. Let's just forget it, shall we?'

'Yes, but I think we need…' started Katy.

'No, Katy,' he said firmly. 'I don't want to talk about it any more.'

'I know, but about this trip to Australia—'

'I said enough, Katy,' he replied, slightly raising his voice. 'The subject is closed. Go to Australia. Go and do your job and then, maybe, finally, we can start looking forward to Christmas.' He looked grim and determined. 'That's all I want to do now.'

'But I—' began Katy again.

'I don't want to hear another bloody word about Australia,' he said. 'Do you hear me? Not a word.' He walked out of the room with just a towel wrapped round his middle. Moments later she heard him next door talking to Millie.

🎄

Several times in the days that followed she wondered how she had got it so wrong as her trip remained firmly the elephant in the room. She contemplated numerous times trying again to share with Ben the job offer, but as Australia was now the root of all evil she felt sure that any rational conversation would be immediately rejected. Her going away was risking a mother not seeing her daughter and husband deliver the best Nativity of all time, and Cooper White was a nasty villain trying to steal Ben's wife. How could they possible live there? It was an evil, evil place.

Besides, she wasn't actually going to take the job anyway, was she? So why cause further upset? Ben was right: she should just go over there and then come back so they could all start finally looking forward to Christmas. Forget the job offer, it was never going to happen. Cooper's comment about gender did, however, occasionally prey on her mind. If their roles were reversed and Ben had been offered the job of a lifetime overseas, they would have jumped at it. But then Ben wasn't racing against a ticking clock to have a baby. She would just have to shove those thoughts to the back of her mind and not be flattered into anything by the sunshine or Cooper White. She was going on a work trip as requested and would return and resume normal life. That was how it had to be.

🎄

The mood was sombre on Christmas party day in Ben and Katy's house. Katy glided the iron over the crisp new white dinner shirt she'd bought Ben to go with the hired monkey suit hanging on the back of the door. He was lying on the sofa in jeans and T-shirt, pretending to watch football on the telly, but she noticed he kept glancing at the disparate ironing pile that Katy was currently working her way through. Floaty, summery dresses passed over the ironing board in between heavy jeans and thick woollen jumpers. She felt herself wince every time she bent down to fold a T-shirt and put it into the suitcase open next to her.

The mood was not helped by the tearful farewell she'd had earlier with Millie, who had gone for a sleepover with Ben's mum and wouldn't be returning until after Katy had left for the airport the following day. Ben had watched as they had both worked themselves up into a state, saying nothing to soothe either of them. Katy couldn't blame him of course – he had every right to be sulking. The onus was very clearly on her to smooth over the inconvenience of her trip.

'There,' she said, holding up the crisp white shirt. 'Do you want to try it on?'

'No,' he replied without looking up.

She draped it over a coat hanger and hung it on the back of the living-room door. 'Your bow tie is on the chest of drawers upstairs,' she said over her shoulder. 'Daniel said he would help you tie it when you got there if we're struggling. I've never done one before, have you?'

'No,' murmured Ben, staring at the long flowery skirt she'd picked up from the pile.

Silence descended again as she ran the iron over the bright patterned fabric. The material was thin and ironed easily. She remembered wearing it last summer in Cornwall. Her, Ben and Millie had gone out to find food in the early evening and had ended up on the beach eating fish and chips. She'd kicked her sandals off and buried her toes in the sand. It had felt good, as she'd munched on salt-and-vinegar-drenched food. She would never have thought the next time she'd be wearing it would be in Australia. Never in a million years. She bent down and placed the skirt in her suitcase. She glanced over at Ben. He was already looking at her; he held her gaze for a moment then looked away.

'By the way, I've asked Mum if she'll babysit one night while she's here,' she said to Ben in an effort to get a conversation out of him. 'So we can have a Christmas night out together. On our own.'

He looked over. A small smile crept on to his face for the first time in days.

'Thought we could go to Fever,' she continued. 'Dance to "All I Want For Christmas is You" again. Do you remember?'

He nodded and the smile grew a bit more. Their first Christmas together they'd met up in a pub in Leeds at lunchtime on Christmas Eve with Braindead and some other mates. Happy drinking had followed until about 4 p.m. when everyone left in a panic to do some last-minute drunken shopping. Ben and Katy, slightly the worse for wear, had wandered down the street and heard Christmas music coming from a bar. They'd dashed in and stormed the deserted dance floor, wobbling and gliding to Mariah Carey's classic Christmas track and meeting together for the last chord with a full-on festive kiss. Two middle-aged men supping pints had clapped and they'd taken a bow, leaving the pub without even buying a drink. They'd both agreed that it had been without doubt their best Christmas Eve ever. Only improved by a Chinese on the way home and a hangover by 9 p.m.

'I'd like that,' he said.

'Great.' She nodded. 'It's a date.' She bent down and grabbed some of Millie's costume to iron, ready for Friday. She was quiet while she concentrated on making sure it was crease-free and spic and span. She turned to Ben as she hung it up.

'I will do everything in my power to make sure I'm there,' she said to him.

'I know,' he replied, not even looking at her.

'Oh and I've booked an electrician to come round on Monday and sort out Santa on the roof,' she said. 'Can't have him saggy for Christmas Day, can we? He said he'd put some more lights up as well while he's up there.'

'Really?' said Ben, turning to look at her wide-eyed. 'I've got loads. I went to the discount place again,' he admitted.

'Did you?' Katy smiled. 'Well, after Monday our house will look the best in Leeds, I reckon.'

Ben got up from the sofa and walked over to Katy.

'Thank you,' he said, putting his arms around her.

'Call it an early Christmas present,' she said.

'Shit,' he said, slapping his forehead. 'I haven't bought you anything yet.'

'No need,' she replied. 'All I want for Christmas is you – you know that, don't you?

'Me too,' he replied, reaching down to kiss her. 'Me too.'

🎄

Matthew had never felt more uncomfortable in his life than at this precise moment. He was perched on the sofa in the kitchen in just his dinner-suit trousers, his chest bare for all to see. Across the room stood Lena in full make-up and gown, ironing his shirt for him. He didn't know where to look or where to hide. For some reason he was acutely aware of his hairless chest, making him feel more exposed than the mere lack of shirt did. Lena knowing an intimate detail like the fact that he had no chest hair had crossed a boundary he wasn't comfortable with. He imagined her sniggering to her friends. Why had she come down just as he was struggling to iron his dress shirt? There is no man more vulnerable than one standing half-naked behind an ironing board in his kitchen.

'Is it all OK?' she had asked as he'd tried not to stare at her stunning transformation when she'd walked into the room.

'Can't seem to get the iron to work,' he'd muttered. 'Is it broken?'

'But I used it today,' she'd said, walking towards him with a confused look on her face. Standing directly opposite him with only an ironing board between them, she'd picked it up and shook it. His senses had been immediately engulfed in her exotic perfume to the extent that when she'd asked him to move out of the way so she could solve the puzzle of the cold iron, he'd been only too happy to escape her heady proximity. He'd dashed to the other side of the room and watched as she'd smiled to herself.

'The temperature is on low, it would not iron a fly wing,' she'd said to him. She'd set the iron down again and walked over to retrieve the shirt from where he'd slung it on the table, before draping it over the board and picking up the iron again.

'No, no,' Matthew had said, flustered but not daring to move closer. 'Please let me, I didn't mean for you to do it.'

'It will be quicker and better,' she'd said.

He couldn't argue about that.

He'd sat wordlessly on the edge of the sofa until she extended her hand out, a perfectly ironed shirt hanging on the end of it. He sprang up and took it from her as quickly as he could, muttering his thanks before trying hard not to break into a run on his way out of the kitchen.

The tension, however, wasn't much better when he arrived back in the bedroom.

'Look at me,' demanded Alison as soon as he walked in.

He had his defence prepared as to why he had been so long ironing his shirt, but one look at Alison told him that his ironing issues were not at the forefront of her mind at the moment.

'You look lovely,' he said, pulling his shirt on.

'Oh shut up,' she said. 'I passed Lena on the landing. I look like an overstuffed sofa and she looks like she just stepped off the dance floor in *Strictly*.'

He couldn't deny that it had crossed his mind when he'd seen the perfect make-up, elaborate hair, thigh-skimming dress and sequins a plenty. She looked gorgeous; Ian was going to go mental.

'You're eight months pregnant and...' he held his hand up to quieten her protests '... you have never looked more stunning.' Her shoulders drooped. Would she accept the compliment? Matthew held his breath.

'I can't wait for this baby,' she said tearfully, rubbing her belly, 'honestly I can't. But it's rubbish being pregnant at Christmas. I so want to look pretty in a sparkly dress.'

'I bet that's exactly what the Virgin Mary said,' replied Matthew solemnly.

Alison managed a smile. 'It's just hard to feel Christmassy when you're the size of a house,' she muttered. 'Especially when you look at Lena and she looks like the fairy on top of the tree.' She glared into the mirror as she put her earrings in. 'We're doomed at this party, aren't we? I don't even know why we're going. I'll be sat in a corner, sober, miserable and with swollen ankles. You can't even put your arms around me to dance. I'll be left watching Ian get his Christmas claws into our nanny. It's going to be the worst party ever.'

🎄

'Will you please put your trousers on while you're ironing my shirt,' gasped Braindead desperately. 'Jesus Christ, if anyone walked in here now they'd think they'd walked into a photo shoot for Mr Gay UK!'

'You would never in a million years make it to Mr Gay UK,' said Daniel, ignoring his request and taking even more time ironing Braindead's shirt for him.

'I take offence at that,' declared Braindead, sticking out his bare, hairy potbelly. 'I think you're being phobic – not homophobic, the other phobic.'

'Heterophobic?' asked Daniel.

'Yeah. Just because I'm not gay doesn't mean you can throw shade at my body.'

'Throw shade at your body!' exclaimed Daniel. 'What kind of talk is that?'

Braindead shrugged. 'Abby talks like that all the time.'

'Doesn't sound right, coming out of your real-ale-swilling mouth. Now, put this on.' He handed the shirt back over to Braindead. 'How you were ever going to think you could convince a girl to marry you in that crumpled mess, I will never know. Now, where's your tie?'

'In my jacket pocket.'

The trouserless Daniel walked over to the chair where Braindead had slung his jacket. Rooting in his pockets he pulled out what looked like a torch strapped to some elastic. 'What on earth is this?' he asked.

'A head torch,' replied Braindead. 'You put it over your head so you can see in the dark, but your hands are still free. Thought it might be useful for when I'm up in the ceiling. Could be dark up there.' He grabbed the contraption off Daniel and pulled it over his head so the torch rested on his forehead. He reached up and switched it on, nearly blinding Daniel.

'Oh, it's like what the surgeons wear on *Grey's Anatomy*,' said Daniel, blinking furiously. 'But Dr McSteamy you ain't, and it's hardly James Bond, is it? Just don't forget to take it off before you come into view. Everyone will think we're under alien attack if you float down with lights beaming from your head. Now, stand still while I do this tie.'

'Please will you put your trousers on?'

'Oh for God's sake, just stand still, will you?'

Braindead stared straight ahead over Daniel's shoulder as he tied his bow tie.

'There you go,' he said, taking a step back. 'Now I'd consider marrying you.'

Braindead faltered for a moment. 'She will say yes, won't she?' he asked.

'Of course. Who could turn down a man floating down from heaven to propose?'

'But that's not me, is it?' said Braindead. 'That's all the fancy stuff. She still has to say yes to me. She still has to say yes to everything she already knows about me.'

Daniel paused for a moment.

'That is exactly why she'll say yes,' he replied.

Braindead sighed and reached up to switch his light off. 'I really hope you're right.'

Chapter Twenty-Three

Lena's eyes widened in amazement as she stepped out of the house.

'You have got to be kidding me,' said Alison.

'Oh, for fuck's sake!' exclaimed Matthew.

'Your carriage awaits.' Ian grinned as he held open the door to the long black stretch Hummer parked on the drive outside Matthew and Alison's house.

Lena rushed forward and embraced Ian. 'This is amazing,' she gushed. 'All my life I have wanted to go in one of these.'

'When you said you were picking us up, I assumed you'd be driving,' said Alison, looking cautiously around to make sure none of the upmarket neighbours had spotted the car most likely to be driven by a drugs baron parked on their drive. She'd been surprised and relieved that Ian had offered to drive, thinking he would be one for wanting to make the most of the all-inclusive drinks package. It all made sense now. A chauffeur-driven fancy car was guaranteed to sweep Lena off her feet and Ian could indulge in as much alcohol as he wanted.

Matthew stood yet again in awe at Ian's cunning. He too had been shocked by Ian's offer to drive. He should have known he had something up his sleeve. The car was pretty cool, though. Matthew had also felt his heart beat slightly faster at the sight of it. He'd also longed for some time to see inside one and have a ride. This was going to be fun.

'What the hell is that?' said Marlene from the doorway. Marlene was a mum friend of Alison's who had offered to babysit. 'My goodness, you lot know how to live!'

'I have nothing whatsoever to do with it,' said Alison. 'I can assure you I had no idea this is how we were going to get to the party. This is Ian, he's showing off.'

'Well, he can show off to me any time if that's how he treats a lady,' said Marlene. 'When Frank takes me out, there's usually a massive argument first about who'll drive and somehow it's always me. I dream of a man who turns up with a carriage like that. Hello, Ian,' she continued, shouting over at Ian, who already had his arm around Lena's shoulders. 'I'm the babysitter. Love your wheels, you can pick me up any time.'

'Seriously!' said Alison, turning to her friend. 'Are you that easily impressed?'

'After ten years of marriage, definitely.' She shrugged. 'I miss the romantic stage.'

'This isn't romance,' said Alison, getting agitated. 'It's glory seeking.'

Marlene shrugged. 'Don't care what you call it. Whatever it is, it works.' She nodded over towards the car. Lena was giggling at something Ian was whispering in her ear.

'Right,' said Alison. 'Shall we go? Let's get this over with. How do we even get in this thing?'

'Enjoy yourselves!' shouted Marlene as Alison struggled to hoist herself up into the high-wheelbase car. Alison looked over her shoulder and grimaced.

🎄

'Holy Mary, mother of God!' gasped Daniel as they walked into the vast open space of Christmas Party Land. 'This is bad on a scale I haven't even had nightmares about yet.' He shielded his eyes from the bombardment of bright lights that bounced off every wall and the juxtaposition of enormous twenty-foot-high Christmas trees alongside African tree houses, imposing masks, totem poles and the sound of thudding drums. The bar area was already thronging with hundreds of excitable partygoers in ballgowns and tuxedos throwing back the all-inclusive drinks package like it was going to run out at any second. And it was only 6.30 p.m.

'It hurts my eyes,' declared Daniel. 'And none of it makes any sense. How can a classic Christmas aesthetic live alongside a totem pole? And do they even have totem poles in Africa? I don't get any of this, it's utterly ridiculous. Do you get it?' he turned to ask Braindead.

Braindead's jaw was virtually on the floor. But it wasn't the décor, or the jarring, drum-thumping music, it was the crowd that he couldn't take his eyes off. He watched as it swarmed and swelled and shouted and sang and pushed and shoved, everyone desperate to get into the party spirit. The mood was jolly but fraught with anticipation. For many this night made the tedium of spending most of their working lives in a shit job just that bit more bearable: the chance to enjoy one's colleagues rather than despair of them.

The throng terrified Braindead. What was he doing? He was self-employed. He had no scores to settle with colleagues, no crosses to bear. He spent the vast majority of his time alone. What was he thinking doing the most personal thing he had ever done in front of this braying mob? This was insanity.

'I'm going home,' he told Daniel, turning to leave.

'What! You can't go,' said Daniel, grabbing his arm. 'It's all set. We need to go and meet Craig. He's all ready with the harness.'

'I can't do it,' said Braindead, shaking his head.

'Why not?'

'This. It's not me. It's not me at all.'

'Precisely,' urged Daniel. 'It isn't about you, is it? It's about Abby. Don't you see? This is you doing something that isn't you – for her. Isn't that the ultimate show of love? She's going to love this, isn't she?'

Braindead nodded, biting his lip.

'You know this is right up her street. It may not be up yours but that makes it so much more powerful. She'll know you're doing it for her. It'll make her life, Braindead. Imagine holding your grandkids on your knee and Abby telling them for the hundredth time how their grandpa proposed. You will be the coolest-sounding grandpa ever.'

Braindead said nothing.

'This is extraordinary,' said Daniel, waving his hands around. 'Don't propose over a bag of chips, Braindead. Make your proposal extraordinary.'

Braindead swallowed. He took three deep breaths. He closed his eyes tight then opened them again.

'OK,' he nodded. 'Let's do it. For Abby.'

🎄

Lena's jaw dropped for the second time that evening as the four of them walked into the foyer of Christmas Party Land. The vast space, decorated by a thousand fairy lights amongst tree houses and palm trees, was totally magical, if a little bizarre.

'I had not expected this,' she said to Ian. 'It is so big.'

Ian fought back a smutty joke. 'There are bumper cars somewhere,' he told her. 'And a Ferris wheel.'

'Wow!' said Lena, her eyes wide.

'Shall we go to the bar?' he asked, looking around to see where Matthew and Alison were.

'Why is it African themed?' asked Alison, coming up behind them and looking unimpressed.

'Who cares?' replied Ian. 'It's Christmas. Now what can I get you to drink?'

'You do know we've already paid for drinks, don't you?' said Alison. She had sat tight-lipped for the whole journey in the Hummer, grimacing when Ian produced a bottle of Champagne. Matthew had gratefully accepted some until he saw Alison scowl and so he had been forced to pretend not to enjoy it.

'I know,' replied Ian. 'I just asked you what you would like to drink. I can rephrase if you like. I could ask you what you would like from the free bar? Is that better?'

'It's technically not a free bar either, is it?' said Alison.

'Alison, what can I get you from the array of drinks that are part of the pre-paid, all-inclusive drinks package that we've already paid for?'

'Orange juice please.'

'I'll come and give you a hand,' said Matthew, ready to apologise for his wife.

'I must find the bathroom,' said Alison.

'Will you be OK waiting here?' Ian asked Lena.

'Of course,' she said. 'I have so much to see. Don't worry about me.'

Ian nodded. 'Stay here then,' he said. 'I don't want to lose you.'

🎄

'Merry Christmas,' said Ben, raising his pint glass to Katy as they stood amongst the throng at the bar. He glanced round, soaking in the happy, jolly faces bobbing around him. Time for the both of them to enjoy a night out and forget the atmosphere that had existed between them over the last few days. He was tired of feeling awkward and confused. Everything was fine. He knew he had nothing to worry about with Katy going to Australia. Time to party!

'Merry Christmas,' replied Katy, holding up her glass of Prosecco. 'By the way I think there is someone over there waving at you,' she added, pointing over to a beautiful woman standing by the grand doorway. 'Looks like she knows you.'

Ben peered over. The woman looked vaguely familiar but he was sure he would remember if he knew someone that stunning. He looked harder then started to panic as she walked towards him. He couldn't place her. How embarrassing. 'I don't know her,' he whispered to Katy. 'What do I do?'

'Well, she certainly thinks she knows you.'

'Hi,' she said, holding out her hand as she approached. 'Lena. From preschool.'

'Oh God, of course,' replied Ben, slapping his forehead. 'I'm sorry, I didn't recognise you. You look so... so...'

'I'm Katy,' interrupted Katy, holding her hand out. 'Ben's wife.'

'Oh,' said Lena. She looked surprised and momentarily confused. 'Well, your husband is superb with children,' she added, once she'd gathered herself.

Katy nodded. 'Thank you. He has good practice with our child, Millie.'

'Lena, er... Lena, er...' faltered Ben. *Oh shit*, he thought.

'What children do you have?' asked Katy.

'Oh, they are not my children. I am the nanny. I look after twins who are at the preschool, as well as a two-year-old at home, and the mother is also pregnant again. So I am busy,' she said with a dazzling smile.

'She's pregnant again!' gasped Ben.

'Yes. With number four and all under four. It is a very busy house as you can imagine, but I love it.'

Katy was staring at Lena now and at Ben. Ben looked nervously over at her. Had she realised whose children Lena was talking about? What with all this Australia business and Braindead's proposal, the arrival of Matthew and Alison's children at Millie's preschool had been somewhat overshadowed.

'And who are you here with?' asked Ben, an awful thought suddenly striking him.

'Well, kind of strange actually but I am here with a friend of my employers.'

Ben nodded. 'Oh good.'

'And my employers.'

'Oh,' said Ben, his eyes suddenly wide. 'How very nice for you.'

'Actually I should get back. They went to get drinks and told me to stay by the door. They will think I have got lost. It was so nice to meet you,' she said to Katy. 'Maybe see you later?'

'Yes, great,' replied Ben.

They both watched in silence as she turned her back and moved away. When there was enough distance between them, Ben grabbed Katy's hand and pulled her behind a pillar.

'Did you realise who that was?' he hissed.

'Was it Matthew and Alison's nanny? You never said how stunning she was.'

'She doesn't collect the kids looking like that, I can assure you,' said Ben. 'What do we do?'

'We'll just have to try to avoid them,' replied Katy.

'Can you believe she's pregnant again?' said Ben, wide-eyed. 'Four kids!'

'I know. Can you imagine?'

'Nearly a football team. Just amazing.' What had he and Katy been playing at? How come Matthew already had two more children than him and another on the way?

'Look, let's go and find Braindead,' suggested Katy before Ben could mention the fact that tonight would be the perfect time to 'make babies' as Millie was out of the house staying with his mother. 'They must be behind the scenes somewhere,' she continued. 'Hopefully we'll be seated at the opposite side of the room to Matthew and Alison, and if she's pregnant they won't be stopping long. With a bit of luck we won't even see them.'

🎄

'You will not guess who is here,' Lena said to Alison when she arrived back from the bathroom and they were still waiting for Matthew and Ian to appear with drinks.

'Who?' asked Alison, looking round hopefully for a chair. She was desperate for them to call dinner so she could sit down, although she wasn't hopeful about the culinary delights dreamed up by someone who thought an African-themed Christmas party was wise.

'Master Elf,' she said excitedly. 'From school. He is here.'

'Master Elf is here!' exclaimed Alison. '*The* Master Elf?'

'Yes, yes! He was just over there. But he is gone now.'

'Well, you must find him and introduce me,' said Alison, feeling instantly uplifted. This was the best news she had heard all day. With Master Elf here there was an outside chance that Ian could be kicked off his perch and Lena could end up with a man more suitable for her, and indeed for Alison. If she could get Lena to introduce her then she would be in prime position for a little matchmaking. This was brilliant news.

'Master Elf is here,' said Alison, beaming as Matthew finally approached her with an orange juice. A look of confusion passed over his face until the possibilities dawned on him.

'Master Elf is here, at this party?' he asked.

'Yes,' chimed Alison and Lena.

'Who is Master Elf?' asked Ian.

'You remember, Master Elf is the most marvellous teacher at George and Rebecca's school, isn't he, Lena?' said Alison.

'He is very good. So good with children,' she agreed.

'You've all taken such a shine to him,' added Alison. 'Haven't you, Lena?'

Lena blushed slightly. 'Oh yes. We all like him a lot.'

'So did you meet him?' Matthew asked Alison.

'No, Lena saw him. She's going to find him so she can introduce us, aren't you, Lena?'

'He works in a preschool and calls himself Master Elf?' questioned Ian, looking knocked off balance for the first time that evening. 'Sounds like a bit of a dweeb.'

'What is a dweeb?' asked Lena.

'Well, you know… er… he sounds unusual. I'm imagining a short tubby man who wears a hat with a bell on it.'

'Oh no, he is tall and very athletic, I would say,' said Lena.

Ian nodded. 'Right.'

Alison grinned at him. 'Shall we go and root him out after dinner,' she said, 'and then we can all meet Master Elf, can't we, Ian?'

Chapter Twenty-Four

'Oh my God,' screamed Abby the minute she saw Ben and Katy. 'I'm so excited you're here too. Have you seen any lions yet?' She practically ran at them, engulfing them in a heady mix of alcohol fumes and perfume.

'Isn't this just brilliant?' she gasped. 'I luuuurve the palm trees! I so want to take one home.'

Katy couldn't help but notice that Abby was swaying slightly. 'Are you OK?' she asked, grabbing her as she tilted dangerously to the left.

'Oh, I'm fine,' she giggled. 'I'm just peaking a bit soon, but I'll be OK. I'm now alternating between bottles of water and bottles of wine. Slowing me down a bit. Just need some food,' she said, looking around vacantly. 'I can't remember the last time I had any food.'

'You look lovely, by the way,' said Katy, grabbing hold of her arm again to stop her falling over.

'Took me all morning to get ready. I was up at nine. On a Saturday! What's that all about?'

'All morning? What do you mean, all morning?'

'We've been out since twelve,' said Abby. 'We've had such a laugh. But I tell you what – I'm knackered now. Where's Braindead? He's coming, you know. With Daniel. But this isn't him, is it?' she said, looking around. 'Not all these people and the theming shit. He'll have something to say about those totem poles, won't he? Oh, I wish he was here now,' she whined before resting her head on Ben's shoulder and closing her eyes.

Ben looked at Katy.

'She's hammered,' he whispered.

'I know,' she hissed back.

'What do we do?'

'We've got to try and sober her up.'

'How do we do that?'

Katy looked at Abby. She still had her eyes closed; she could well be passed out on Ben's shoulder.

'Why don't I take her to her table and force-feed her water and see if I can get some bread rolls into her or something? You go and find Braindead and warn him. Perhaps you should suggest they ditch the dancing bit. The less involvement from Abby in this proposal the better, don't you think?'

'Definitely.'

'Abby,' said Katy, shaking her shoulder. 'Abby, let's go and find you some food, eh? Will you come with me?'

'Eh? Yeah, good idea,' she replied, blinking her eyes open and allowing herself to be guided away from the vast foyer and into the dining area.

'Good luck,' said Ben.

'You too,' replied Katy. 'Hurry up!'

🎄

Ben asked a security guy by the door where he might find the technician for the show. The man shrugged. Ben wanted to shake him, but he was bigger than him.

He ran into the main dining hall where he could see Katy and Abby stumbling across chairs at the far end of the room. There was a stage set up at the near end with ropes and bars hanging from the ceiling as well as trampolines lying on the floor that had to be part of the evening's entertainment. There was only one thing for it. He leapt up on stage and strode confidently through the wings into the backstage area.

He was met with a tangle of people dressed in a variety of African costumes, including acrobats dressed as monkeys and dancers dressed as every animal you might expect to see on safari. Such was the throng that they didn't notice a smartly dressed man push his way through, looking for any sign of his friend.

'Don't touch my balls!'

He heard a shout coming from somewhere towards the back. That had to be Braindead. He dashed towards where he sensed the commotion coming from.

'Will you look at what they're doing to me!' Braindead cried as Ben approached. Ben fought the urge to laugh when he caught sight of his friend being trussed up like a chicken as some bloke in a black T-shirt manhandled him into a harness. Daniel was watching from a distance, clearly also fighting hard the desire to laugh.

'You all right?' Ben asked, wondering how he was going to break the news that there was a spanner in the works.

'Fucking terrified,' said Braindead. 'This had better work or else I'm going to kill the pair of you for landing me in this position.' Fortunately he was distracted by a six-foot-tall female dancer gliding by. Ben took the opportunity to take Daniel to one side and explain that Abby was drunk. Perhaps the news would be better coming from Daniel.

'Slight problem,' Ben told him.

'Don't bring me problems!' exclaimed Daniel, clearly a little tense. 'Bring me solutions.'

'We're not in the office now, you know,' bit back Ben. 'We are backstage with a shedload of safari animals, some ridiculously tall women, Braindead doing an impression of Hannibal Lecter in his straitjacket and… and… and…'

'And what?' demanded Daniel.

'Abby is completely hammered. She's been out drinking since lunchtime. She can barely stand.'

'What!' exploded Daniel. 'Are you serious? The selfish bitch! What the hell is she doing, getting pissed before she's about to be proposed to in the most spectacular fashion you could ever imagine?'

'She wasn't to know, was she?'

'All these weeks of planning completely wasted,' wailed Daniel.

'We only thought of it on Monday,' Ben reminded him.

'How bad is she?'

'Katy's trying to sober her up now. She thinks we need to ditch the dancing, just go straight for the proposal. She'll fall flat on her arse and probably drag Braindead down with her if they attempt any coordinated movement.'

Daniel nodded. 'Katy's right, all is not lost. We can salvage this. Just ditch the dance. Let's tell Braindead.'

'Shall we not tell him she's drunk? I think he'll totally bottle it if we do,' said Ben.

Daniel nodded. 'Absolutely. We need to make sure something good comes out of this shambles. If Braindead isn't engaged after all this, well, I'm giving up on romance.'

'What are you two whispering about?' shouted Braindead. 'You're not setting me up, are you? Is this some elaborate plot to make me look like an idiot? Because if it is then I think you'd better come clean now.'

'No, mate, no,' said Ben, walking back over towards him.

'We were just saying,' said Daniel, 'that having seen the dance floor, we don't think it has the right intimacy to carry off the dance, and we thought you should consider not doing it and going straight for the proposal.'

Braindead stared back at them. *Please say yes*, thought Ben.

'Thank you, thank you, thank you,' said Braindead, heaving a huge sigh of relief. 'I never liked that idea. Thought I was going to look like a twat, to be honest. So I just float to the ground, someone will unhook me and I'll call Abby on to the dance floor and get down on one knee?'

'The crowd goes wild, applause, applause, applause, and we all live happily ever after,' said Daniel, looking sideways at Ben.

'Exactly,' agreed Ben, crossing his fingers that it would just be Braindead on his knees in the middle of the dance floor in front of 700 people and not Abby as well.

A loud bell chimed backstage and a momentary hush fell.

'What's that?' gasped Braindead. 'What does that mean?'

'It means they're calling everyone to dinner so it's ten minutes until showtime,' said the technician, still adjusting straps. 'We need to get you up there pronto.'

'Oh shit,' said Braindead. He looked over at Ben, the colour having drained from his face. Ben wondered if it was the height he was about to scale, being dangled on the end of a rope or proposing to Abby in front of hundreds of people that Braindead was most afraid of. Probably all three. Braindead rarely strayed outside of his comfort zone; in fact he made it his mission in life to stay firmly *in* his comfort zone. It was really only Abby who had managed to cajole him into experiences you never would have dreamed he would partake in. This was certainly one of those experiences.

'Good luck, mate,' said Ben, slapping his friend on the back.

'Cheers,' said Braindead. 'See you on the other side, eh?'

'Yep.' Ben nodded. 'I love you, you know.' He bent forward to give him a hug.

'Give over,' replied Braindead when Ben released him. 'Don't get all sentimental on me now.'

'I'm there for you, mate,' he said and turned to walk away. 'I think you might need me,' he muttered under his breath.

Chapter Twenty-Five

By the time Ben and Daniel emerged from backstage, 700 people were trying to find their table. People jostled past each other, eager to check they had their fair share of wine waiting for them and that they were sitting next to the right person, whether that be their partner, or someone they wished to be their partner by the end of the evening. It was a noisy mass of shiny satin and eager faces.

Ben and Daniel had no idea where their table was, so after some time swimming against the tide and looking for a familiar face they decided to head back out to the bar area to refer to the seating plan.

'Table thirteen,' said Daniel, finding it first. 'Unlucky for some.'

'Don't say that,' said Ben. 'I hope Katy's managed to sort Abby out. This could all go so wrong.' He was beginning to regret not having told Braindead to ditch the entire idea. 'We should never have pushed him this far.'

'When you want to pull off something this big then you have to take a risk,' said Daniel.

'We should have at least done a risk assessment,' mumbled Ben. 'We should have predicted that the biggest risk could be Abby turning up drunk.'

'Katy will be dealing with it,' said Daniel confidently. 'This is what she does. This is why she's so damn good at her job – she manages mini-crises all the time.'

'Well, I hope so or else Braindead may never recover. And he'll definitely never ever get married.'

The room was starting to calm down now as people took their seats and ceased their gossiping about who was wearing what. Finally Ben could see across the room and spotted Katy urgently beckoning them over to table thirteen.

'Over there,' Ben told Daniel, pointing at Katy. 'Can you see Abby?'

'No,' said Daniel. 'But she'll be sitting with her colleagues, won't she? She's on table ten – we checked when we came in so Braindead knew where to head once he landed on the dance floor.'

'You're right,' said Ben, feeling relieved. He tried to look for table ten as they continued their journey to Katy. He'd just like to catch a glimpse of Abby to see that she could at least stand up.

'Is she OK?' asked Ben as they finally got to table thirteen.

'Take a look for yourself,' replied Katy. She lifted the tablecloth. Abby was lying on the floor, fast asleep.

'Wake her up!' exclaimed Daniel. 'Wake her up!'

'You try.'

Daniel bent down and shook her shoulder vigorously. 'Abby! Abby! You need to wake up. Now, Abby!'

'Nooerrr. Leave ma alone,' she muttered, batting him away.

Daniel looked up at Katy, pure fear written all over both of their faces. Ben was also staring at her.

'Do something!' they both exclaimed.

'What am I supposed to do?' asked Katy.

'I have no idea, but we need to do something. This is a disaster,' said Ben. 'Braindead can't swoop down from the sky and propose to that.' He pointed at the slumped lump that was Abby. 'We have to stop him, we have to stop this farce now.' He turned and fled back towards the stage.

'I'll go too,' said Daniel, getting up from the floor and chasing after him.

Katy looked down at Abby and dropped the tablecloth over her. The only answer was to let her sleep it off. She'd tried everything bar chucking water over her, as she didn't think Abby would ever forgive her if she ruined her make-up.

As she looked up, the lights in the venue suddenly went down, leaving the ceiling to appear to be lit by hundreds of twinkling stars. The noisy crowd hushed their voices as the African drumbeat picked up pace, getting louder and louder until it resembled a drum roll. The effect was to fill the room with an enormous sense of anticipation. There was almost complete quiet by the time the drum roll reached its crescendo then stopped before a spotlight beamed on to the ceiling revealing a masked man in a dinner suit, holding a yellow rose between his teeth.

They didn't get to him in time, thought Katy, her heart now beating as fast as the African drums had been. This was happening. Braindead was about to propose to thin air. What could she do? She saw Ben and Daniel freeze halfway across the space; mouths open, gazing up at Braindead. By now people in the crowd were pointing and nudging each other, wondering what on earth a man was doing, dangling from the ceiling.

The fiasco lurched to the precipice as the unmistakable music from *Beauty and the Beast* began to fill the room and Braindead began his descent. Bizarrely, he appeared to be enjoying himself, smiling and waving from behind his Zorro mask at the hundreds of faces gazing up at him in awe. So much so he began to work the crowd, encouraging them to clap and cheer so that when his feet hit the floor the sound of applause was deafening. He grinned from ear to ear, bowing to all corners of the dance floor, then confidently strode over to table ten, searching for signs of his future fiancée.

Katy ran her hands through her hair. Ben and Daniel were still rooted to the spot. No-one knew what to do as Katy spotted a flicker of confusion fall across Braindead's face.

'I'm here,' shouted Katy, standing up and staggering towards Braindead, who was now stranded on the edge of the dance floor. 'What are you doing?' she declared. 'I can't believe my boyfriend would do something so cool,' she shouted, throwing her arms around his neck and engulfing him in an enormous hug.

'Propose to me,' she hissed in his ear. 'Abby is too pissed.'

'What?' he said, trying to pull away but she just gripped him tighter.

'She's passed out. Propose to me and then we'll get you out of here.'

She let him pull away so she could look into his terrified eyes and then gently put her hands on his shoulders and pushed him down to his knees.

The entire room let out oohs and ahhs as they caught on to what was happening.

Braindead looked around warily and saw a sea of 700 faces looking at him expectantly. He looked at Katy as she tried to smile encouragingly.

'Will you... will you... marry me?' he stuttered before throwing his arms in the air in utter confusion. The room was silent as it waited for Katy's response. She looked around nervously. Hundreds of sets of eyes were now focused on her.'

'Yes,' she said nodding and forced a smile. 'Yes!'

The entire room went crazy. People stood and cheered. Women cried. A man from table twenty-eight walked over to Braindead and shook his hand.

This is terrible, thought Katy. And then it got a whole lot worse. Suddenly the sound of Bing Crosby filled the room, declaring his dream of a white Christmas. Braindead was encouraged to his feet by the man who'd shaken his hand, and he and Katy stared at each other awkwardly as the delirious crowd went mental with happiness around them. And then the fake snow started to fall.

'What the fuck?' said Braindead, looking up into the roof as globs of foam floated to the ground. 'What just happened?' he asked Katy. 'I don't have to marry you now, do I?'

'No,' replied Katy. 'Let's call this damage limitation. I think we do have to dance though.'

'Seriously?'

'I'm afraid so.' Katy grabbed him and attempted to whirl him round the dance floor. 'You need to pretend to look pleased,' she urged.

'I have no idea what just happened. I think I'm having post-traumatic shock.'

'Abby is asleep under table thirteen. Get this dance over with and I'll take you over, and we'll get you both out of here.'

'This is the worst experience of my life,' he wailed. 'When I see Daniel, I'm going to kill him.'

Katy was dimly aware of people taking pictures of the happy couple. She decided not to point this out to Braindead.

'I should have known anything that required me to dangle from a ceiling was doomed.'

'It's not Daniel's fault Abby got drunk too soon.'

'You can't blame Abby for any of this. She wasn't to know. It's her Christmas party, she had every right to be drunk. I had no right to assume she would be sober just because I was going to propose. Can we stop now?'

Braindead stopped abruptly and stormed off the dance floor while Katy tried to grab his hand to indicate that they could possibly be a blissfully happy, newly engaged couple.

Chapter Twenty-Six

'Is that... is that... is that Katy?' said Matthew half to himself, shielding his eyes from the light to try and get a better look. He hadn't said her name in a very long time and even now it sat guiltily on his lips. Alison hadn't heard him. She was too busy moving her seat grumpily because Ian had politely asked her if she would swap with him so he could sit next to Lena.

It is *Katy*, thought Matthew. He'd know her anywhere. Simply by the way she held herself. Why was she standing in front of a man on his knees who had just dangled rather ridiculously from the ceiling with a rose between his teeth? It looked like a proposal, but surely not? The man wasn't Ben. He was wearing a mask, but Matthew could tell it wasn't him. Had Katy dumped Ben and moved on to someone else? Either way, this type of proposal didn't feel like Katy – she was far too sophisticated for this.

'Is that who I think it is?' said Alison when she'd settled herself into the seat next to Matthew after much huffing and puffing.

'I think it might be,' said Matthew.

They were both silent as they watched the spectacle unfold. Katy nodded and embraced the mystery man, and the crowd went wild.

'Did they just get engaged?' said Alison. 'Who *is* that? It's not Ben, is it?' She looked over at Matthew in confusion.

'So romantic,' said Lena, clapping her hands together in glee, watching the delicate foam snowflakes drift to the floor. 'A proposal in fake snow, I have never seen anything like it before.'

'That's impressive,' agreed Ian. 'He's certainly done it in style. She must be worth it.'

'It's Katy,' Matthew told Ian before he could stop himself. Ian had been his sounding board when he'd got into a right pickle with Katy before. The only person he had ever confessed his one-night stand to.

'What? *The* Katy!' exclaimed Ian.

'What do you mean, "*the* Katy"?' asked Alison.

'She looks so happy,' said Lena dreamily.

Ian took in Matthew's horrified glance.

'Katy Charles, from Gilpin,' said Ian. 'I assume you mean her, Matthew? It's Matthew's bitch of a client. He can't stand her,' he told Lena.

'Oh, but she looks so nice,' said Lena.

'No, it's not that Katy,' said Matthew, relieved at Ian's quick thinking. 'A different one. You've never met her.'

'It's Matthew's ex,' Alison said bluntly. 'We've had some run-ins with her in the past, and let's just say it's been awkward.'

'Oh, I see,' replied Ian. 'Exes can be like that.'

'As well you know, Ian,' said Alison.

'Thank you, Alison,' replied Ian, getting up and grabbing a bottle of white wine from the ice bucket and reaching over to fill Lena's glass. 'Now let me introduce you, Lena, to all my long-suffering colleagues. As you can probably detect, we are on the tax-department table. Hence, allow me to present to you a lot of single male losers,' he said, casting his arm round the table. His colleagues heckled and Lena grinned. Meanwhile Katy was now dragging the mystery man around the dance floor to the croonings of Bing Crosby.

'Whoever he is, he doesn't actually look very happy about what he's just done,' muttered Alison to Matthew. Meanwhile Matthew's mind was in overdrive. He'd never had much time for Ben, but Katy clearly did. None of this made any sense, and it looked as though it didn't make any sense to the two on the dance floor either.

'I hope they're not sitting anywhere near us,' added Alison. 'I really don't need to make polite conversation with your ex-girlfriend tonight.'

'No,' said Matthew, shaking his head. He didn't need that either.

'Let's watch where they sit and then avoid that side of the room,' suggested Alison.

'OK,' said Matthew, still mesmerised by the weird couple.

She dug him in the ribs. 'Don't forget you must make sure that you ask Lena to go and find Master Elf as soon as dinner is finished,' she added. 'It's all going far too well for the lovebirds over there.'

Lena was gazing into Ian's eyes as he held court over the opposite side of the table. He cracked a joke, causing the entire group to fall about laughing. Including Lena.

Matthew and Alison watched as the couple abruptly left the dance floor at the opposite side of the room.

'Thank goodness for that,' said Alison. 'All we need now is to avoid Katy and find Master Elf.'

🎄

'He's gone,' said Daniel, walking back into the deserted bar area where Katy and Ben were sitting with Abby, who was slumped on a sofa. 'Can't find him anywhere.'

'He was really pissed off,' said Katy.

'He'll have gone home,' said Ben. 'He'll be on the PlayStation by now, trying to block out the mortification.'

'Nobody spotted, did they?' asked Katy.

'That he asked the wrong person to marry him in front of a cast of thousands?' said Daniel. 'No, no-one spotted, apart from him, of course. Stupid girl,' he said, prodding Abby.

'I mean, he didn't look stupid in front of everyone, did he? We spared him that?' asked Katy.

'I think you just about got away with it,' said Ben. 'If you were looking closely, you could totally tell something was up, but everyone was either too pissed or totally caught up in how romantic he was being.'

'Quick thinking,' said Daniel, slapping Katy on the back, 'very quick. It did cross my mind of course to steam in myself, but I think Braindead would have thumped me, don't you?'

A couple passed by on their way to the bar. They spotted Katy and dashed over.

'That was sooo romantic,' gushed the woman. 'You are sooo lucky. Let me see the ring – come on, let me see it.'

'Er, I-I didn't get a ring yet,' stuttered Katy, hiding her hands.

'Are you going to choose it together?' she asked.

Katy nodded. 'Yes.'

'Such a good idea,' she enthused. 'Look what hideous piece of junk I got stuck with.' She stuck her hand in Katy's face to show her the triple sapphire set in gold that adorned her ring finger. 'But it's the thought that counts, isn't it?' she said, grabbing the hand of her husband, who was standing gormlessly next to her. 'Be sure he spends shedloads,' the woman added. 'He clearly thinks you're worth it. Where is he, by the way? I need to tell him that every woman in that room totally fell in love with him.'

'Oh, he's in the loo,' said Katy quickly.

'Well, you give him a smacker from me,' she said. 'He's a keeper. Well done, love.' She staggered off towards the bar, her husband stumbling behind her.

'Is it going to be like this all night?' said Katy. 'I can't spend the evening accepting congratulations. And how do we explain where Braindead is?' She glared down at Abby, snoring contentedly. 'What have you done, Abby?'

🎄

'I'll explain to everyone that we're leaving,' Katy told Ben as they slunk along the back of the hall. Daniel had offered to take Abby home – anything to end Christmas Party Land early. Katy and Ben decided this was the ideal excuse for an early exit too. 'You grab my bag from under the table,' she said.

'Great,' replied Ben. 'Hey, we don't have to go home. We just have to get out of here, don't we? Shall we go into town? Let's go to Fever – see if they'll play us some Christmas tunes.'

Katy grinned. 'Brilliant idea! Tell you what, why don't you grab a bottle of wine and we can drink that in the cab on the way over?'

'You are such a bad influence,' said Ben proudly.

'After tonight, I think we deserve a drink, don't you?'

'Master Elf, Master Elf!' they heard a shriek come from behind them. Ben automatically swivelled round to come face-to-face with Lena before spotting Matthew and Alison sitting with her.

'This is Master Elf!' cried Lena, leaping up from out of her seat and pulling him over towards the table. Ben noticed that her cheeks were a little flushed and she looked highly excitable.

The look of absolute astonishment on Alison and Matthew's faces was a sight to behold.

'Hi,' said Ben meekly, raising a hand. 'Fancy meeting you here.'

'You!' said Alison, pointing a finger at Ben. 'You are Master Elf? But that's impossible.'

'It *is* him,' said Lena, jumping up and down excitedly. 'Ian, this is Master Elf. From George and Rebecca's preschool.'

'The one everyone's been going on and on about,' said Ian, getting up and shaking Ben's hand before turning to Katy. 'And you just got engaged!' he said. 'May I buy the bride-to-be a drink?' He did a double take and then glanced over at Matthew with a quizzical look.

'It's a free bar!' exclaimed Alison for the fifth time. 'And... and... it's Ben. I don't understand. What are you doing here, and why are you with her, and why is Lena calling you Master Elf?' she added, getting up. 'I don't understand any of this.'

'Bloody hell, Alison!' exclaimed Ben. 'You're enormous!'

'I don't think that's relevant right at this point, do you, Ben?' she said. 'Please tell me you're not Master Elf.'

Ben had forgotten how scary Alison could be when everything had just spun out of control and she was desperately trying to make sense of things.

'Yes,' he said, bracing himself. 'I am Master Elf.'

'Master Elf? As in the Master Elf at George and Rebecca's preschool that they go on and on about every day?' said Matthew, getting up.

'Yes, Matthew,' said Alison, sounding frustrated. 'Ben is Master Elf. Do you have any idea of the implications of this?' she said.

No-one said anything. Katy was wondering if now would be a good time to talk to Ben about Australia as an escape route from this chaos. She could see, however, that Ben was totally mesmerised by Alison's bump. As for Alison, as usual she was completely overreacting to the news that Ben was in charge of her precious children's Nativity.

Little could Katy know that Alison was also suffering from the extreme disappointment that Master Elf was no longer in the running to rescue Lena from Ian. Katy could see, however, that Matthew was looking at her in a weird fashion.

'But you just got engaged?' he said in wonder to Katy.

'Who cares about that!' said Alison to Matthew. 'That is not the issue here.'

'He wasn't supposed to ask me,' said Katy. 'I had to stand in for his real girlfriend because well… because she was too drunk.'

Alison looked incredulously at Katy, then at Ben. Then she shook her head.

'I really don't need to know the details,' she said.

'So you two are still together?' asked Matthew. He had to ask.

'Yes,' said Ben, feeling the need to reach down and grab Katy's hand. 'Of course we are. It was all just a big screw up, what you saw. Katy and I are actually married now.'

'Oh, congratulations,' said Alison sarcastically. 'I'm so happy for you, and in the meantime you've been masquerading as Master Elf the whole time and never thought to say anything?'

'I haven't been masquerading as anything,' replied Ben. 'I've just been doing my job.'

'He's very good at his job,' interrupted Lena.

'I don't care if he's the best teacher in the universe. He's been teaching my children and I didn't know about it.'

'But… but… why is this a problem?' asked Lena.

Ian stood beside her and laughed. He'd sussed out the problem by now and had a huge grin on his face.

'Lena,' he said, taking her hand gently. 'Let me take you outside to look at the Christmas tree. It's the biggest in Yorkshire, I've been told.'

'Is it really?' gasped Lena, allowing herself to be led away. Ian glanced over his shoulder and gave Alison a wink and a thumbs up.

'Oh no!' groaned Alison. 'Now look what you let happen,' she told Ben. 'Why did you have to be Master Elf?'

'What was I supposed to do?' he cried. 'Refuse to teach George and Rebecca because every time we all get tangled up in each other's lives it ends in tears?'

'You could at least have alerted us,' said Matthew.

Ben shrugged. 'And say what? I'm doing your kids' Nativity. Sorry about that.'

Alison gasped. 'You're doing the Nativity!' She put her head in her hands. 'What have we done?' she wailed to Matthew.

'You were the one who wanted to pull them out of the other school,' he said.

'I know,' whined Alison. 'But I couldn't bear the thought of them being donkeys in the Nativity.'

'You pulled them out of school because they were going to be donkeys?' asked Katy.

Alison nodded. 'Yes, the school refused to treat them as individuals. You can't victimise them for being twins by casting them both as donkeys.'

'I'm so sorry to interrupt,' said a woman, tapping Katy on the shoulder. 'Just wanted to say congratulations on your engagement. You must be over the moon. Seeing your man do that has made my Christmas.'

Katy grimaced. 'Thank you, it's really made mine as well.'

'Did you have any idea he was going to do it?' she pressed on.

'No,' said Katy. 'No idea at all.'

'Just amazing! I bet you can't wait for the wedding if he pulls off that kind of stunt just for the proposal?'

'That's right,' said Katy. 'Should be amazing.'

'Well, all the best then. Er could I just get a selfie? With him too, if that's all right,' she said, looking round to see where Braindead was while reaching inside her bag for her phone.

'No, er, no, if you don't mind. That's not really my thing. I'd really rather you didn't,' said Katy, backing away rapidly.

'Oh, OK, suit yourself,' said the lady huffily. She turned and walked off in a strop.

'Why is your life always so complicated?' Alison asked Katy.

'No, it isn't.'

Alison shrugged. 'Whenever we meet it always seems to be shrouded in confusion and deception somehow.'

Katy looked over at Matthew, who had gone very pale.

'I thought we were talking about the Nativity,' said Ben, stepping in to deflect the wisp of cold air that had whistled through the atmosphere.

'Yes, we were,' said Matthew, also keen to deflect any attention. 'Look, we can't do anything about George and Rebecca's preschool now. At least Ben has cast them as Joseph and Mary. That's something, isn't it?'

'Along with all the other kids,' said Ben.

'What!' said Matthew, turning to look sharply at Ben. He was trying to salvage the situation here.

'All the boys wanted to be Joseph and all the girls wanted to be Mary so I came to the obvious conclusion: to let them all be Joseph and Mary. It *is* Christmas after all.'

'You did *what?*' exclaimed Alison.

'Cast them all as Mary and Joseph. We have thirteen Marys and ten Josephs.'

'I think I need to sit down,' said Alison.

'Are you OK?' asked Matthew, panicking. 'Don't stress yourself. It's OK, just sit down and breathe.'

Alison took the seat that Matthew placed behind her and he gripped her hand.

'It's OK,' he said. 'It's only the Nativity.'

She was breathing heavily now. A flush had spread over her face.

'Are you OK?' asked Ben, kneeling down, a look of concern on his face.

'One of thirteen Marys!' she breathed. 'That's worse than being cast as a donkey alongside your twin brother.'

'I think I'd better take you home,' said Matthew, pushing Ben out of the way. 'You're just getting yourself into a state. This is no place for a pregnant woman.'

'But what about Lena?' she gasped. 'And Mary and Joseph, and oh no...'

'Lena can look after herself,' said Matthew, pulling Alison up out of her chair. 'She's a grown woman, she's not your daughter. You've got to let her work it out.'

'But Ian could ruin her Christmas!' she muttered, shaking her head. 'I was relying on you, Master Elf,' she said to Ben as Matthew led her gently away.

'What's she talking about?' asked Ben.

'Let it go,' said Matthew to Alison.

'You were supposed to make Lena's Christmas, not ruin my children's Nativity!' she said, stabbing Ben in the chest with a finger.

'Come on, Alison,' said Matthew. 'This is neither the time nor the place. You need to go home and lie down.'

'I will see you at the Nativity,' said Alison grimly, glaring at Katy and Ben before she allowed herself to be led away.

🎄

'What the hell was all that about?' said Ben as they watched them walk off out of the room.

'I have no idea. What did she mean about Lena?'

'I haven't a clue. This has been the weirdest Christmas party ever, like ever in the history of man. Please can we get out of here?'

They weaved their way through the tables while people shouted their congratulations at Katy as she smiled inanely back. At last they were out in the main foyer again. They were just about to head over to the cloakroom to collect Katy's coat when Ben stopped in his tracks.

'What's wrong?' asked Katy.

Ben didn't say anything for a moment, just bit his lip.

'Are you OK?'

'Let's not go out,' he said eventually.

'Why not? Come on, it'll be fun. We haven't been out as just the two of us in Leeds for ages. And it'll be all Christmassy. Come on.'

'Let's go home,' he said. 'And…' He looked down at his feet. Then he looked up again. Katy's heart contracted. She knew exactly what he was going to say.

'…and make a baby.'

He smiled at her, and she tried to smile back but a million thoughts whooshed into her head – so much so she felt dizzy. She didn't know if she wanted a baby. She might want to live in Australia. Neither of these things could she talk to Ben about right now. She looked back at him. She could tell that with every bone in his body, all he wanted to do right at this minute was to go home and extend the family. His certainty was equal and opposite to her uncertainty, and it looked like at that precise moment there was no option but to collide those two thoughts.

She swallowed.

'But I'd really like to go out,' she whimpered.

'I'd really like to go home and make a baby.'

She looked at the floor.

'Is there any way we can just wait until after I've been on this trip?'

'Why? What's your trip got to do with our family?'

'Just come and sit down a minute,' she said, leading him over to the sofas where moments earlier they had sat with a drunken Abby.

'What?' he said, looking quizzically at her. 'What's going on, Katy?'

'I've been trying to tell you, but I was hoping there would be nothing to tell.'

'What do you mean? For fuck's sake, Katy, what's going on?'

'This trip to Australia,' she said slowly. 'Well, I'm going there to see Boomerang Airlines, but there's also a job there if I want it. If *we* want it.'

'What do you mean, a job?'

'Cooper White has offered me the role of brand director for Boomerang Airlines. In Australia.'

'You've been offered a job in Australia… but… why didn't you say? Why not tell me?' He lay back, his hand on his forehead, trying to take it all in. 'That could be all right, couldn't it? I'd need to think about it, of course, but I could be up for Australia, I think. Never thought about living abroad, to be honest, but I wouldn't dismiss it, I don't think. I don't know. But why are you only telling me now?'

'Because if I take the job, if we moved to Australia, then we probably wouldn't be able to have another baby for a couple of years.'

'Oh right,' said Ben, screwing his forehead up.

'And then I'd be kind of old for a baby. So there's a greater risk I may not conceive.'

'Right, I see.' He was nodding, but she could see his brain was struggling to keep up with the implications of what she was saying.

'So… so… what are you saying?' he said eventually, sitting back up. 'I'm sorry, Katy, you'll have to spell it out for me. I can't compute all of this. One minute you seem to be telling me we could be moving to Australia, and the next minute you're telling me we might not be able to have any more kids?'

'That is kind of exactly what I'm saying. We may not be able to have both. A new life in Australia and kids, I mean. We may have to choose. It's why I haven't said anything. I was hoping that I could go to Australia and it would be clear to me that actually the job and the lifestyle isn't what I want, then I wouldn't even have to trouble you with it.'

Ben leaned back on the sofa again in shock, both hands clasped over his forehead now. She reached out to touch his knee, but he instantly reached down and shoved it off.

'What about what *I* want?' he said. His face was angry.

'I think I know what you want,' she said tentatively. 'You want another baby. I was trying to avoid this. I didn't want to talk to you about it until I knew what I really wanted. I'm confused, Ben. I didn't think it would help to decide what we should do if my head is all in a mess over it.'

'Don't you want another baby?'

'Yes – well, I think so.'

'What do you mean, you think so?'

'It's just, well, it's tempting, isn't it? Moving to Australia? And the job would be amazing.'

Ben was shaking his head.

'Come on, even you said a minute ago you'd like to live there.'

'I didn't realise we were talking about a choice then. It's a no-brainer, isn't it? It's got to be a baby. I can't even believe you're considering it. I've been the stay-at-home parent for your career. I made that sacrifice. Now you're asking me to sacrifice having another member of our family for your career. Screw your career, quite frankly.'

Katy recoiled in horror.

'It's a no-brainer surely?' repeated Ben.

'I think it is,' said Katy. 'I guess I just want to be sure.'

Ben stared at her as though he couldn't believe his ears.

'I don't understand,' he said.

She took his hands, and thankfully he allowed her.

'This would be a different conversation if I were a man,' she said.

'Why would it?'

'If you were being offered the job in Sydney, we could just go, couldn't we? Get on a plane; I could have a baby – everyone's happy. But we can't do that, can we? I have to make a choice. Sorry, *we* have to make a choice?'

He stared back at her. 'Yes,' he said eventually. '*We* have to. Not you, *we*. I still don't understand why you're only telling me now. I understand that it's tough making these decisions but it's a whole lot tougher if you don't talk to me about it.'

'I tried to tell you but you wouldn't even let me talk about going to Australia, never mind living there,' she pleaded. 'And I didn't think there was going to be anything to talk about. He offered me the job and I'd decided it was a no. Definitely a no. Then he asks Andrew if I'll go and see the operation in Sydney. I couldn't refuse, Ben. It's part of securing the contract. I know it's a stealth move on Cooper's part. He's trying to convince me to take the job. I didn't want to have this conversation. What I wanted was to come home having rejected the job offer and have it clear in my head that I want another baby.'

'But why not tell me that?'

'Because you are so damn sure, Ben. I couldn't bear the thought of telling you I wasn't. Admitting to you that I'm not sure about another baby… it felt like a massive deal.'

'It *is* a massive deal.'

'Exactly. So before I told you I wasn't sure, I wanted to be sure I wasn't sure.'

'This isn't making any sense. Either you want another baby or you don't.'

'I'm trying to explain, Ben. I don't know, I just don't know.'

'And you think swanning off to Sydney with Cooper What's His Face is going to help you decide more than actually talking to me about it?'

'No. I mean yes. I mean I didn't mean to shut you out – honestly, I didn't. I was trying to protect your feelings, not make you angry.'

'Tell you what,' he said, getting up. 'You go to Sydney and talk to Cooper about whether or not we have another child, and you let me know when you get back, will you? Can't wait to hear what Cooper thinks is in my future.'

'No, it's not like that!' exclaimed Katy, chasing after him as he strode towards the door. 'I promise you it isn't like that.'

He paused, turning back to face her. 'I'm going to see if Braindead is all right. I'll see you in the morning.'

'No, Ben! You need to listen.'

'Oh, you want to talk to me about it now, do you? Well too damn late, Katy!'

She watched as he left the building. She felt hot tears instantly well up in her eyes. What a screw up. How could she have been such an idiot?

'Oh look, it's the woman who got engaged,' she heard someone cry from her left. Before she could make her escape the woman engulfed her in a drunken hug. 'I was in bits,' the woman breathed down her ear. 'That was the most romantic thing I have ever seen. You are so lucky. Please tell me where you found him?' she asked, pulling away. 'Does he have any friends? I would kill for a man like that.'

Chapter Twenty-Seven

'You are a crazy lady,' Ian told Lena as she stepped off her bumper car. 'Remind me never to get into a car with you behind the wheel.'

Lena laughed. 'You expected to be better, huh? At bumping? You expected me to hold back? To be shy? To be kind?'

Ian paused for a moment and looked at her. 'No, actually,' he said eventually. 'I think you are more than capable of holding your own. Despite what Alison might think.'

'I can take care of myself,' she said and nodded, giving him a knowing look.

'I know you can,' said Ian. 'Look, you know, don't you, that Alison doesn't want you to get involved with me? I can't blame her. My record isn't great. But… but…'

'I can take care of myself,' repeated Lena, smiling.

Ian swallowed. 'That's what frightens me.'

She threw back her head and laughed.

For the first time possibly in his whole life, Ian was at a loss for words. Lena was making him think things he had not thought in a long time. Normally he would just move in for a kiss, but somehow he was paralysed. Petrified of making the wrong move. In normal Ian mode he would have slept with her by now, and if he hadn't then he would have dumped her. But Lena was different: she was extraordinary and called for extraordinary measures.

'I am so cold,' she said eventually when Ian didn't speak. 'What is it with you Brits that you insist on standing in the cold with no coat?'

'Is it cold?' Ian asked. 'I hadn't even noticed.'

'Please no,' replied Lena, collapsing again with laughter.

'No really, I meant that line. No honestly. I hadn't realised it was cold. I'm not cold.'

'Your nose is red. You look like Rudolph.'

'You are so not kind!'

'A cute Rudolph.'

'Is that supposed to make me feel better?'

'No,' said Lena, shaking her head.

'Will you spend Christmas with me?' he blurted out suddenly. He realised he didn't want to just have sex with Lena – he wanted so much more than that.

'You are not serious,' she replied.

'No, I have never been more serious. I'll, er… I'll cook a turkey, or do you even have turkey in Lithuania? What do you have? Tell me and I'll cook it for you.'

Lena took a step back. Her smile had disappeared. 'You are lonely, I remember. You are alone for Christmas. This makes people say weird things.'

'No!' Ian exclaimed. 'Yes – I mean no. I mean yes, I am alone this Christmas, but that isn't why I'm asking you. I just want to spend time with you. Really I do.'

Lena raised her eyebrows, a distinct look of suspicion on her face. 'You have a bad reputation,' she said.

'Look,' said Ian. 'You've probably heard all sorts of stories from Matthew. But this isn't like that, I promise you.'

'You just want me to come over on Christmas Day and you want to cook me a meal,' she said as though she didn't believe him.

'Yes, I honestly do. How can I convince you?' Ian looked around in despair. 'No-one ever has sex on Christmas Day, do they?' he said eventually. 'I mean, it's so not sexy. Kids up at the crack of dawn, hands up turkeys' backsides before breakfast, stomachs bloated by too much food and alcohol, exhaustion from weeks of celebrating. All you want to do on Christmas Day is spend time with the ones you care about. I'd very much like to do that with you. If you would like to, that is.'

Lena looked at Ian for a long time.

'Fish,' she said.

'What?'

'We often eat fish at Christmas.'

'Right – fish. Great, fish it is.'

She broke into a smile then leaned forward and kissed him delicately on the lips.

'I think all my Christmases have come at once,' he gasped when he opened his eyes and met her gaze. He leaned forward to kiss her again but she sidestepped quickly.

'Will you dance?' she asked, a wicked smile on her face.

'Are going to make me sweat, literally, for another kiss?' asked Ian with a bigger smile on his face.

'Come on, Rudolph,' she said, grabbing his hand and dragging him back towards the main hall. 'We will dance because it is Christmas, and because that is what you do. We will dance a happy Christmas dance. And you can tell me all about how you will cook that fish for me on Christmas Day.'

Chapter Twenty-Eight

'Is that what I should have done then?' said Braindead, slumped on the sofa next to Ben. 'Learn a bloody foreign language?'

They were watching *Love Actually*, sipping from cans of Fosters. They hadn't intended to watch it, but it happened to be on because it was Christmas and it was always on at Christmas. They had already watched Kris Marshall arrive in America and walk into a bar where all the stunning women thought his accent was the sexiest thing on the planet. Braindead had commented on the unfairness of this scenario. 'What kind of warped world do we live in when you have to go overseas to be sexy?'

They were now watching Colin Firth's proposal in bad Portuguese. They both squirmed, thinking about the catastrophe of Braindead's efforts earlier in the evening.

'Hope there was no-one I knew there,' muttered Braindead, 'or else I'm going to have to spend the whole of Christmas explaining why I swung from the ceiling and proposed to your wife. They put you in a straitjacket for less than that.'

'You might have had a lucky escape, mate,' Ben mumbled back. 'Struggling to see the point of marriage myself right at this moment.'

'Mmm,' agreed Braindead as the entire Portuguese restaurant erupted as Colin Firth's ex-cleaning lady agreed to marry him.

'It's bloody love, isn't it?' muttered Braindead.

'Actually…' huffed Ben.

'What?'

'*Love Actually.*'

'Yeah that. It's dangerous.'

'What is?'

'Love.'

'*Love Actually?*'

'Actually, yes. It is.'

'It messes with your brain.'

'It sure does.'

'Is there a cure?'

'I doubt it.'

'So we're screwed.'

'Pretty much.'

Chapter Twenty-Nine

'I know you're in Australia but please will you call Gabriel and invite him for Christmas dinner. I've asked him, but he is so polite that he doesn't want to impose. Will you just call him? Is it too much to ask for Carlos to have his son with him at Christmas?'

Katy was just about to send an angry text back to her mother, who couldn't seem to understand that she had other things on her mind apart from the well-being of her new boyfriend, when Millie appeared on the tablet that was balancing on her knee.

'Have you seen a kangaroo yet, Mummy?' she asked immediately, bouncing up and down while stuffing toast into her mouth.

'Hello Millie,' she replied. 'No kangaroos yet.' She knew Ben would be hovering somewhere out of sight listening to every word. 'I'm not sure there are any in Sydney.'

'When are you coming home?'

'Not long now. I'll be back soon.'

'I'm Mary in the Nativity,' she said.

'I know, I can't wait to see you.'

'Who is that, Mummy?'

'Who do you mean?'

'That person standing behind you.'

Katy swivelled her head round.

'Next to the swimming pool,' Millie added helpfully.

Katy could see that Cooper had drifted into shot behind her, busy chatting to the HR director from Boomerang Airlines.

She swivelled back round and could see Ben and Millie now staring back at her expectantly.

'These are the people who've been showing me round,' she said. She tried really hard to stop herself going pink as though she'd been caught doing something she shouldn't. It was her second night in Sydney, and Cooper had invited her to his house along with his senior team. When she'd walked through the enormous French doors out on to the patio her jaw had literally dropped. Beyond the pool lay the glittering expanse of the Pacific Ocean. It could not be more spectacular.

'Not bad, eh?' Cooper had said.

She'd nodded. 'It's nice. Quite nice.'

'Can I get you a drink? How about a Chardonnay from a winery not far from here?'

'Thank you,' Katy had replied, thinking those were words you'd never hear in Leeds.

She'd stood awkwardly gazing at the view until Cooper had returned with a glass of wine that looked so delicious she just wanted to look at it. The soft yellow had glowed through the glistening, condensation-soaked glass. She'd sipped and found it truly did taste like the best wine she had ever had. Far better than the special-offer wine from the supermarket that she normally drank. Or that rubbish that Ben had purchased at the discount warehouse.

'I could take you to the vineyard tomorrow evening if you like? I know the owner. He'd lay on a tasting, I'm sure.'

Katy had looked at Cooper, horrified. She should have stayed at home. This had been such a mistake.

'We won't have time, will we?' she'd said. 'I thought you were taking me to see the facility in Brisbane tomorrow?'

'Oh we'll have plenty of time. We'll be back by five, and then we'll take the chopper up there. Robbie has a landing pad. No worries.'

'The chopper?'

'Helicopter.'

'Right.'

'You'll like it, I promise.'

Katy hadn't doubted that. She hadn't doubted it at all. In fact she'd known she would love it and that was entirely the problem.

'Well, we'll have to see what my jet lag is like,' she'd said. 'I might be ready to pass out by then.'

'Of course,' Cooper had replied. 'We can play it by ear – not a problem. Now let me introduce you to Bradley.'

Katy had spent the rest of the evening making small talk with various members of Cooper's team at Boomerang. Cooper hadn't told any of them that he'd offered her a job so they treated her as a visitor from the UK touting for their communications business. As such, they spent most of the time telling her how much better at sport the Aussies were than the British, a conversation Ben would have embraced no doubt if he'd been there. She missed him; she'd missed being able to talk to him about all of it. She'd wanted to laugh with him about the macho posturing of the men surrounding her then go back to the hotel and gossip about Cooper's taste in furniture (white leather!) and his state-of-the-art gym, clearly visible from the patio. That afternoon, when she'd had a couple of hours to explore Sydney, she had guiltily seized the chance to go inside the famous opera house, and several times she'd turned to point something out to him. As much as she'd been stunned by its incredible architecture and her good fortune in being able to see it, when she'd sat outside a café drinking lemonade, overlooking the soaring archways, she had never felt more alone.

When Ben had texted to say that Millie wanted to do FaceTime, she had jumped at the chance, despite the fact that it would be in the middle of Cooper's barbecue. She could hardly say it was inconvenient – she hadn't seen either of them since the horrible scene at the Christmas party. Ben had texted in the early hours of the morning to say he was staying at Braindead's and wouldn't be back until after she had left for the airport. She'd already said her goodbyes to Millie and didn't want to upset her again by turning up at her mother-in-law's for one last hug. She longed to see their faces, however as she looked at them staring back at her now, she knew she should have somehow found a way of doing it in a less glamorous situation.

'Have you been in the pool?' asked Millie.

'No, darling. We're here to have some food.'

'Aren't you allowed in the pool?'

'I'm sure if I asked I would be, but it's not really what I've come for. I've come to meet some people and have a meal. I'll be going back to the hotel soon.'

'We had spaghetti hoops for tea last night,' said Millie.

'Brilliant,' said Katy, smiling at Ben. He looked stony-faced. She pulled the screen towards her so that she blocked out the stunning view behind her and hopefully the sight of the other guests.'

'Do they have spaghetti hoops in Australia?'

'I've no idea.'

'Does Santa go to Australia?'

'Yes, he actually comes here first because it's one of the first countries to wake up on Christmas morning.'

'But it looks hot there. Won't he be too hot in his red suit?'

'Perhaps he has a warm-weather outfit for here?'

'Does he wear shorts? Have you seen pictures of him wearing shorts?'

'No, Millie. I actually saw a model Santa in a shop window, and he was wearing his full red suit.'

'Really? Poor Santa, he'll be so hot.'

'I know. But I'm sure he'll be OK.'

'Do kids in Australia leave ice lollies instead of mince pies so he can cool down?'

'I don't know.'

'Ask someone.'

'I will tomorrow.'

'Ask that man behind you.'

'What, now?'

'Yes, ask him. Has he got kids? Are there kids there?'

'No, I don't think he has kids,' she said, glancing at Ben.

'Ask him anyway.'

Katy turned and cleared her throat. 'Excuse me, sorry to interrupt but my daughter would like to know what children in Australia leave for Father Christmas when he comes to bring them presents.'

Cooper walked towards Katy and to her horror bent forward to address Millie directly.

'Hi, it's Millie, isn't it?' he said.

'Yes,' muttered Millie, looking in amazement at the stranger bearing down on her.

'I'm so sorry to have dragged your mum away, but she'll be back soon, I promise, and to answer your question, I used to leave Santa Claus a cold beer when I was your age. Merry Christmas to you both.' He stood back up and walked away, and Katy was left with the sight of Ben and Millie looking slightly awestruck. Millie in a good way, but she wasn't quite so sure about Ben. He abruptly got up and disappeared from the screen.

'Beer?' questioned Millie. 'Can I leave Santa a cold beer this year?'

'If you want to,' replied Katy, hoping that Ben would reappear soon. 'I guess it would save us buying sherry that we never drink,' she said distractedly.

'You don't drink it – Santa does.'

'You're right. Of course he does.'

Millie looked up, away from the screen.

'Daddy says I need to go to school now,' she said after a moment.

'OK, darling. Can't wait to see you. Can I speak to Daddy just before you go?'

'Daddy!' shouted Millie. 'Mummy wants to talk to you.' Millie disappeared and all Katy could see was an empty cereal bowl and the backside of Millie's teddy. She waited patiently, but it was a couple of minutes before Ben appeared.

'We need to go,' he said, pushing the bowl and teddy to one side. 'Last rehearsal today.'

'I know. I, er, just wanted to wish you good luck. Shall I call you before I get on the plane?'

He shrugged. 'If you like,' he said. 'You are coming home then?'

'Of course I am. What's that supposed to mean?'

He shrugged. 'Nothing.'

'We'll talk later then, shall we?' she asked.

'Yeah,' he replied. She could see his finger already reaching forward to cut her off. 'Bye,' he said before the screen went blank and Ben and Millie both disappeared into their day on the other side of the world.

Chapter Thirty

'Be quiet!' shouted Ben. His heart was racing. He had never been more terrified in his life. Why had he done this? Twenty-seven children surrounded him in various states of costume and it had turned them mental. Turned him mental as it happened. Now they were all standing backstage (aka the quiet reading room), and he was having the most monumental attack of stage fright. He peeped through the curtains for the fifth time and looked at all the expectant faces starting to file in. Glowing, cheerful mums and smiling dads shaking hands with each other, pumped and primed to watch their little treasures perform the rite of passage that is the Nativity play.

He was going to screw it up; he knew it. In fact, he probably already had. He'd been too cavalier from the very beginning. Deciding on a whim to reject the customs of the Nativity play for a wholly more contemporary take on the matter. An interpretation, shall we say, not shackled by the constraints of tradition. An interpretation focused on truly getting to the nub of the story in a fresh and surprising way. An interpretation developed in collaboration with the performers. When he'd asked them all who they wanted to be, most of them had requested to be Mary or Joseph. Why not, he had thought. Who was he to make someone play a donkey or a sheep? Let them all have the main parts. Didn't that teach them that in the eyes of God we are all equal and should be treated accordingly?

Right at that moment, however, he was feeling less Kenneth Branagh and more like a blundering idiot who was going to be the biggest disappointment the school had seen in many years.

'It keeps falling off,' Millie said, arriving at his elbow and pulling at his arm.

He bent down to pin her tea towel in place. Oh God, he thought. Poor Millie was going to get it in the neck as well. Millie with the loser dad who couldn't even put on a decent Nativity. He wanted to crawl under a stone and die.

He took his phone out of his pocket to put it on silent.

'I'll be there. Katy Xxx'

That was the last message he'd received from Katy. He was half-angry, half-terrified. Angry that she wasn't there already, terrified that she wasn't there to tell him it was all going to be OK. He'd been on the brink of calling her to see where she was, but every time his finger hovered over the call button he pulled it away. Calling her felt needy – she should be the one to call him, not the other way round.

He peeked his nose through the curtain again just as Alison and Matthew took seats in the front row. He watched as a couple, rather begrudgingly, gave up their seats to the heavily pregnant lady and her husband. *That's all I need*, he thought. Alison was going to have an absolute field day with his version of the Nativity. Nothing short of a classic religious fairy tale would satisfy her, and this was way short of a classic religious fairy tale.

Alison looked up just as Ben was staring at her. She raised her eyebrows. She expected him to fail, he knew it.

He turned and faced his army.

'Right!' he whispered loudly. 'Let's all sit down and channel our inner Nativity.'

'What's that mean Master Elf?" someone asked.

'It just means that we're going to sit here quietly for a few seconds and pray for a good performance. Now put your hands together, children.'

🎄

Katy was having a shocker. A humdinger. An outrageous disaster. Her flight home was delayed. Obviously. It had to happen, didn't it? How could she have been so stupid to think it wouldn't?

She'd sat in Singapore Airport waiting for her connecting flight, staring so hard at the announcement board she feared her eyes might laser beam right through it. What started as a thirty-minute delay ended in a ninety-minute delay, just at the point when she was about to throttle the poor woman on the Singapore Airlines desk.

'I have my husband's Nativity to get to!' she had shrieked when the woman refused to tell her when the plane might be taking off.

'Your husband's?' the woman had asked.

'Yes,' replied Katy on the verge of tears. 'If I'm not there, well, it's entirely possible it will end in divorce.'

'What part is he playing?'

'Master Elf,' she replied. 'Now tell me when this flight will be taking off.'

When she finally got on to the plane, she hadn't slept a wink of the fourteen-hour flight, so craving the knowledge that she would get home in time that she daren't shut her eyes for one minute.

Also, the minute she shut her eyes, she knew all she would picture was the blue of the ocean and the feel of the warmth of the sun on her skin, and it made her want to cry. The trip couldn't have gone much better, and Cooper couldn't have played it more cleverly. He'd put zero pressure on her, leaving his beautiful country and vibrant yet laid-back colleagues to do the work for him. The minute the HR director told her that it was normal to finish work by five thirty, no questions asked, in order to enjoy the great outdoors... well, that in itself was enough to make her want to flee the workaholic shores of the British Isles immediately.

She had, of course, ended up flying to the winery in the helicopter. She couldn't resist. It was heaven sitting on the side of a mountain with an array of glasses in front of her as she pretended to know what she was talking about. Pure heaven. Well, it would have been, if Ben and Millie had been there. Sure, she had enjoyed Cooper's company. He was pleasant, even quite fun, and obviously he was a joy to look at, but he wasn't Ben. She'd spent most of the night wanting to call Ben and reassure him that Cooper wasn't him, feeling certain that Ben would be comparing himself unfavourably, especially having seen him up close. But that would have been an admission of guilt, wouldn't it? That she had fancied him even though nothing more had ever crossed her mind. Hard not to, but marriage was about so much more than a great suntan and a killer smile.

She'd braced herself for the hard sell that night from Cooper. But he was the perfect host. Never mentioning the career opportunity, leaving her wondering if he'd changed his mind and whether she should check the job was still on offer.

He'd picked her up the next morning to deliver her to the airport, and still it hung in the air. She was terrified, as she didn't have an answer. Terrified what would come out of her mouth if put on the spot by him, but as it turned out, he didn't do anything of the sort. Handing her carry-on case to her as she was about to go through security, he merely said, 'I hope you've enjoyed yourself and seen enough to convince you that you and your family would be very welcome here in Sydney. Call me after Christmas when you have had time to think about it.'

Then he'd turned and left.

She could have burst into tears there and then. A masterstroke. No begging, just an open welcome.

The trip had done nothing to give her any clarity. It had merely achieved exactly what Cooper had intended – given her a taste for a lifestyle that on face value appeared irresistible. How could she say no to glorious weather, beaches by the bucketload, a more laid-back pace of life and a dream job to boot? Everything about it screamed an easy yes, and yet it felt impossible. Eventually, in total desperation on the plane, she got out her laptop and set up a spreadsheet. She had to do something to fight this impasse in her head and spreadsheets normally helped solve all her problems in her work life.

She started to type in the list of pros for Australia, of which there were many. Not so when it came to cons, but as she typed she realised that the reasons weren't equal. Some held greater weight than others. You couldn't say that 'eating outside all the time' had an equal value to 'leaving Daniel'… or maybe you could, she pondered momentarily. And how much value do you put on having another child? You couldn't, she realised. It was impossible. She slammed down the lid of the laptop. She was back to square one, alone and totally confused.

🎄

She could see the rain slamming against the tarmac as she touched down in Manchester and switched on her phone

*'Gabriel is coming for Christmas! Thank you for texting him, but
I would have thought you could have phoned! Where will he sleep?
He could have the spare room and you could sleep in the lounge.
See you tomorrow! Mum x'*

The last thing she cared about now was the Christmas sleeping
arrangements. She had less than an hour and a half to get to the school.
She couldn't afford to hang around for her luggage – she'd have to
work out a way of coming back to collect it at a later date. As soon as
the seatbelt sign clicked off, she was up and out of her seat, her heart
already hammering in her chest. There was no time to think about
moving to Australia now, she had a Nativity to get to.

🎄

'Good morning, everyone,' said Ben. He'd changed into a full-blown
elf costume complete with hat, a bright green and red suit and winkle-
picker-shaped overshoes with tinkling bells. He could sense the dads
sniggering already. He peered over their heads to see if he could catch
a glimpse of Katy.

Still no sign.

'When I asked your children what parts they wanted to play in
the Nativity, almost all of them said Mary or Joseph. One of them
wanted to be Spider-Man and two others requested peeping penguins.
I wondered how we could put a penguin in Bethlehem at the time of
Christ's birth. And where would Spider-Man show up? I needn't have
worried.' He paused. Everyone looked worried.

'Your amazingly creative, funny – no, scratch that – hilarious, bright,
unfiltered children worked out their own Nativity, complete with
thirteen Marys, ten Josephs, one Spider-Man, two peeping penguins

and Freddie, who just wanted to be Freddie. They've worked really hard. I hope you enjoy it.'

🎄

Katy was close to tears in the back of the cab. She didn't give a damn about the fare racking its way up through the £100 then the £200 mark. If the driver had said, 'Give me a thousand pounds and I'll get you there on time,' she would have gladly handed it over. They were crawling through the dregs of rush hour as she tried very hard not to look at her watch. Why on earth did they have Nativities in the morning when the world and his wife were trying to get somewhere? It was just cruel.

They drove past shop after shop with cheerful messages and seasonal greetings, but nothing could distract her from the sick feeling in her stomach that she was going to miss her family's finest moment yet. She didn't dare think of the consequences if she did: flying to Australia while leaving their whole future in the balance was one thing, but missing the Nativity? That was a whole different level.

They were getting closer now. If she got out of the car and ran there was a chance she wouldn't miss the beginning. Cars were lined up in front of her as far as the eye could see, and there was some movement but precious little. Should she sit here and pray for a break in traffic or jump out and leg it? She looked at her watch – only five minutes to go.

'Stop the car!' she shouted.

'I'm already stopped,' the driver said over his shoulder. 'We're in a traffic jam.'

'Right, yes. Well, I'm getting out. Here you go.' She pushed a wodge of notes that she'd hastily got out of the cash machine at the airport through the squat little hole in front of her.

'Oh,' he said. 'Right, you want a receipt?'

'Keep the change,' she shouted over her shoulder, making a dive for the door. It opened and she was out, running as fast as she could up the sodden streets of Leeds.

🎄

'We're having a baby!' cried a mob of children running on to the small makeshift stage along one side of the preschool room.

'We're having a baby!' they shouted again.

'And it's going to be the best baby ever,' said a Mary.

'The best there has ever been,' said a Joseph.

'Because he will be the son of God,' shouted Spider-Man from behind his mask.

'Everyone line up and sing a song,' said another Joseph.

The thirteen Marys sat on the floor while the ten Josephs stood in a line behind them and they sang their hearts out to 'Can't Stop the Feeling' by Justin Timberlake. Freddie break-danced in front of them.

It had been a dramatic start to this year's Nativity play. Half the parents were sitting with their mouths open while the other half wiggled in their seats in time to the music and started to clap. I might have won some of them over, thought Ben, observing from the side of the stage. Maybe. But clearly not Alison yet. She was staring, stony-faced, as Freddie performed the terrible dance routine that he claimed to have been practising every night.

🎄

Katy could see the school looming up ahead. Her hair was plastered to the side of her face and the rain had already soaked through her hoody and jeans so she felt like she was carrying an extra five pounds just in water. She didn't care though – the finish line was in sight, she could see the gate. She was going to make it! She hurled herself at it then came to an abrupt halt: it didn't move. She grasped it with both hands, rattling it like a caged animal, but still it wouldn't open. She spotted the secured padlock on the other side: she was locked out of the Nativity. So near and yet so far. What on earth would she do now?

🎄

Three Marys and one Joseph sat behind the manger. The Marys were passing a baby doll between them in turns as though Jesus were Pass the Parcel and at some point the music would stop and whoever was holding the doll would be declared the real mother. In the meantime the two peeping penguins had declared that Jesus was born and would be accepting visitors and presents. Master Elf had announced the commencement of 'The Reindeer Games' and that gifts of gold, frankincense and myrrh were hidden in the room, and that the first ones to find them would be the first ones allowed to visit the baby Jesus. Chaos ensued as twenty-three children charged around the room searching out gifts to lay before the parcel-passing tableau on stage. Ben scanned the audience's reaction to the mayhem. To his amazement, parents shouted encouragement to their offspring, eager for their children to win the game by finding the treasure and be first up on stage with the newborn.

'Gold!' shrieked Rebecca from somewhere inside the craft corner. 'I got gold!' she shouted, running past the audience and standing on the stage as victorious as though she had won first prize in a major competition. To look at Alison you would have thought she had in fact become an Olympic gold medallist, as she raised both hands in proud victory, glancing around at the other parents as if to say, 'That's my daughter, and yes she is amazing.'

Then there was a streak of blue and white as George dashed on to the stage clutching a purple-painted box with FRANKINCENSE written on it in large letters. He had a look of total euphoria on his face. 'I found it!' he cried. 'I found it!' Matthew and Alison stared at him in astonishment then began clapping with all their might. There was their son standing on a stage in front of a sea of strange adult faces as though he didn't have a care in the world. Everyone joined in to cheer and clap as he beamed right back at them without the slightest trace of anxiety.

Just as the clapping started to die down he took a small bow and scuttled to the back of the stage area and sat down next to his sister. She wrapped him in an enormous hug. Ben looked over at Matthew and Alison beaming down at their son. Maybe he had managed to win Alison over. A Christmas miracle indeed.

🎄

'I'm assuming you will be picking us up from the airport. We land at 8.15 a.m. We have four large suitcases. Mum x'

Katy shoved the phone back in her pocket. She'd only looked at her phone hoping for a message from Ben but as usual it was her mother sending yet more Christmas demands. She leaned heavily on the bell next to the school reception. To her dismay she'd found that the office was empty when she'd finally worked out that it was the only way to get into school. What if they were all watching the Nativity? she thought in panic. What if she stood there until it ended? She pressed again, wiping the rain out of her eyes. *Please come*, she prayed. *Please come and just let me in*. If someone comes and lets me in now then I'll... I'll go to church on Christmas Day, honestly I will. I'll do anything, just please come and let me into the goddamn school so I can see my daughter and husband in their Nativity play.

'Can I help you?'

Katy snapped her head up from where it had been resting on the glass in despair.

'Yes!' she gasped. 'Please let me in – I'm late for the Nativity.'

'And you are?'

'Millie's mum?'

'Do you have any ID?'

'Seriously?'

'I'm sorry, but I don't recognise you.'

Katy didn't have time to think about how upsetting it was that she wasn't recognised at her own daughter's school as she scrabbled furiously in her bag for her wallet. She rifled through for her driving licence as quickly as she could, pulling it out and thrusting it into the overzealous secretary's face.

She took it from her and seemed to spend an age studying the unflattering picture.

'And your daughter's name is?'

'Amelia. Amelia King.'

To Katy's dismay the secretary made a big show of sitting down and tapping it into a computer as though she was deliberately trying to slow her down. Katy wanted to ram the computer down her throat. After what seemed like an age, and without even looking up, she reached under the desk and Katy heard the sweet sound of a small buzzer as the door was unlocked. She barged through it without a backward glance and began to run again.

🎄

The children were just launching into 'Away in a Manger' as Katy barged through the double doors at the back. Everyone looked round to see a dripping wet woman appear at the door, panting heavily. Eyes were cast up and down before turning back to the front to continue watching their little angels.

'That's my mummy,' Millie told her fellow actors on stage. 'She's been for a barbecue next to the sea.'

Ben watched as Katy mouthed 'so sorry' then moved to position herself in a place where she could see.

The children were singing their hearts out, and there wasn't a dry eye in the house. Even Ben's eyes were damp. He'd got away with it, he thought. Or rather the children's enthusiasm and honest delivery had charmed everyone. Even Mrs Allcock had given him a thumbs up from the back of the room, having glared at him for at least the first ten minutes. He stepped forward and attempted to gather himself before the grand finale.

'Thank you, children,' he said before clearing his throat. 'We've talked a lot about the story of the Nativity in class while preparing our performance for you today. And we've talked a lot about the meaning of Christmas. I asked the children what Christmas meant to them and this is what they told me.'

'PRESENTS!' they all screamed at the tops of their voices.

'I don't think they heard you,' Ben said to them.

'PRESENTS!' they all screamed even louder.

There were a few titters from the audience, as well as a few frustrated sighs.

'So I asked them all what they would have given to Jesus if they had been around at the time of his birth. I asked them what the most important gift that you could give anyone is.'

'It's not a Play-Doh Ice Cream Castle,' piped up a Mary.

'Or a Spider-Man outfit,' added Spiderman.

'Or frankincense,' added George with a grin, holding his box up.

'What is the best present of all?' asked Ben.

'LOVE!' shouted every single Mary, Joseph, peeping penguin, Spider-Man and, of course, not forgetting Freddie.

'Now you went out and found gold, frankincense and myrrh in the room earlier today to give to the baby Jesus,' Ben said to them. He paused as they all looked up at him expectantly. 'Now all of you go out and find love.'

Without exception every child leapt up with grins on their faces and ran towards their mum or their dad or grandparent or guardian. A chorus of 'I love yous' filled the room as eyes filled again with tears. Families hugged hard, all confirming their gift of love.

Ben watched as Millie squealed with delight as she launched herself into her mother's arms after days without seeing her. Katy smothered her with kisses while the tears poured down her still-wet face. As she let her back down to the floor, Millie grabbed her hand and pulled her over to where Ben was still standing on the stage.

She fell into his arms and he felt her wet clothes soak through on to his Master Elf suit.

'I'm so sorry,' she gasped. 'For everything.'

They'd kissed until Millie pulled at her hand and Katy realised everyone was watching them. She backed away quickly and apologetically as Ben fixed his gaze on her before remembering where he was and that he had a Nativity play to finish.

He pulled himself up straight then clapped to summon all the children back on to the stage. There was ample jostling until they were standing in two rows, holding hands and facing their wet-cheeked parents. A familiar tune struck up, causing everyone to reach for their hankies yet again as the golden sparks in their lives launched into a rendition of the Beatles' classic 'All You Need is Love'. It wasn't long before everyone in the room was singing along in one of those precious moments of festive comfort and joy.

🎄

'I was wrong,' Alison told Ben as the parents filed out. 'I could not have made a better choice, sending my two children here. That Nativity, well,' she said, wiping away a stray tear, 'it could not have been better. You made them both shine like stars.'

Matthew reached forward and shook Ben's hand. Ben looked down in astonishment. He was painfully aware that Matthew had never approved of him and certainly never thought he was good enough for Katy.

'What you did…' he said, almost struggling to get the words out. 'Well, it was amazing. Especially seeing George up there.' He paused. 'Thank you,' he said eventually. 'I really mean that.'

Ben nodded. He knew he did.

'I found the frankincense!' cried George, running up to them both.

'You did!' exclaimed Matthew, scooping him up in his arms.

George leaned forward and whispered in his dad's ear. 'Master Elf told me where it was but told me not to tell anyone,' he said, loud enough for Matthew and Ben to hear.

'Did he?' said Matthew. 'Well, he is a very clever Master Elf indeed then, isn't he?'

Ben smiled at the admission. 'See you next term, buddy,' he said to George. 'Well, I assume we'll be seeing you next term?'

'Definitely.' Matthew nodded. 'Time to, er… leave some stuff in the past and move forward, I think.'

Ben glanced over at Katy, who was appreciating some of Millie's artwork on the other side of the room. 'I agree,' he said to Matthew. 'We shouldn't let the past ruin our future, should we? Merry Christmas, mate.'

'Merry Christmas to you too.'

🎄

'And you did this all on your own?' Katy said to Millie as she observed the splodge of green paint doused in multi-coloured glitter.

'Mrs Allcock said it was the best Christmas tree she had ever seen,' replied Millie.

'Of course it is,' said Katy, fighting the urge to engulf her daughter in her arms yet again. It had never been so good to see her and hold her, having been starved of that feeling for days. And to see her standing on that stage, shouting out the words to 'Away in a Manger', well, it was all she could do to stop herself breaking down in wracking sobs at the thought she could have missed out on this moment of utter bliss. It was the best Christmas gift anyone could have, she thought as she glanced over at Ben, also glowing with pride. It filled her up until she thought she might explode with happiness. This was what life was really all about. It wasn't about beaches or barbecues, or having a brand to call your own: it was about people. It was always about people. No wonder she couldn't put a value on having another baby on her spreadsheet. It was priceless.

🎄

'We're going to have a baby,' said Katy when all the other parents had finally left and she could talk to Master Elf alone.

'That was the first line of the Nativity,' replied Ben, looking a little confused. 'Actually, Millie thought of it. I think she might grow up to be a screenwriter.'

'No. I mean us, me and you. I want a baby. Another one of yours please.'

'What? Really? Are you sure?'

'Yes, very sure. Never been more sure of anything.'

Ben fell on her, clasping her in his arms.

'That's the best news,' he said, pulling back for a moment and wiping tears from his eyes. 'Was it the Nativity?'

'Yes, no, I don't know. Does it matter? Yes it does, doesn't it? Your brilliant Nativity reminded me what was important. Reminded us all, I think.'

'But what about Australia? I thought... well, everything looked so amazing. I thought there was no way you could come home and not want to move out there.'

'Well, it was amazing,' she told him.

'Oh.'

'But nothing could compare to this,' she said, casting her hand around the empty room. 'Not the sunshine, not the beach, not the job, not the wine...'

'Not the wine?'

'I know. Not even the wine.'

'Wow,' said Ben, looking truly stunned. 'And not him?'

'Of course not him.'

'You never said he looked like a Ken doll.'

She had to smile – Cooper did look a bit like a Ken doll. 'You're right,' she agreed, 'a bit plastic. Not a patch on my genius husband.' She moved forward to put her arms round his neck. 'What you did today was brilliant. I wouldn't be surprised if there was a baby boom in the area in about nine months' time!'

Ben laughed. 'I guess if a Nativity doesn't make you broody then nothing will. Should I have just played you "Away in a Manger" months ago?'

'Maybe. Who knows? Maybe it's because it's Christmas, but what you did was remind everyone what matters. And it's love.' She took his hands and looked him square in the face. 'It's you and Millie and the owner of that stocking you bought, back in November. Everything else, well, it's meaningless, isn't it?'

Chapter Thirty-One

'I'm here!' said Daniel, letting himself in the front door when no-one responded to his knocking. The hallway was empty but he could hear the sound of sleigh bells coming from the lounge so he pushed open the door, brandishing a bottle of Champagne.

'Merry Christmas,' he declared, stepping into the room.

'Uncle Daniel!' squealed Millie, getting up from a wrapping-paper-infested floor and grabbing him round the legs. 'Did you bring a present? Did you bring a present?' Daniel observed she was dressed in a *Frozen* onesie. He knew he should have stayed home alone on Christmas Day watching classic French films with a bottle of gin.

An enormous man hauled himself up from the sofa and extended his hand out to Daniel. 'I am Carlos,' he announced. 'The boyfriend.'

'I am Daniel,' replied Daniel, taking in his gigantic frame. 'The unloved single man with nowhere better to go.'

Carlos cocked his head to one side and smiled. 'You must meet my son,' he replied. 'I believe he is the same as you.'

Daniel leapt back in horror. He was sure no son of this man could be anything similar to him – it just wasn't possible.

'Daniel!' came the cry behind him, and he swung round to see Katy's mum in a dress that looked like it was made of tinfoil. It reflected so much light he wished he'd brought his sunglasses. 'So good to see you again. It must have been the wedding since we last had a good old gossip about my daughter.'

'Rita,' said Daniel, reaching forward to embrace her. Despite all of Katy's moaning, Daniel had a soft spot for Rita, as she was just as blunt as he was when it came to Katy's failings, and it was highly entertaining to compare notes.

'You brought Champagne!' said Rita, spotting the bottle he was carrying. 'I knew we could rely on you. Why don't we all go through into the kitchen and have a drink? Gabriel is in there preparing vegetables. Dinner is somewhat delayed, I'm afraid.' She raised her eyebrows but turned and left the room before Daniel could ask her to elaborate.

Bloody hell, thought Daniel as he followed Rita down the hallway. He was about to get roped into chopping carrots or peeling potatoes or some other hell. Not in my Paul Smith suit, he decided. There was no way – he was a guest after all.

He only saw Gabriel's back as he entered the room, as he was hunched over the sink. He wasn't large like his dad, he noted – that was something at least. Perhaps they would all fit round the dinner table after all.

'Gabriel,' said Carlos from behind Daniel, placing an enormous hand on his shoulder. 'This is Daniel, Katy's lonely single friend.'

Daniel was just about to protest at Carlos's chosen description when Gabriel turned his head round over his shoulder and cast a smile in Daniel's direction. Daniel stood frozen to the spot as Gabriel reached for a towel to dry off his hands before extending one of them for a warm handshake with the awestruck Daniel. Just as he did, the sun emerged from behind a cloud and shone a ray of light across his face.

'Gabriel, you say?' gasped Daniel.

'Yes,' he nodded, grinning, 'as in the angel. My mother's choice apparently. It so doesn't suit me.'

'It so does,' replied Daniel, stuck for words in front of the awesome chiselled beauty of the man in front of him.

'He is like you, no?' Carlos asked Daniel.

'I very much hope so,' sighed Daniel, unable to take his eyes off him.

'What a cosmopolitan group we will be at our dinner table,' chirped Rita. 'Two gays, two Spaniards, two toy boys – who would have thought it? The most exciting Christmas dinner table I will have sat at,' she said, handing the bottle of Champagne over to Carlos to open.

'Totally,' said Daniel, thinking he might explode with joy. This was turning out to be maybe not the most cosmopolitan but certainly the best Christmas he had ever had.

Rita took Champagne flutes from the shelf and handed them out while Gabriel and Daniel didn't take their eyes off each other. Daniel prayed with all his heart that he was getting a positive appraisal.

'May I… may I help you with the vegetables?' he found himself saying, suddenly feeling jittery and nervous as Carlos filled their glasses.

'That would be excellent,' replied Gabriel, raising his glass. 'You can do the sprouts, whatever they are?'

'My daughter really is unbelievable,' said Rita, indicating to Carlos to be sure to fill hers to the top. 'I mean, fancy inviting us all over for Christmas dinner and then expecting us to prepare it. I really wonder where I went wrong with her, you know.'

'You did a beautiful job,' said Carlos, throwing an arm around her. 'She is a credit.'

'Well, I did my best,' muttered Rita, taking a large gulp of Champagne.

'Where are they?' asked Daniel, realising he hadn't seen Katy or Ben since he'd arrived. Not that he cared any more.

'Still in bed,' huffed Rita. 'They showed their faces to see Millie open her presents then disappeared. So rude.'

'They are busy,' Carlos grinned. 'Ben is getting his Christmas present, I think.'

'But… but…' said Daniel, suddenly realising what Carlos was suggesting, 'on Christmas Day! Surely that's not right, is it? Isn't it in the Ten Commandments or something?'

'Thou shalt not have sex on Christmas Day?' said Gabriel with a sexy smile.

Daniel felt his legs go to jelly. 'Yes, well, rules are there to be broken, I guess…' he added, feeling himself start to blush.

As if on cue, Ben and Katy burst through the door all rosy cheeked and grinning from ear to ear. They smelt of pine and perfume, clearly both fresh from the shower. It was entirely obvious to everyone what they'd been up to.

'Sorry,' Katy giggled, 'we were… we were…'

'Merry Christmas,' said Daniel, lunging forward to save her embarrassment and his. He engulfed her in a hug so tight she thought she might have to stop breathing.

'Does this mean you're staying?' he breathed in her ear.

'Yes,' she whispered.

He pulled back and looked in her eyes. 'That's all I wanted for Christmas,' he said as tears prickled his eyes. 'But thank you for bringing me Gabriel as well,' he added with a wink.

She laughed. 'You're very welcome. That's all you're getting, mind you!'

'But I gave you so many hints about the wallet display in Harvey Nichols,' he protested.

'Ho ho ho,' came a sudden boom from the hallway. 'Glad tidings we bring to you and your kin,' two voices chimed as the kitchen door opened.

'We're getting married,' said Abby, appearing in the doorway, sparkling finger held up for all to see. She was jumping up and down, a look of pure excitement on her face. Braindead peeked over her shoulder, grinning from ear to ear.

'Thank God for that,' roared Daniel, Katy and Ben all at the same time, rushing forward to shake their hands and hug and admire the ring.

'So spill the beans then,' said Daniel when it had all calmed down. 'I want to hear every detail of how you finally managed to pop the question, Braindead.'

Ben laughed. 'So impressed you managed to ask the right person this time.'

Braindead shrugged. 'I didn't have to.'

'I asked him!' squealed Abby, still jumping up and down like an excited child. 'Well, I had to, didn't I? When he told me how I had totally screwed it all up for him by getting wasted, well, I couldn't believe it. I cried for days, thinking about how I'd missed seeing him come down from the ceiling looking for me and I wasn't there. I apologised so many times, but I didn't know what to do until Charlene said I should return the favour. So I went out and bought myself a ring and I proposed to him in the way I thought he'd want to be asked.'

'It was perfect,' said Braindead, putting his arm round her shoulder, a smug smile appearing on his face.

'I cannot wait to hear this,' said Daniel.

'Can I tell him?' Braindead asked Abby.

'Go ahead,' she replied.

'It was awesome,' said Braindead. 'She took me to my local last night, which to be honest, I thought was odd because it was Christmas Eve and normally she would want to go into town, but she said no, she wanted to spend the night with me in The Feathers, and she bought me a drink, sat down and the next thing I knew she was on one knee. Next to me. In the Feathers. And she just asked me, there and then.'

'He cried,' added Abby.

'So did she,' said Braindead.

'We got free drinks all night,' said Abby.

'And they had a lock-in. Best night ever. Seriously,' said Braindead. 'You so missed out,' he told Ben.

'We must toast,' said Carlos, handing Braindead and Abby a glass of Champagne each. 'I am the toy boy,' he added to clarify.

'Of course you are,' said Braindead.

But before glasses could be raised, the door to the kitchen opened yet again, and to everyone's shock, there stood Matthew, looking very harassed.

'I knocked and knocked,' he said. 'I'm so sorry, it's just that...'

Before he could finish George, Rebecca, Harry and Millie had raced into the room, running round people's legs like a bunch of excitable Collie dogs.

'I am the toy boy,' said Carlos, approaching Matthew with a glass of Champagne.

'Oh no, no, please I have to go, it's just, well...'

'Matthew!' said Rita. 'What on earth are you doing here? It *is* you, isn't it? I've not seen you since you were a teenager, but I'd spot that wonky ear anywhere.'

'Hello, Mrs Chapman, it's nice to see you, but... but Alison has gone into labour...' he said, looking round in bewilderment.

'What!' cried everyone in unison.

'Yes, yes,' continued Matthew, casting a concerned glance towards the door.

'We're having a baby, we're having a baby,' chanted Rebecca, George and Millie.

'Is it Jesus coming?' asked Braindead.

'Noooo,' said Matthew, looking at Braindead as though he were a lunatic.

'Sorry, I've just got engaged,' said Braindead.

'Oh well, congratulations,' replied Matthew. 'Aren't you the man from Christmas Party Land?'

Braindead grinned. 'Yes.'

Matthew looked around, confused, then shook his head. 'I haven't got time to ask.' He turned to Ben. 'We gave Lena the day off, you see. To be with her new boyfriend, and George and Rebecca, well, they insisted they come to Master Elf for Christmas. George has had the mother of all tantrums, and I didn't know what to do, and I have Alison in the car and I realise this is such an imposition...'

'Get in that car and get your wife to hospital now,' said Ben, stepping forward. 'There is room at the inn here for your children.'

'Really?' said Matthew, looking as though he were about to burst into tears with relief. 'Are you sure?'

'Of course we're sure. Go and give birth. Go on, off you go. Get out of here now.'

'OK, great. So, bye, kids!' he shouted then turned and ran out of the door, leaving a gathering of bemused adults.

'That's Katy's ex-boyfriend,' Rita told Carlos helpfully.

'Time for that toast, I think,' said Katy, stepping into the middle of the room and raising her glass high in the air before her mum could fill him in on any more of their difficult history. She spun round slowly, taking in the people surrounding her. First, her mum, who grinned back at her cheekily, clearly happy for the first time in a long while with her caring and devoted toy boy. Then on to Gabriel, who had arrived and charmed her daughter into eating peas, a battle Katy had fought and lost at many a tea table. He'd also insisted on sleeping on the sofa so that Ben and Katy could have the privacy of the spare room. Thank goodness. They had a baby to make. Then she turned her gaze to Daniel, who raised his glass to her and murmured another thank you. Whether it was for Gabriel or for being invited to share Christmas with them, or the news that she wasn't leaving him, she didn't know, but she murmured a thank you back, for his special friendship. She was so glad he was there.

Braindead and Abby spilled into her vision, bubbling over with excitement and happiness. Boy, was she glad they'd be around to share their joy next year. It was bound to be a hell of a ride.

And finally, Ben. She watched as he reached over and handed Braindead a beer knowing he'd prefer that to Champagne. Then he scooped up a passing Millie, who screamed with excitement at his tickles while George, Rebecca and Harry grabbed hold of his legs and began their chant again: 'We're having a baby, we're having a baby…'

Ben glanced over at Katy and winked. She raised her glass towards him.

'All you need is love,' she said. 'All you ever need, in fact.'

'All you need is love,' they all chimed in. 'Love is all you need.'

A letter from Tracy

I want to say a huge thank you for choosing to read *No-one Ever Has Sex on Christmas Day*. If you did enjoy it, and want to keep up-to-date with all my latest releases, just sign up at the following link. Your email address will never be shared, and you can unsubscribe at any time.

Sign up to Tracy Bloom's email list

I hope you loved *No-one Ever Has Sex on Christmas Day*, and if you did, I would be very grateful if you could write a review. I'd love to hear what you think, and it makes such a difference helping new readers to discover one of my books for the first time.

I love hearing from my readers – you can get in touch on my Facebook page, through Twitter, Goodreads or my website.

It has been such a joy to spend time again with Katy, Ben, Matthew and Alison, and of course not forgetting Braindead and Daniel. If you'd like to read more about their loves, lives and laughter then you can catch up with them in two other novels, *No-one Ever Has Sex on a Tuesday* and *No-one Ever Has Sex in the Suburbs*.

Thanks,
Tracy Bloom

 tracybloomwrites

 @TracyBBloom

www.tracybloom.com

Acknowledgements

This book would not have been written without the encouragement and sharp stick waving of two people. My editor, Jenny Geras, wanted me to write this book three years ago, and when she asked me again this year I felt I had enough ideas to do it justice. I've so enjoyed writing this book, Jenny, so thank you for all your continued support and pestering! Also, my thanks must go to Peta Nightingale, who listens and cajoles and thinks and works stuff out. So glad you have my back professionally and above all, so proud to have you as a friend. Thank you.

Many thanks to Madeleine Milburn, my agent, who did not hesitate when I approached her and who has buoyed me up tremendously with positive words and encouragement. We are on our way!

I also want to thank my readers, who continue to send me lovely messages. I cannot tell you how good that feels. Thank you for reading, and I hope you like this one just as much as my other novels.

Finally, to everyone who I have shared my Christmases with: Mum and Dad, Andrew and Helen, Gillian, Laura, Rebecca and Hannah, Marc, Emma and George, Chris and David, Gillian, Chris, Jack and Sam. Good times and laughter. Long may it continue!

For Helen Wilkins, who takes us in every Christmas Eve and organises the 'food critics' annual Christmas party with Christine – you are a star and Christmas would not be the same without you.

And finally, to my husband, Bruce, who every year puts up with Christmas being the excuse for everyone ignoring his birthday in January. Sorry. Will try harder this year... promise xx